Let Me Go

LILY FOSTER

Also by Lily Foster

LET ME SERIES

Let Me Be the One

Let Me Love You

Let Me Go

Let Me Heal Your Heart

Let Me Fall

When I Let You Go

BLACKBIRD SERIES

When the Night is Over

Your Hand in Mine

Ghost on the Shore

All Your Life

Shorefront Books

Let Me Go

Chapter One

DYLAN

I was bored silly, sitting in the living room of our frat house watching Sports Center, nursing a hangover and listening to a bunch of clowns argue over which one had the hotter girlfriend.

A guy who belonged to a neighboring frat, thought his name was Evan or Ethan or something like that, cleared his throat loudly. "I'm gonna shut all of y'all up right now."

Virginia was an odd place in that Yankees like me, who spoke with our crisp New England accent, intermingled on a daily basis with southern boys who dropped the *y'all* and *I'm fixing to* a lot. I guess I liked the sound of it for some reason because it always got my attention.

Whatever he was showing off on his phone had made an impression on the five or so guys sitting on the other side of the room.

I opened my palm without looking his way. "Toss it over."

He got up and walked it over. Looked like a damn puppy waiting for a pat on the head before backing away. The move was weak and pathetic on his part, but to be fair, I wasn't exactly Mr. Congeniality.

I was fiercely loyal and good to my friends, to the people close to me, but I didn't feel the need to give everyone and their grandmother the time of day. Most people approached with caution, and for good reason.

I had to control myself—couldn't give this loser the satisfaction of a reaction—but what I saw on that screen blew me away. The picture was a bona fide work of art. This dipshit was the Ansel Adams of phone-snapped nudie pics.

Before me was a stunning blond with flawless skin. Curled onto her side and sleeping like an angel, you could see the sweet curve of her ass and the round fullness of her breast. She had a beautiful face from what I could see of her profile, and her rosy lips were parted in a way that made my imagination run wild.

In an attempt to appear bored and disinterested, I looked back at the television before asking, "Who is this?"

And I was itching to slap that stupid, smug look off his face when he bragged, "My girlfriend."

"How long have you been going out with her?"

"Started hanging out with her at the end of last semester."

"Tapped that yet?"

My bullshit detector was spot on, so I could tell this little coward was toying with the idea of lying before his conscience got the better of him. He looked down at the floor before muttering, "Nah...Soon though."

Hmm...a good girl.

Ethan wisely decided to stand down when I started messing with his phone, deleting the picture, wiping the contacts clean and returning it back to its original settings.

"So you're the kind of guy who takes pictures of his girl when she's passed out cold and then shows them to other guys?"

"N-n-no."

With that, I popped out the memory card, put it on the floor next to me, took one of the dumbbells that Justin left all over the goddamn house, and gently smashed it to bits.

"What are you doing, man?"

I tossed his phone back to him and gestured towards the door. "You'll have to re-enter your contacts. Sorry 'bout that. Now get out."

"What the hell?"

Brian smelled like a brewery, and I assumed he'd been sleeping as he laid face-down on one of the couches, but apparently he was awake. He growled, "You were told to get out. Are you deaf, motherfucker?"

Brian was a giant. I don't recall the guy ever getting into an actual fight because he'd only have to look at his opponent and maybe bark out a few angry words before they were sure to back down. Always good to have a friend like Brian who has your back.

As Ethan moped his way out of the house, Christian commented, "Always the hospitable one, aren't you, Cole?"

"Would you like someone to do that to your sister?"

"Good point. Whatever, I never liked the guy anyway."

I looked over to the other guys, mostly juniors and sophomores, and asked, "Any of you know her?"

Matt reluctantly answered, "My girlfriend is good friends with her."

"About today—"

"I know, I won't say anything."

"You *don't* know, Matt, so don't interrupt. And you *will* tell your girlfriend what happened here today, understand? Whoever this girl is, she shouldn't be walking around clueless, thinking she's dating Prince Charming."

Christian tossed a football from across the room. "Come on, don't you think that's a little harsh?"

"Fuck him, he's a scumbag."

Tossing the football back, I smiled, fully aware and proud of the fact that I was the reigning king of the scumbags, because you *know* I sent that picture to my own phone before I deleted it from Ethan's.

I was planning on studying every pixel of that photo like a goddamn art critic tonight.

* * *

KASIA

I couldn't eat and I was running on next to no sleep. I was convinced that every guy who passed me on campus had seen the picture—or pictures.

When Bernadette came over Sunday night and told me what Ethan had done, I dropped my water glass and walked right over the shards like a zombie to get my phone. I think Bernadette screamed when she saw my foot bleeding, but neither the sound nor the pain registered.

Hands trembling, I nearly dropped the phone as I waited for the call to connect. He stayed silent on his end, no greeting. No one else could have been responsible, but his silence was confirmation of his guilt.

"How could you do this to me?"

Given a moment to regroup, Ethan changed tack and decided to play dumb. *What? Huh?* That age old strategy: deny, deny, deny. He knew exactly what I was talking about and he was to blame.

I cut him off. Couldn't listen to him babble and flip-flop. Couldn't tolerate his feeble attempts to vindicate himself and placate me. My voice was flat and dead when I told him not to call me or come near me ever again. Then I spent the next two days alternating between crying and being angry at myself for being such a poor judge of character.

Two boyfriends. I wasn't naïve but I wasn't exactly worldly. Ethan was the only person I'd dated besides Patryk, who was my first in every way that's important.

Patryk and I grew up together in Brooklyn, and our families were close in the way that immigrant families often are. We started dating during senior year of high school and stayed together until the end of sophomore year. Pat was at Columbia and I was away at school in Virginia. The distance wore on us both. The fact that my parents all but assumed I was going to marry Patryk also grated on me. I loved him but he was almost too familiar.

I've always had to navigate my way between two worlds. I grew up in Greenpoint, a neighborhood in Brooklyn, New York, known as Little Poland. My parents came to this country not speaking the language, and they remained tied to Poland while being immensely proud of their American citizenship. They held on to tradition but wanted their children to assimilate and thrive. My parents expected hard work and good grades, and as a result, all of us were granted acceptance into the most prestigious specialized public high schools, or in my case, a scholarship to private prep school.

So I, little Kasia Mazur, would spend her days among the most privileged kids in Manhattan before going back home to our tidy rowhouse on Lorimar Street, where I would sit around the dinner table enjoying gulasz or bigos with my parents and three older brothers. My life was different from my classmates, who spent winter break hitting the slopes in Courchevel or Sun Valley and then summered in the Hamptons or the Vineyard. The Mazurs "summered" in Coney Island.

Oh, but now the familiarity of home and Patryk were luring me in like shelter from the storm.

Did I miss something? Ethan came off as a nice person, and his carefree, breezy attitude was a breath of fresh air compared to Patryk's more serious nature. I guess this is what I get for taking a walk on my version of the wild side.

My mother has this seventy-two hour rule. She always says that no matter what happens, no matter how awful, no matter how bad you feel, you'll see things in a better light seventy-two hours later. In the past it's held true, but I still felt like hell and I was forty-eight hours in already.

Bernadette didn't spare any details Tuesday night when she sat on my bed, relaying the story again at my insistence.

I questioned every detail. "What *exactly* could you see in the picture, Bernadette?"

I had to know, because although I'd had a few drinks, I didn't make a habit of being drunk and I did not recall being totally naked at any time with Ethan.

"He said you were *practically* naked in it, Kasia. I'm not sure what Matt meant exactly. If it's any consolation," she cracked a smile as she tossed a pillow my way, "my *boyfriend* said you looked really good."

"It's no consolation."

"But it is pretty wild that Dylan Cole came to your rescue, right? He never struck me as the warm and fuzzy type, but I think his knight in shining armor side is pretty hot. Doesn't hurt that he also happens to be insanely gorgeous."

"Come again?"

Bernie threw her head back, exasperated. "I told you all of this the other night. You were a total basket case, though, so I guess you didn't process much beyond the basics." She was all starry-eyed as she clutched her hands to her chest. "Dylan got a hold of Ethan's phone, deleted the picture and wiped the phone's memory clean. He reemed Ethan, basically calling him a pathetic pervert, and then kicked him out of their house."

I was speechless and confused. To be fair, I'd only observed Dylan Cole from afar, but he came off as a snotty, entitled jerk, not the upstanding citizen my friend was describing.

He's one of *those* guys. Someone you notice in a room even though you want to smack yourself for paying them even one iota of attention.

There's something detestable about a guy who's trying his best to look unkempt, but try as he might, he still looks hot—so hot you want to take a bite out of him. That's Dylan, with his sandy blond hair cut in that expert way so that it falls just slightly over one eye. Just enough so that you're tempted to reach over and smooth it back to get an unobstructed view of those eyes, which happen to be a freakishly awesome shade of sea green. He's so smug, with his never messy longish hair, his slender, muscular build, and an air of superiority in those sea-green eyes.

From his looks alone you know he's ridiculously wealthy. He's like so many of the kids I knew in high school—entitlement and privilege seeping from his every pore. And Dylan didn't come off as the least bit friendly. No, his icy demeanor made you wary of him.

Knight in shining armor, my ass.

Walking into the cafeteria on Wednesday, among the packed tables I saw several of Matt's frat brothers eating lunch. I'd been avoiding this place for the past few days for this very reason. But two days of eating practically nothing but chips and granola bars from the vending machine had left me feeling light-headed, so I stopped in to grab something more substantial to scarf down during my Marketing Strategies class.

I snuck in the side entrance to avoid walking up the center aisle, and I was just a few steps away from sneaking back out the way I'd come in when Valerie hollered my name so loudly she could have shattered all the windows in the place. Val was a rowdy girl and I loved her, but in that moment I wanted to take my grilled veggie wrap and shove it down her throat just to shut her up.

Out of the corner of my eye I saw a few of the Kappa brothers perk up at the sound of my name. *What to do, what to do?* I decided to suck it up, squaring my shoulders and holding my head up high as I made my way towards Val, Bernadette and Trish. Just my luck, today of all days they were sitting only two tables over from those guys.

I forced a smile. "Hey."

Bernadette beamed. "Looking good, Kasia."

"I feel better."

Trish reached over to feel my forehead. "Were you sick? You didn't answer my calls. I just figured you were studying or something."

She was a true softie who wanted to take care of everyone. "Nothing major, Trish." I gestured towards Valerie. "It's a good thing Bernadette was there to nurse me back to health because I haven't seen my roommate in days."

"Nice, I feel like a turd now. I'm sorry, but Coop is always begging me to stay," Val shot me a wicked grin, "and I see no reason to leave his bed most days."

Bernadette wasn't amused. "If you keep this up you're going to fail. I mean it. You haven't been to Modern Lit for like, two weeks. He doesn't take attendance but you're going to bomb the midterm."

She waved her off. "I'll manage."

Valerie was one of those people who had A—most likely read every book on the syllabus years ago, and B—could ace the test without hearing so much as one lecture. She was *that* kind of smart. I didn't struggle academically but I envied how easily everything came to Val. She was just on a different level than most people.

And the seventy-two-hour rule stood as law because I was able to tell the girls what happened, fairly confident that I wouldn't make a spectacle of myself by crying in public. I waved them in closer. "I know Bernie didn't spill, but something crappy happened over the weekend and that's why I've been missing in action." I looked directly at Val. "Don't react and do not get loud right now. I don't want any attention."

I gave them the abridged version, while Bernadette, the eternal optimist, added on the Dylan to the rescue bit.

Valerie kept her voice low, thankfully, but looked like she could spit nails when she said, "Ethan...that little-prick motherfucker. And now I won't feel bad spreading that *little* piece of information around."

Trish was giggling. "You snuck a peek, Val?"

Valerie answered back, waving her off as if it was nothing, "I did Ethan freshman year. He was nothing special. I actually felt bad when you hooked up with him, Kasia. Worst lay ever. I can't wait to run into that jackass."

I met her eyes, my warning clear. "You say nothing to him, understand? I just want this to go away."

Trish took my hand. "Relax, this has probably blown over already. Naked pics are a dime a dozen in a frat house."

"I don't think I was totally naked." Oh crap, I could feel the tears coming on again. "Someone change the subject, please."

"Sorry," Trish said, squeezing my hand. "You know, I'm not surprised about Dylan, though. I know he comes off like a badass but I think he's nice. We had a class together last year and there was this one kid with some sort of disability. He wore leg braces. Anyway, I noticed Dylan would hang back a few extra minutes just like the other kid did, and then I'd see him helping with his bag and holding the door for him on the way out."

Valerie raised an eyebrow. "Maybe he does a good deed now and then, but he's no boy scout. That dude will screw anything with a pulse."

Bernadette chimed in, "After what he did for Kasia, I've decided I like him."

I was still working on processing the Dylan Cole angle of this story. What he did was kind, but I had no plans to issue a personal thank you. If I had it my way, I wouldn't run into him, Ethan, Matt, or anyone else involved in this mess for the rest of the year.

As talk moved on to the party at Cooper's place this weekend, I knew I'd be skipping it. I'd be laying low for the foreseeable future.

Great way to kick off my senior year.

* * *

DYLAN

I was taking in my surroundings with more care than usual. This campus was big and I'd never crossed paths with her before, so it shouldn't surprise me that I was having trouble finding her now.

I didn't even know her name.

I could have asked Matt or one of my other fraternity brothers, but that would have implied some level of interest on my part.

Was I interested? Let's just say that picture had set off an obsessive-like need to track her down, to see her in person. My mystery girl had starred in my dreams for the past two nights. Rolling over to face me and lacing her fingers around my neck, she always whispered the same line: *I want you.*

I scanned the crowd quickly before sitting down and turning my attention to Brian and Christian. "What's up?"

Christian answered, "You know we have to meet with Coach at four, right?"

I let out a tired breath. "Yeah, I know. I'm not looking forward to it this season like I have in the past. Just don't feel particularly into it, you know?"

"Why is that?"

"Dunno," I answered, shrugging. "We won the conference title last year. It all just feels so...been there done that. And I'm busy working on some plans for my father. My head is already in that world."

Brian chuckled. "Always the businessman."

I smiled back. "Exactly."

Christian leaned in. "You're the strongest midfielder on the team, so I hope you're not planning on quitting. And as for your *business,* we've officially started workouts so you're going to have to make some changes. Random piss tests will be heading our way before you know it."

"Got it, Mom."

"I know *you* can weasel your way around any test, Cole, it's the other morons I'm thinking about. Don't want their shit landing back on your doorstep."

"I'm not worried."

I wasn't a dealer per se, just sold to my frat brothers and friends. And I had a conscience about it. I considered myself the Wholesome Foods equivalent of the suppliers. I sold weed and shrooms only—nothing hard, nothing I considered addictive.

Looking around the cafeteria again, I saw a raven haired beauty scowling in my general direction. She was the girlfriend of one of my customers. I remembered with a smile that I'd tried to get with her once last semester while her boyfriend was in the next room. She'd shot me down cold.

I gestured to her. "What's that girl's name?"

Brian made a face like he was mid-orgasm. "Oh, that's Valerie, Cooper's girlfriend. I heard those two basically never leave his room and just fuck all day."

"I knew I liked her."

Christian lit up. "That reminds me, you just missed the subject of that lovely photo. She was sitting with Valerie."

I tried my best to sound bored. "What photo?"

"The skin pic? Ethan's girl?" Christian added, "And just for the record, she's even better looking in person. I'd say she's in my top ten."

Now there were a lot of beautiful women at this university, so saying she was top ten was high praise. I was getting restless. It was already Wednesday and I wanted that girl in my bed by the weekend. The fact that Ethan couldn't seal the deal meant nothing. I played dirtier.

"Gotta go, gentlemen."

As I exited, I saw a blonde walking about a hundred yards ahead of me. Trying to find a specific blonde on this campus was like looking for a needle in a haystack, but I had a gut feeling it was her. When I got to within ten feet, I slowed my pace and fell into step behind her.

I followed her across the quad and then into the bookstore. I was all set to approach but then stopped. Something about her was different, told me I couldn't pull out the same tired bullshit that worked on the sort of women I usually kept company with. So I just watched.

Her face was perfect, with full rosy lips and eyes that were an unusual shade of pale, cool blue—almost grey. Her blonde hair fell halfway down her back, and it wasn't the stick straight 'do that every other girl around here sported. She was slim but curvy in all the best places, and the way she dressed was different, edgier. A fitted, cropped black leather jacket fell open over a tight black pullover—awesome rack—and her tight black jeans were tucked into black boots that laced up almost to her knee. Prairie girl meets Marilyn Manson.

When she got to the register, I busied myself looking at the prominently displayed selection of condoms, listening in as the cashier chatted my girl up. She smiled patiently, tolerating this guy who had no game whatsoever, but her downcast eyes were sad.

I moved in closer and leaned right over her shoulder as the cashier handed back her debit card. "Kasia. That fits. I've been wondering what your name is."

She turned, and after looking startled for a nanosecond, she collected herself and shot back, "Not Kah-see-ah. It's pronounced Kah-shah. And what, you've been wanting to put a name to the face in the picture?"

I couldn't help but smile. "Yeah, a name to go with the...face." Her cheeks colored as she fixed her eyes on the floor. She was ashamed and I was immediately annoyed with myself for teasing her. "I'm sorry."

She shook her head. "Yeah, it's still too soon for the whole 'look back on this and laugh' thing."

Gesturing to her clothes, I said solemnly, "I should have been more sensitive. I can see you're still in mourning."

After looking down at her all-black ensemble, she laughed and offered me a reluctant smile. "I suppose I do owe you a thank you. Bernadette told me you defended my honor, or defended women in general."

"It was nothing. I never liked your boyfriend anyway."

"Not my boyfriend. Not my friend. Not anything."

"Figured that. Are you ok, though?"

"I wasn't for a few days, but now I'm all right. It helps to know that the picture isn't making the rounds. Really, thank you."

"Don't mention it again, I mean it." I noticed her textbook purchase then and was truly surprised. "How are you a business major and we've never had classes together? Am I that unlucky?"

She smiled with no trace of the sadness I saw in her eyes just a few moments before. "Guess so."

"What are you doing this weekend?"

"My plan is to lay low."

"Screw that." In response to her wide eyes, I toned it down. "I mean, you're not going to Cooper's? Your friend Val is with him, right?"

"Yep, but I'm not up for any fraternity parties just yet."

"Well, if you change your mind, and I hope you do, maybe we'll run into one another."

"I won't. I'm sure."

I shrugged my shoulders, doing my best not to seem too eager. "Well then it's goodbye, Kah-shah," I said, emphasizing the pronunciation. "It was nice to finally, officially meet you."

Turning to leave, she said, "Nice to meet you too, Dylan. You're not what I expected."

Don't know what that was supposed to mean, but I took it at face value. She didn't expect me to be decent, nice or considerate. My reputation had preceded me once again.

My plan to have her by this weekend was no longer in play. I could tell this one was a challenge. I liked challenges, and I liked Kasia.

* * *

KASIA

By Friday morning I was feeling a whole lot better. The girls rallied around, assuring me it wasn't such a big deal, and I reminded myself that thanks to Dylan, the picture wasn't being circulated. I was feeling so much better that I considered going to Cooper's party.

I did like Cooper. He was nice, extremely laid back—likely due to the heavy weed habit—and I could tell that he really cared for Val. Valerie gushed about him as if he was Bill Gates, Orlando Bloom and Ghandi all rolled into one: smart, hot and enlightened. He was a good guy, but the two of them were entirely too wrapped up in one another lately. Laughing to myself, I wondered if they would even make it downstairs during the party.

And I hate to admit it, but the possibility of seeing Dylan again was the main draw. I nearly started to hyperventilate when he all but pressed into my back and said my name the other day. I was taller than average but he still towered over me, invading my space and my senses. He smelled so good, and I imagined lean muscles rippling beneath his clothes. Try as I might to put him out of my mind, I'd been daydreaming about the boy since our encounter in the bookstore.

By the time I was leaving my last class of the day, I made the decision to go with Valerie, Trish and Bernie to the party. I was smiling to myself thinking about what I would wear, deciding that I would tone down the all-black angry city chick look. But my smile fell when I turned the corner and saw Ethan sitting on my front steps.

I could barely contain my anger. "I have nothing to say to you."

He stood and took a few tentative steps closer. "I just want to tell you how sorry I am. Got caught up in some dumb conversation and I acted like an idiot. I never meant to hurt you and I'm sorry."

"You're sorry for what, Ethan? For showing people a picture of my practically naked body? Or are you sorry for taking a picture like that without my consent in the first place?"

"I was wrong—"

"No shit you were wrong, and I'm not interested in your apology. I can't believe I actually liked you and thought we were good together."

"We are good together. Please, just please let me make it up to you."

"Never gonna happen. I want you to go."

He waited a beat before he lowered his head and walked away. And like an idiot, I stood there feeling bad for the guy.

People make mistakes, and Ethan isn't a monster. I'm sure he was being sincere when he said he was sorry, but I meant it when I said we were done. What he did wasn't just disrespectful to me, it also showed how immature and insecure he was. I could fault Patryk in some areas, but the boy was self-assured. He'd never be looking for a seal of approval from anyone, let alone a bunch of smug frat boys.

Running into Ethan took the wind out of my sails. The only outfit I wanted to change into was my pajamas, and I suddenly had a strong urge for sushi and a night of sketching and pattern cutting.

Designing and making clothes is my passion. I've been sewing since I was ten. My mother could probably make garments that were far better tailored than mine, but she used her skills for making curtains, slipcovers, pillows and things like that. She taught me the basics on our old sewing machine, as well as some detailed work with adding zippers and pleating, but otherwise I was self-taught.

In high school I started devoting more time to my hobby, and once I was in college I used what I'd learned in my marketing and e-commerce classes to launch my brand, Sweet Betty Threads. I sold my vintage-inspired dresses, tops and skirts to a mostly hipster, northeastern demographic. I certainly wasn't making enough money to call it a career yet, but I knew that's what I wanted. I was using Sweet Betty Threads as my senior thesis project, and it was a true labor of love.

I wound up spending the entire weekend and the days that followed working on designs, and I was up until the early hours of the mornings tweaking my website. I had an early class Friday, and was yawning as I waited in line for some much needed coffee.

I sensed his presence before he came right up close and whispered in my ear, "It's really Kah-zjah, right?"

Damn, my whole body felt scorched when he was near. I took a deep breath and tried my best to sound casual. "You don't have to do the full-on Polish accent, Dylan. I'll think one of my brothers is calling my name."

He rested his hand on my shoulder in a way that felt like I was being branded. "Well, I definitely don't want you to think of me in a brotherly way." He was playing with me and I liked it. "Did you say brothers, plural?"

"Yes, I have three older, rather large, overprotective brothers."

"That's good, I like protective. So, you never made it to Cooper's. Did you spend last weekend home knitting or something?"

"Close. I was sewing."

He looked confused but pressed on. "So, uh, is there any way I can persuade you to come to a party at my place tonight? I know it was the scene of the crime and all, but I can guarantee you that no one will so much as mention it." He put his hand on his chest. "You'll have your own private security detail."

"That's a nice offer, but *your* frat house is pretty much number one on the list of places I plan on avoiding this year."

He pulled his best wounded face. "All year? Come on, Kasia, you're killing me."

"It's not the same for guys. You don't care who sees you naked. How would you feel if you were in my shoes?"

"First of all, not like I looked carefully or anything, but you weren't completely naked. Second, if that was me in the picture and I looked like *that*, I'd have made a damn billboard out of it."

I closed my eyes and kneaded the heel of my palm into my forehead. Dylan had obviously seen the picture. Who was I kidding? Every guy in that house had seen it.

His tone softened. "Hey, if you won't come then I'll skip it too. Let me take you out."

"I don't get it. You don't seem like the type who pursues."

He shrugged. "I just want to get to know you." He looked down at the floor then, a move that made him look uncharacteristically timid. "There's something about you."

"I don't know."

"Come on, I won't bite...or photograph." He smiled and bumped my shoulder. "Still too soon to joke about it?"

I bumped him back, smiling. "Yeah, too soon."

"Please, will you let me take you out tonight?"

I wanted to go, I knew that much at least. "All right, but it's not like a date or anything."

"Tone down the enthusiasm, would ya? You're crushing my ego, but I guess I have to take what I can get. I'll pick you up at seven?"

"Ok." As he turned to leave, I asked, "Aren't you getting coffee?"

He shook his head. "Nope, I was just following you."

I got absolutely nothing out of Business Ethics, as I spent the entirety of class thinking about Dylan Cole.

* * *

DYLAN

My reaction took me off guard.

Normally I'd be assessing a girl's looks, her body—that's all. When Kasia answered the door, though, it made me feel…happy? I was light-hearted and excited for some possibility. I wanted to talk to her, to make her laugh, to impress her. And believe me when I say that I never cared about impressing anyone.

She did look beautiful. The biker chick look was gone, replaced by something decidedly more "sexy hipster." I took her in from head to toe and then teased, "Nice specs."

"You like?" she teased back, smiling. "My eyes are irritated from lack of sleep. The contacts aren't happening."

She really did look cute in her retro-nerdy glasses. "I *do* like. You look like the sexy librarian who's going to punish me for being too loud in the library."

She blushed. "You have *some* imagination, Dylan."

"You have *no* idea, Kasia."

She asked where we were going as we made our way to the lot.

"Dinner." I raised my hand to silence her before she could speak. "Not a dinner date, so don't go getting any ideas. Just dinner because people need to eat."

"Oh-kay, boss."

I took her to an Italian place in town where we talked for two hours straight over dinner and a bottle of wine. Best date I've been on in I don't know how long. And I don't care what she said, it was a date.

Before we ordered desert I was already thinking about where I'd take her to eat next time. No movie, no concert or play—I was taking this girl out to eat again. Let's just say that I'm into girls who eat, and watching Kasia eat was like watching high-quality porn. Most of the girls I knew subsisted on juice fasts and laxatives, so I couldn't help but smile as she cleaned the last bit of sauce on her plate with a piece of bread.

When she noticed me smiling, she blushed, suddenly self-conscious. "I know. My brothers tell me I can put away food like a linebacker."

"Don't stop. I like watching you eat." She cocked her head to the side, doubtful. "I can't stand it when girls act like they're not hungry and then starve themselves. It's weird…You're normal."

Kasia eyed me like I'd said the strangest thing, then shrugged and said, "I'm lucky. Apparently, I inherited my mother's metabolism. She's still slender after a lifetime of pierogis."

"Good to know."

In that moment, a vision of Kasia as a slim, hot older wife flashed in my head. I laughed to myself, shaking off the thought, knowing this girl was already having an effect on me.

"So, at the risk of hearing something terrible about myself, can I ask why you were so reluctant to go out with me?"

She looked uneasy for a second but then smiled. "I'm not usually drawn to the big man on campus type, that's all."

"Is that me? Is that my type?"

"Frat guy, lacrosse star," she looked up to meet my eyes, "someone who's rumored to have a different girl in his bed every weekend. That type."

"Ouch. I sound like a total dick."

She laughed. "Yeah, you do."

"So who is little Kah-zjah usually drawn to?"

"I don't know…Nice guys."

Walked right into that one, sweetheart.

"Like Ethan? You have to admit, that book wasn't well judged by its cover. Maybe you have me all wrong."

"You've got me there, Dylan."

Driving home, I gave myself a mental high five. I was making some serious progress with this girl. I considered reaching across the console to take her hand, but figured that wouldn't be a good idea. Better to play it smart, to leave her wanting. I couldn't help it, in business and in life I was always strategizing.

"Thank you for dinner, Dylan."

"You're welcome. I had fun."

She gave me a shy smile when we reached her door. "Yeah, me too."

The air felt like it was crackling between us in the ensuing silence. That would typically be the moment when I'd ease my way in, kiss her senseless and press into her until she was begging for it. But no, I was throwing out the playbook for this girl.

I smiled and turned, looking back over my shoulder to say, "I'll see you around."

Her eyes stayed on me as I got into my car and drove off.

Take that, sweet Kasia. I hope you're lying in bed as frustrated as I am tonight.

* * *

KASIA

"I heard you were out with Dylan last night," Valerie challenged as she came bounding in the door.

"If I knew that's all it would take for you to actually leave Cooper's bed and make your way home, I would have gone out with him the first time he asked me."

"Very funny. Seriously, what's going on? Did he actually take you out on a date?"

"Is that so unbelievable? Am I an ogre or something?"

She flopped onto my bed. "You know exactly what I mean. Dylan doesn't date. He just summons chicks, you know?"

"It wasn't a date. He kind of badgered me into hanging out with him and I gave in."

She looked to the ceiling. "Holy shit."

"What?"

"I don't know. I feel, like, afraid for you. I know what he did for you was really nice and everything, but there's something about him. He's dangerous."

"I think that icy, uppity vibe he gives off is just an act. I was with a genuinely nice person last night. He was thoughtful and funny." I paused and thought for a moment, thought back to something I remembered from last year. "I'm attracted to him, but you're right, there is something…"

"Just be careful."

"He dropped me off without so much as a kiss goodnight, so obviously he's not that into me."

I didn't believe the words as I spoke them. I knew he wanted me. I could feel it. And I wanted him too.

Val wasn't fooled either. "The fact that he *didn't* kiss you says so much more, don't you see? He's drawing you in like a spider to his web. Presenting this persona, making you see him as something he's not, leaving you wanting. I'm telling you to run, he's devious."

Maybe Val was right, but she was starting to irk me. And for some reason I was feeling oddly protective over Dylan.

"Come on, let's not over dramatize this. He's not some Svengali and I'm not a blind, mindless female, ok?"

"I didn't mean it that way."

"I know, but I can make my own decisions. I like him and I might go out with him again if he asks."

"All right, I'll keep my nose out of it. And I guess you could be right. I mean, maybe there's another side to Dylan Cole. Maybe you bring out a better side."

"After what happened with Ethan, don't worry, I'm going into everything with my eyes wide open. I'll be fine."

Trish and Bernadette trailed in then, one looking more hung-over than the other. Trish rubbed her head and moaned. "I need some greasy food, stat. Let's go to Burger Den."

Turkey club on toasted wheat bread. The same meal I ate practically every Saturday afternoon at this greasy dive. I had yet to sample a burger at the Burger Den and had no desire to do so. The turkey was oven roasted like you'd have at home, not deli meat, and they fried the bacon just right—not too crisp, not too soggy. Usually I relished every bite of my sandwich, but today I just couldn't focus enough to enjoy it.

I assumed Dylan went back to the party at his house after dropping me off, and Bernie and Trish had been there. I desperately wanted details but didn't want to seem overly eager in front of Val.

After half an hour without one mention of the party, though, I started fishing. "What were you girls drinking last night? You both look like you're in pain."

Bernadette grimaced. "I was sampling all sorts of cocktails last night and I think I also drank beer. That's never a good idea."

Valerie was also digging for intel, but no doubt she was just looking to prove to me that I was in over my head with Dylan. "So, anything crazy happen over there last night?"

"Standard frat party," Trish said on a yawn. She brightened when she teased, "Kasia, your smokin' hot knight in shining armor was asking about you."

I played dumb. "Huh?"

"Dylan Cole, remember? He was asking lots of questions, wanted to know all sorts of things about you."

"Like what?"

Trish cocked her head to the side. "Hmm...I don't remember exactly."

"God Trish, I hope you didn't tell him anything awful or embarrassing."

Eyes wide, she said, "I would never!"

"I know. Just forget it."

"I definitely think he likes you," Bernadette paused, lowering her voice, "but what's up with Melanie Pierce? I know she's Christian's girlfriend and all, but it's beyond weird. She hangs all over Dylan, and I mean she does it right in front of Christian. I get this weird feeling that they both, um…Like maybe they're sharing her?"

Valerie spoke around a mouthful of fries. "That's gross but I wouldn't put it past her. Definitely wouldn't put it past him."

Trish chirped, "Nope, he's definitely looking to get with Kasia."

I locked eyes with Valerie, annoyed and a little embarrassed. "That won't be happening."

As much as I didn't want to admit it, Val was right, with him I'd definitely be in over my head.

Sunday came and went, then Monday. I didn't hear from him and I was glad for it. I didn't want to play those flirty games anymore. I just wanted to focus on my designs, my classes, and life without Dylan Cole.

Nearly a full week had passed when a large hand gripped my shoulder, stopping me in my tracks. I turned to see an out of breath Dylan smiling down at me.

"Damn, you walk fast. I've been chasing after you since you left lower campus."

Nope, not getting sucked back in. "What's up, Dylan?"

"Um, same old thing, I guess. I did start practices this week so I've been busy with that. Hey, I was wondering if we could grab dinner again tomorrow night."

"Sorry, I've got plans with the girls tomorrow night. Can't make it."

He crossed his arms over his chest and cocked his head to the side as if he was studying me. "Are you mad at me for some reason?"

"No."

"Ok, then what's with the ice princess act?"

Crap. Figures he'd be the type to call me out. I really didn't know what to say so I stalled. "Excuse me?"

He shrugged. "You're blowing me off. I just want to know why."

"Look, I had a nice time with you last week. It's just that I don't see this going any further, ok?"

"No, not ok, but can you at least tell me why?"

"I'm not what you're used to. I'm not the kind of girl you want."

He gave me a knowing smile that was more mean spirited than friendly. "What kind of girl do I want? You must know, right, because you know me so well?"

"Your usual...Someone willing, a pretty plaything who's down with being used then tossed away."

His hand went to his side as if I'd struck him. And his pained expression had me wishing I could suck those bitchy words of mine right back in.

"Why would you say that?"

"I'm sorry, it's just that you may not have noticed me before this year, but I've noticed you." I motioned between us. "We don't fit together."

He stared down at the floor for maybe thirty seconds, then acted as if I wasn't standing right in front of him when he brushed past me and said, "Screw this."

I watched him walk away. He was taller than most, so his head was clearly visible as he strode the entire length of Spencer Hall. I saw him fist his hair with one hand, seemingly in frustration. As he made his way further down the corridor, his posture straightened, he raked his hand through his hair to straighten it, and then gave his head one vigorous shake.

He was shaking me off.

It's what I wanted, but it left me feeling hollowed-out and alone.

* * *

DYLAN

What exactly did Kasia see that made her so sure I wasn't worthy of her?

Who was I kidding, it could have been one of a million moments from my very sordid past. Hell, if she was my sister I'd make certain she never set foot within ten miles of a guy like me.

I'd live. Getting hung up on her was ridiculously stupid. She was beautiful, but so were more than a third of the girls on this campus. I told myself it was just the idea of wanting what I couldn't have. It would pass. No girl, not even someone as hot as Kasia, would be leading me around by my manhood.

After being denied in such a spectacular fashion, I was on a mission to start the weekend a-sap. I skipped my Thursday afternoon class and thought about smoking a bowl when I got back to the house, but decided that chilling out in solitude wasn't what the doctor ordered.

Coming in to find Matt, Justin, Christian and some under-classmen flopped on the couches, I announced, "I haven't been laid in three weeks. I know for some of you fucktards that's nothing, but for me it's a dry spell of epic proportions. Needs to be rectified." I looked at the two freshmen. "Clean the first floor and then you're in charge of booze. See Christian for the cash." Then I looked to Matt, Christian and Justin. "Start reaching out."

I knew within an hour that anyone worth knowing on campus would hear about our place tonight. I put in a call to my supplier, whose brother fronted a local indie band with a hot back-up singer. We were set.

By ten o'clock our place was packed, with the overflow spreading out into the front and backyards. Just what I needed. *Kasia who?* I surveyed the scene as I nursed a beer. More beautiful women here than any man could hope for, the sweet aroma of weed wafting through the house, and the band was cranking. I was pleased and it was time to join the fun.

Justin was lining up shots of whiskey and I knocked back two in quick succession. I could feel it taking effect immediately, oozing its way through my system all warm and comforting. I went back to my room and took out the stash that I rarely broke into. *Just one line*, I told myself. I wanted that extra buzz. Needed it to fake the energy and charisma required to lure in some girl other than Kasia. As I went to leave my room, I stopped and reconsidered, turned around and went back in for one more line.

I walked, or more like bounced down the stairs, stopping a few feet from the bottom to survey the scene again. I saw several sure things, but tonight I wanted to prove to myself that I could bag a challenge. Towards the make-shift stage I saw Isabelle, a dark haired beauty with a smoking body. She also just happened to be practically engaged to the star pitcher on our Division-one baseball team. Perfect. Even better that he was here with at least five of his buddies. The odds were against me, making it my favorite kind of challenge.

I'd been getting off on this type of thing since I was sixteen, hell bent on proving something to my father. It was really more like a pathetic, passive-aggressive way to get back at him. Didn't matter that he never found out about it—the fact that I could take something from right out under his nose was enough.

"Isabelle, what's up with that boyfriend of yours? Look at him over there sucking back shots with his boys. I'd never leave you unattended. Half the men at this party are thinking about what it would be like to run their hands over that fine ass of yours."

She drawled, "Jesus, I could come just listening to that mouth of yours."

I'm in.

I leaned in and whispered, "Meet me upstairs in five. No one will ever know."

She let out a laugh—no, a guffaw. "You aren't being serious, are you?" When she took in my expression, hers changed. Shit, she looked hurt. "Do you think I'm one of those stupid girls who go for your bullshit? Ohmigod, I actually thought we were cool, that you were a friend of mine. You're such an ass, Dylan. Get the hell away from me."

"I'm sorry, Isabelle. You're right, that was a shitty move."

She wasn't buying the apology and I wasn't in the mood to grovel. I turned to walk away and ran right into Val. She looked like she'd just hit the lottery, a toothy grin on her smug little face.

"That was priceless."

I nodded towards the stairs. "Are you hoping for an invite now that Isabelle's out of the picture?"

She flipped me the bird. "I'd rather contract herpes. Come to think of it, I most likely would contract an STD if I got with you."

"Who knew you were such a bitter little cunt, Val."

She rolled her eyes, nonplussed—the foulest word didn't even shock her. "Wow, Kasia really missed out, didn't she? Look at you, all tooted up. Even have a little stray glitter on your collar, you slob. You really think someone like her would go for a loser like you?"

I don't know if it was the combination of shots and drugs, but it didn't feel like I was talking to Val anymore. No, she was now my inner voice, castigating me. Why *would* Kasia be interested in me? I was rich...and smart, I guess. Feeling down on myself, I thought that's about all I had going for me. I *was* a loser. But arrogance had been coursing through my veins since birth, so it wasn't long before I was kicking that notion to the curb. Fuck that, I'm rich *and* I'm smart. Why would I want to be with *her*? Kasia was not even in the same stratosphere, social or economic, as the girls I normally associated with.

Val was still standing there staring me down, so I tapped the face on my watch. "Better run along. I hear Cooper likes to get laid every hour on the hour. You're running late."

I turned and meshed into the crowd before she could land a comeback.

I'm sure Val hated me, but I actually liked her. She had balls, she could take it and dish it out better than most guys I knew, and I liked that Kasia had friends like Val who looked out for her. It kind of sucked, though, that looking out for Kasia meant keeping her away from me.

The night wasn't turning out the way I'd planned, so I changed my strategy and settled for a sure thing.

And reality hit like a bitch when the sun streamed through my window the next morning, momentarily blinding my cocaine-addled, bloodshot eyes. Rolling over to escape the glare, I came face to face with the wide-eyed girl in my bed. She didn't look too thrilled, and I'm sure my look expressed something along the lines of: *What the fuck are you still doing here?*

Now that's true love.

"That was a crazy night." She grabbed her clothes from the floor, wiggled her jeans over her hips and then ducked completely under the sheets to wrangle her shirt back on. Shame-faced, she said, "Um, I've gotta get going. We can keep this just between us, right?"

I played the indifferent part well but was slightly insulted. She made it, what, three girls in the span of twenty-four hours who wanted nothing to do with me?

"I don't spill, Kristy. Brendan won't hear it from me."

"I *never* do that." *Sure you don't, honey.* She looked over her shoulder, smiling as she slipped back into her jacket. "But it *was* fun, Dylan."

She didn't pick up on the sarcasm when I rolled over, dismissing her. "Glad I could be of service."

Kasia called me on my bullshit, she all but annihilated me. And I was such a jackass, storming off all miffed and indignant, all *Who the hell does she think she is?* I'm above it all, the smartest guy in the room, right? Yeah, I'm so smart that I went right out there and proved her point.

The shots, the lines, Isabelle's horrified expression, Val's victory lap, waking up next to some other guy's woman in my bed—the images came together like my very own *This is Your Life* montage from hell.

Kasia was right.

I was nothing but an asshole with a superiority complex.

Chapter Two

KASIA

Fighting my attraction to him was useless.

All week I told myself I'd dodged a bullet, made a good call where Dylan was concerned. So why were my eyes searching, scanning every face, looking for him everywhere I went?

I found him in the library reading the Wall Street Journal, and had to clear my throat when he ignored my first attempt to say hello.

I flinched when he finally said, "What's up, Kasia?" without even taking his nose out of the paper. His posture, his tone—he wanted me to know my presence wasn't welcome, that I was tiresome and he was bored.

This was the Dylan Cole I always thought I knew, the one I observed from a distance, but this wasn't the person I got to know over dinner last week.

Struggling against the strong urge I had to walk away, I stood my ground and swallowed my pride. "I want to apologize about the other day. I have no right to judge you, and maybe my delivery wasn't the best. But I meant what I said...I don't think I'm right for you."

Dylan lowered the paper. "How so?"

"I'm really low key, like to the point of being boring. I wasn't joking that day in the coffee shop. I actually do spend long stretches of time just sewing."

He stood up, towering over me. His smile, genuine and kind, softened his features and sucked me right back in. "Then we'll just have to be friends, but not in that bullshit kind of way where we just say 'hi' as we pass each other on campus."

I played along. "What are you suggesting?"

"We'll hang out sometimes, have lunch, talk. It's been a long time since I've had a friend who's a girl."

"I'd say you have plenty of girlfriends, Dylan."

I was fishing, looking for some reassurance. God help me, but I wanted to be more than what every other girl had been to him.

"Nope, I have plenty of girls. Correction...I've *had* plenty of girls. It's entirely different."

I liked his emphasis on the past tense and his honesty. "Ok, friends."

"So I'll see you tomorrow?"

I backed up a step but then smiled. "Tomorrow? Easy tiger."

"I was just going to suggest we grab lunch. Wow, look at you assuming I want more than lunch. You have a dirty mind and a mighty high opinion of yourself."

He was a tease and I loved it. "I'll see you tomorrow."

"I'll pick you up at one?"

"Sure."

"See you then, Kasia."

* * *

DYLAN

Friends, my ass. I was biding my time.

I practically skipped over to her place that next day. My plan to have Kasia was back in play. And I was feeling confident until the door opened and I was face to face with my bitchy, albeit sexy nemesis.

Shit.

"Hello, Mr. Cole. Long time, no see."

"Oh, Valerie…You here to crucify me publicly?"

"Nope. Kasia's a big girl. She can make her own mistakes. I'm sure she'll look back on you as one of the biggest learning experiences of her life."

With that, Kasia came out of her room into the common area and Val said her goodbyes, extra chipper. I did my best to shake her off.

"So, is this where the Sweet Betty Threads magic happens?" Kasia looked surprised—no, alarmed. "I always do my research."

"You research your friends?"

"I always perform my due diligence."

"You're a freak."

"Please, everyone does it. And don't change the subject. I was surprised when I came across your website and I'm majorly impressed. Can I see some of your work?"

She shrugged. "Sure."

Her room looked like a very organized sort of chaos: fabric swatches pinned to a board, sketches taped to the wall, a table with a sewing machine that looked like it had been abused for years. The room was jam packed but tidy. I was drawn to some samples hanging on a garment rack, and as I took each individual piece in, I gotta say I was awestruck. *She made all of this with her own hands?*

"You're amazing, Kasia."

She was blushing. "Thanks."

Stupid, bossy and right back to business, I forged ahead. "I think you need a different logo."

She choked on the water she was sipping and then laughed. "Really now? Thanks, but I'm a sole proprietorship. Don't come in here with all these grand ideas and expect a cut, Dylan."

She was so damn cute. "Wouldn't dream of it. This is free advice."

She teased, "From the heir apparent of Cole Industries?"

"Hah, I knew you were stalking me!"

All wide eyed and embarrassed, she squeaked, "No!" Then Kasia laughed and admitted, "Well, maybe just a little."

She went to her desk and turned on the computer. When her website was up she asked, "What's wrong with the logo? And be careful, I designed it myself."

"No, it's good. It gives off that funky downtown vibe and all, but it doesn't express the vintage quality of your designs."

"How do you know so much about my designs?"

"I told you, I do my research. And I notice your clothes, a lot." When she blushed, I added, "Just friends. I notice your clothes only... I don't even *think* about what's underneath."

"You're terrible."

"Back to the logo? I was thinking with the black and white dress image you already have, you could write the company name in red, using a font that looks like stitching with a needle dangling at the end."

"I don't want to make this," she gestured around the room, "seem like more than it is. I'm hardly getting any orders."

"You will, and once it takes off you'll need to hook up with manufacturers. You can't keep custom making every order, Kasia."

"I like your confidence in me."

"I have nothing but confidence in you. With the logo, though? I know a really talented graphic artist. Can I have her do a mock-up?"

"Dylan, you don't have to do that."

"I know, but I want to. No pressure, though. I know this is your baby."

"I'm not at the point where I can start paying people yet."

"Oh, I wasn't angling for a salary," I teased. "And as for the graphic designer, she's already well compensated by Cole Industries, so don't worry about her. And before you say no, this job will probably take her all of twenty minutes, ok?"

She looked uneasy but smiled. "Ok. If you're sure it's no problem."

* * *

KASIA

"Wednesday lunch three weeks in a row? This is becoming like Wednesdays With Dylan...Maybe we should write a book."

"It should be a juicy erotica novel, but since we're just friends," he made a nauseated face, "this lame book will be made into a nice, chaste buddy flick."

"Ouch! You know I'm sensitive about being cast as the boring old seamstress."

He studied me for a moment before shaking his head. "You're definitely not boring. If you were, I wouldn't be following you around like a damn puppy."

I got up and took our trash to the bin. "I can't figure you out, Dylan."

Resting back onto the grass with one arm behind his head, he looked up at the clouds. "What is it about me?" When I didn't answer, he turned to me. "What is it that makes you scared of me?" Before I could say anything, he added, "And it's not that big man on campus, frat house, lacrosse guy crap you fed me." I didn't know what to say. "Please, I really want to know. I *need* to know."

I didn't want to get into it, but at the same time I wanted to hear his side of things. So I swallowed, took a deep breath and just put it out there.

"Sophomore year I was at a party at your place." Dylan pinched his eyes closed for a moment, bracing himself. "I saw you talking to some girl and her boyfriend. You gestured to one of your friends, almost like you'd concocted some plan together in advance to distract the guy. Then you were really pouring it on with the girl, and a few minutes later I saw you take her upstairs." I poked him gently. "It's not like I was standing in one spot watching your every move. I mean, all that happened within the span of a few minutes. But then I happened to be talking to someone near the staircase, and you caught my eye when you came back downstairs about twenty minutes later. The girl didn't look disheveled or anything, just a little flushed and... guilty. You looked smug. Maybe I'd gotten it all wrong, but it looked to me as if you took her upstairs and..." I waited for him to fill in the blanks but his eyes stayed fixed on the clouds. "Maybe I assumed incorrectly, but if you did, then...Well, it just seems sinister or, um, devious, you know?"

"It was."

"Why would you do that, Dylan?"

He laid his forearm over his eyes. "Can you handle the truth?"

"I don't know." I tousled his hair to lighten the mood. "But if I'm truly your friend then I want to be able to handle it."

By then I was lying down next to him on my side, my elbow propping me up. He rolled over onto his side and looked at me as if he was asking for understanding.

"The first time I did that I'd just turned sixteen." He laughed in response to my wide-eyed reaction. "Don't look so shocked, little Kah-zjah, or else I won't be able to tell you." He flopped down onto his back again. "I'm an only child...Crown Prince of Cole Industries, as you said. I grew up idolizing my father. He was like this uber-powerful, confident, but nice guy."

"Reminds me of someone I know."

He smiled at me and teased, "A compliment, Kasia? Don't hurt yourself."

"That's not fair. You know I think you're a good person."

"Sorry, I'm being a jerk. Anyway, I worshipped my dad. I loved going to his office and watching him take command in business meetings—decisive and fair but iron-fisted. I knew from a young age that everything I had—the luxury box seats at the stadiums, the first class travel, the homes, the staff that catered to our every need—it was all because of him. I respected him. And the way he treated my mother?" Dylan looked to me again but his expression was filled with sorrow. "He made it seem like she was his world. Sometimes I'd catch them dancing slow or kissing when they thought I was up in my room. At first I thought it was gross, but then when you're about thirteen or fourteen and you start to notice how distant and cold some of your friends' parents are, then you start to appreciate it. You know what I mean?"

I nodded. More than understanding him, I wanted Dylan to know I was here with him, for him.

"So I'm just turning fifteen, and my dad makes plans to take me to a Rangers game. I was supposed to be there at five, but I ditched my last two classes and caught an early train to the city from Connecticut. Get there about an hour or so before I'm expected. I breeze right by the first receptionist and head back to his office. My dad's personal secretary wasn't at her desk, though, and I'd typically wait to be let in. I'd met her once before. She was probably no more than twenty-two, just out of college. So I wait a few minutes and then I'm impatient."

I kept my eyes fixed on the blades of grass I was pulling from the earth one by one.

"So you know how this story goes, right?" He barely got the next words out, and I felt sick for him. "I felt like...It was..."

He covered his face with his forearm again, so I ran my fingers through his hair, wanting more than anything to soothe him.

"Hey."

He uncovered his face a few seconds later, brushing my hand away in the process. And just like that, his voice was steady and his mask of relaxed control was back in place.

"A year later, a new secretary, another one hired for the assets my father appreciates. But this time *I* had her bent over his desk. I mean...I couldn't confront him, couldn't hate him, couldn't walk away. Guess that was me staging my own little lame rebellion.

"And after that I became more aware. I watched and learned. Saw how he was with women, how smooth and phony. My hero was nothing but a cheating bastard. It was all a farce."

"What was a farce?"

"Happily ever after, love, my parents' marriage. And then I didn't really care. I looked at it as a game, a challenge—the riskier, the better."

"I don't think you really believe that."

He took a deep breath. "I don't." He rolled over onto his stomach and pushed himself up to a stand before he looked down and offered a hand to pull me up. "I shouldn't have told you all that." He looked at his phone and then turned away as he muttered something about having to get to class.

"Don't do that."

He raised his eyebrows and smirked. "Do what?"

I didn't know what to say or how to reach him. He was suddenly busy, texting back and forth with someone while patently ignoring me.

When I pushed his hand away from his phone, he stared me down. "I know what you think of me," he shook his head and shrugged, "and I don't blame you. We're from different worlds, mine decidedly more jaded."

I bumped his shoulder, trying and failing to lighten the mood. "You're wrong. I've been around jaded my entire life. I like jaded."

But Dylan was gone, lost in his own thoughts. He made the short trek back to my dorm alongside me, but his silence and rigid posture made it clear that he would rather have been anywhere else on earth at that moment. He broke the uncomfortable silence with, "See you later," before he turned and walked away without a backward glance.

His fraternity was known for throwing the biggest, most outrageous Halloween party, which was now only two days away. Guess an invite was not coming my way.

Bernadette, Trish and Valerie were all crammed into my room Thursday night picking through their costume shop purchases and requesting I make alterations. Val's zombie-angel outfit needed a tight bustier apparently, and Bernie's punk rock chick outfit needed some slashes cut into it to show more skin. Even Trish, the most prudent and modest member of our group, was wearing a roller derby costume with shorts that practically exposed her cheeks. What was it about Halloween that turned normal girls into Kardashian wannabes?

As Trish stood peering over her shoulder at her ass in the mirror, she whined, "Kasia, you *have* to come!"

"Yeah," Bernadette agreed as she flopped onto my bed. "You know he wants you there."

"He didn't mention the party, and anyway, I really don't want to go."

"You're going to stay home?" Valerie took my hand in hers. "Come with me and Cooper. I promise we won't leave your side. If it's not fun, I'll bail with you."

"No, you go with Cooper. I'm good."

I was so not good and they all knew it. After Bernadette and Trish left, Valerie set about painting her toenails as I finished shortening the hem on her flimsy white dress.

"I'm surprised you're pushing me to go. I know you don't think much of Dylan."

"I'm not going to say I fully endorse him because I never will, but it does seem like he cares about you. Anyway, who am I to judge? I'm certainly not perfect."

He cares about you.

Does he? When I first met him, I viewed every nice word and gesture as insincere—everything said and done in an effort to play me. Lately there have been times when he's let me in and I start to feel as if I truly know him, but then he can shut down and cut me off without warning. He was giving me whiplash.

"Val, something happened the other day. He told me some things that were really personal, and then it was like he regretted it immediately and backed away."

"He confided in you?" When I nodded, she whispered, "Wow." Given a moment to regroup, she had a plan. "Then I'd go to him. Show up and face it head on. What's the worst possible thing that could happen?"

I cringed as I thought of him pressed up against someone, kissing them. "He could be hooking-up with some random girl when I walk in the door."

She crossed the room and sat next to me on the bed. "That's the worst?"

I nodded.

"If that's what you see, and you very well might, then I guess you'll know to run like hell before you get in too deep."

* * *

DYLAN

The house was buzzing with activity. A few pledges were rolling up the area rugs, the couches were being pushed out against the walls, kegs were being iced in those big industrial garbage cans, and the older brothers were doing a good job of making the place into a quasi-haunted house. Every surface was draped in black, skeletons hung from the ceiling, and a fog machine completed the creepy vibe.

By ten o'clock there were more semi-naked people crammed into our house than on any other night of the year: sexy kittens, bad angels, naughty nuns. The guys were no better. We had a few tighty-whitey clad Stewies, one Adam wearing nothing but a fig leaf, a Baby New Year and several practically naked cavemen. I wasn't into it, but did throw on some board shorts and flip flops to create a lazy surfer dude costume.

I wasn't totally anti-social but I wasn't feeling the drunken scene. The sloppy guys spilling their beers irked me and I wanted to slap away some random girl's hand when she pawed at my chest, making a play for me. When Trish skated over I had my first genuine laugh of the night, as she practically broke her neck trying to come to a turning stop in front of me.

"Roller skates and drinking don't mix," she giggled as I held her up.

"No, I'd say they don't."

"Hey," she whined, clearly buzzed, "why didn't you invite Kasia?"

Because I can't face her.

I never should have spilled all that shit the other day. She played the role of understanding friend to a tee, but I knew deep down that she was disgusted. Add to that *this* frustrating little dilemma: I was pretty certain I was in love with Kasia and not altogether comfortable with the feeling.

I shrugged, acting like I didn't give a shit, when in reality I'd spent nearly every waking moment over the past month practically obsessing over her. "She knows she's invited...Everyone is."

"She's sitting home alone right now, probably moping," Trish said with an exaggerated frown.

With that, Brian came over and lifted Trish up into the air. Up and down, up and down, up and down he lifted her. *You're a dirty perv, my friend*. He was practically salivating at the sight of her goodies shaking in her tube top—have to admit I was admiring them myself.

Brian shouted above the din of the crowd, "Roller girl, you look hot!"

Trish slapped his chest and smiled as she squealed the most half-hearted protest, "Put me down, Brian!"

Three was becoming a crowd, and fuck it, I was being a jerk. I grabbed some cat ears off a girl by the front door—she didn't even notice—and walked out of the house. My plan was to go to Kasia and get her to come back here with me. I was, after all, supposed to be her friend.

I wasn't ten feet down the path when my eyes came upon a leggy blond in knee-high, spike-heeled black leather boots, tight black leather shorts, and a black top that looked like a second skin. What a body. Her hair fell in loose waves around her face and lip gloss was the only make-up she wore. She was always the perfect contrast between sin and innocence.

"Where are you going, Dylan?" Her voice was barely above a whisper.

"Kasia? I was...I was coming to get you." I could barely speak, my chest felt tight, and my eyes were bugging out at the sight of her. "You're here."

"I am," she said as she took one step closer.

"I didn't think you'd come."

She took another tentative step. "I wasn't going to come, but then I was sitting home alone, thinking about all of those girls, and I..."

"What?"

"I don't want you touching any of them."

Fuck, my mouth was so dry I could hardly get the words out. I practically stammered, "I wouldn't. I didn't. I don't want any of them."

She was a mere foot away from me when she breathed the words, "Who *do* you want, Dylan?"

Backing her against the side of a neighboring house, I practically growled, "I want you. You know I want you." I crushed my mouth to hers and she moaned when I pressed myself between her legs. "Fuck, I've never wanted anyone the way I want you."

She wrapped one leg around my waist, pulling me into her, and I grabbed her ass to press in even closer. We went on like that for a few minutes—kissing, grinding, fucking with our clothes on—before she lowered her head. "Dylan," she panted, "we should stop. I-I'm sorry. I shouldn't have—"

I let out a few ragged breaths resting my forehead against hers. "Don't say you're sorry." I kissed her gently as I lowered her leg. "I shouldn't be mauling you out here where anyone could see." I willed my member to behave, backing away from her a few inches, but still close enough to cradle her face in my hands. "I'm so glad you're here, Kasia. I've been feeling so messed up since Wednesday...Needing you."

She looked unsure when she said, "I think I need you too," and she smiled when I laughed.

"Come on." I took her hand and led her back inside. "I want to show you off *and* prove to you that I'm now well behaved at social events."

People were dancing, carrying on, and most were fairly drunk by then, but eyes were definitely on us as we came back into the house.

Trish squealed Kasia's name and waved us over. "Look at *you*! What a cute couple you two make!"

I laughed but Kasia cringed. "Trish, shut up."

"Brian, I'm going to get Kasia a drink. She's not out of your sight, you got me?"

He looked her up and down, taking in the outfit, knowing it wouldn't be more than two seconds before some guy would be looking to have at her. Brian nodded, dead serious. "No one comes near her."

Melanie stopped me with a firm hand to my chest when I entered the kitchen. She arched an eyebrow and smiled. "Who's the dominatrix? Christian and I could be into a little fun and games later on if you're interested."

"Never gonna happen, Melanie. She's not like that."

Fuck. There were times I wanted to erase entire years of my life and start over.

"That's a pity," Melanie said as she took my chin in her hand, forcing me to look at her. I shook her off.

Justin was next. "I just saw that girl, the one from the picture? She's here and she looks hawt!"

My hand tightened on the bottle. "She's with me, Justin. No one says a fucking word to her. Make sure that's understood."

He waggled his eyebrows. "Nice score, Cole."

"No score, moron, she's a friend of mine."

"Very interesting."

Bringing Kasia here no longer seemed like a good idea. I was relieved when I made my way back and saw Brian with the two girls practically caged in between his massive body and the stairs.

"Here you go," I said as I handed her a vodka cranberry. "I wasn't sure what you like to drink."

She smiled at me as if we shared a secret. "This is good."

With that, Trish's skates slid out in front of her and Brian caught her right before her ass hit the floor. She giggled, "I think I better skate on home."

Brian held her up around her waist. "You're not going anywhere alone dressed like that, sweetie. I'm taking you home."

There was definitely a love connection happening there, and Kasia was amused looking on at her friend and the boy who was obviously smitten with her.

As they made their way out I took Kasia's hand. "Can your

private security detail escort you upstairs?" I immediately held my hand up to explain. "I'm not looking for anything to happen. I just want to be with you and away from everyone else."

She nodded and followed me upstairs. The air was buzzing between us when I stopped outside my bedroom door. "I mean it, nothing is happening tonight. I'm not looking for that, all right?"

"Relax, Dylan," she said as we walked into the room. She took a seat on my bed and reached down to undo her boots. I watched as her delicate fingers slid the long zipper down her leg once and then again. She looked up at me with a shy smile. "I do feel a little ridiculous in this outfit, though. I don't know what I was thinking."

I sat on the floor at her feet and slid one boot off, tracing my fingers down her leg, and then went for the other. "You were thinking that I would notice you in this, as if I hadn't just spent the past six weeks lusting after you?"

Her eyes lit up with amusement. "*The* Dylan Cole, lusting after *me*?"

I was still on the floor at her feet. I tossed the boots aside and then leaned back and planted my palms on the floor behind me. "I lust after you in sweats and a t-shirt, so yeah, the boots and leather hot pants were entirely unnecessary."

She laughed, her smile reaching her eyes. "And they're uncomfortable."

My chin practically hit the floor when she stood up and started to shimmy out of the shorts. "Kasia, wait...I mean, don't." I rose up a little and put my hands on her thighs to ease her back onto the bed. "Are you doing this because you think I expect it? I don't."

"Maybe I'm doing this because I want to." She moved my hands away and stood before me, peeling the shorts down her legs and then wriggling a little as she struggled to free her breasts from the tight shirt. When she was down to nothing but lace, she sat back down on the bed. "Well?"

* * *

KASIA

He was the perfect physical specimen, all hard, lean planes. His hip bones peeked out from his low slung board shorts, and my breath quickened thinking about what was situated just a bit lower.

What was the matter with me? Here I was, teetering down the street dressed like a hooker, and now I was fantasizing about tasting him? The whole night was crazy and out of character for me.

Was I trying to be the kind of girl I thought Dylan wanted? Someone reckless and forward? Dylan definitely came to that conclusion, and as a result he tried to put the brakes on us several times.

When I sat myself on his bed practically naked, basically begging him to take me, he stood up, raked his hands over his face and then went to his closet and grabbed a shirt that he proceeded to pull over my head.

"What are you doing?"

"I'm stopping you from doing something you'll regret."

"I've had *half* of *one* drink, Dylan! I *know* what I'm doing!"

"No, I want to...I want it to be—"

I slid the shirt back up over my head, tossed it aside, then took my time as I unclasped and removed my bra. I wasn't playing fair. I was kneeling on the bed now, knees parted, telepathically willing him to come closer. "You're important to me, Dylan, and I trust you."

When I said those last three words, his demeanor changed. He was quiet for a moment and then smiled at me tenderly as he stood and slowly stripped down to his tight knit boxers. "You trust me?" he asked, and when I nodded, he moved towards the bed. "I trust you, too. I know you won't use me." I laughed as he acted the part of innocent damsel. "I know you won't brag about my giant cock to your friends. I know you won't just use me for sex."

His smile fell when he sat on the bed next to where I was kneeling. He cupped one breast in his hand, slowly passing his thumb back and forth over my nipple, lulling me into a state as he whispered words against my neck. "You're so beautiful. You know that, don't you? You're so, so beautiful." He laid open-mouth kisses and sucked at each breast, and it was like a tripwire connected directly to my thighs. I couldn't help it as my knees inched further apart. I wanted him. "Can I touch you?" I barely murmured my assent as he slid his fingers between the lace and worked me over. My head fell back and I gripped his shoulders hard. It wasn't going to be enough.

"Please, Dylan."

"I've got you."

I reached around him and pushed the little clothing he had on over his ass and down. "I've never wanted this so much. I need you."

He trailed kisses up my neck, torturing me, reaching that spot right behind my ear. "It's more than wanting you, Kasia...I'm in love with you." He stilled then, waiting for my reaction.

"You love me?"

Without meeting my eyes, he shrugged. "I do."

He gripped my hips and nuzzled into my neck again, avoiding me. "Dylan?"

"Please don't say anything. I don't want you to say it back." When I went to speak, he spoke over me before I could get any words out. "I'm begging you, don't say it...I don't need to hear it. I just need you to know how I feel."

I didn't say it back.

I couldn't.

I laid back on the bed with my thumbs hooked into the one scrap of lace still covering me. "Come here, Dylan."

He covered me with his body. So strong, so powerful, but more vulnerable in that moment than I felt. I wanted more than anything to comfort him, but he didn't want that. He wanted to show me how he felt because words were so much more difficult.

And it was better than good. The thrill I felt when his naked hips rutted against mine, when he filled me up, when he uttered dirty words of desire and made me come—it was better than I thought it could ever be. And when I woke the next morning, Dylan was stroking his fingers through my hair and looking down at me...like he loved me.

DYLAN

I don't hem and haw. Fuck it, I loved her and I wanted her to know. I knew it the day I spilled all that shit about my past and she didn't run away.

She looked so peaceful, and having her in my arms was the best feeling I'd had in years. I stayed in bed the next morning with her cradled against me, watching her. Every time she'd kick the sheet away from her body I'd pull it up and drape it back over her. It's not like I hadn't seen every square inch of her up close and personal last night—I had—but it didn't seem right to look at her body now while she was sleeping like an angel.

I barely heard Justin tap on the door before he poked his head inside and caught me gazing at Kasia. I shot him a murderous look as he stood there wide-eyed, laughing silently and pointing at me. I didn't give a fuck about him seeing the emotion on my face. No, Kasia was mine now, and I didn't want him getting so much as a glimpse of her bare shoulder peeking out from above the sheet.

"Hi," she whispered a little later as she rolled onto her back and looked up at me.

"Hello, beautiful."

"Dylan, last night was—" A tear was forming in the corner of her eye and she stole a breath when she said, "I just want you to know that I'm happy, ok?"

I let out the breath I'd been holding, sure that Kasia was getting ready to launch into a regret-filled speech. I squeezed her against me. "I'm happy, too. I'm really happy."

And from that day forward, Kasia was my girlfriend and I was all-in. This feeling of needing someone was entirely new and I'll admit, it scared me a little. I wanted her in my bed *every* night. The nights she insisted on staying at her place to get some work done, I'd give her space until I couldn't take it anymore. Then I'd steal over there late-night just to sink into bed behind her and pull her close.

Before Kasia, I'd never been with a girl I considered my equal. She was a self-starter and determined. She worked hard, so unlike the insipid country club princesses I was used to. Those girls made sucking up to me a full-time job in the hopes that one day, as my wife, they'd have the honor of running the social events calendar for the CEO of Cole Industries. So Kasia was a breath of fresh air. She had no interest in what she could gain from me. She saw herself as her own entity, with goals and ambitions separate from mine.

I found myself thinking ahead to next year, the two of us together in New York. Kasia would be getting her venture up off the ground with my help, and she would be supporting me as I made my mark on the family business.

Crazy, but I could already see our future.

$$\mathcal{C}hapter\ \mathcal{T}hree$$

DYLAN

Two weeks before Thanksgiving break the texts started to pour in. My Thanksgiving Eve parties have been legend since sophomore year of high school.

My parents and I, plus extended family, always spent Thanksgiving at our place on Martha's Vineyard. My parents went there a day or two before the holiday to prepare while I went back home to Connecticut, threw what had become our annual high school reunion party, and then made my way to the Vineyard early on Thanksgiving Day. My best friends from home, Tom Farrell and Ben Miller, helped me set up every year, and then I had a cleaning crew come in to restore the house back to its original condition afterwards.

Tom was bringing his girlfriend home with him this year and I wanted Kasia there, too. I knew it was going to be a hard sell. Her extended family was gigantic and they were tight. Apparently, days of preparation went into the Thanksgiving festivities.

"I shouldn't have done a group text. My phone is blowing up."

"How many people show up to your party?"

"Over a hundred."

"Aren't you afraid your house will get trashed?"

"My friends aren't animals, but I do take precautions. We put everything breakable away, roll up the rugs, cover the couches, and the upstairs is absolutely off-limits to everyone except a few of my closest friends. They can bring their hook-ups upstairs, just not to my room or my parents' room."

"Ewww!"

I laughed. "It can get pretty crazy." I pulled her over and up onto my lap in the library. Unable to keep my lips off her, I nuzzled into her neck and whispered, "Please, *please* come home with me. I want you to meet my friends, Kasia."

"My parents would freak. My mother cooks for a week leading up to Thanksgiving and I help her. I don't know how she'd react if I told her I wouldn't be home until Thanksgiving Day."

"Come on, baby, you're killing me. I'll have a driver take you down first thing that morning."

She hesitated and then looked at me directly. "It's also because my parents haven't met you yet, and until they do, they won't approve. I mean, they don't think I'm Mother Teresa, but staying over at your house? I know you probably think it's ridiculous but they're traditional."

I couldn't help but laugh. "So mama and papa need to know my *intentions* where you're concerned? Do I need to put a ring on it?" I regretted the words and my flip attitude immediately. I never wanted to cause Kasia pain, and right then she looked truly hurt. "Hey, I'm not making fun of them. I'm just selfish, that's all. I want you by my side. You're sure there's nothing you can say to convince them?"

"I would like to come...I just don't know."

The two of us all alone in my big house. Yeah, I wanted Kasia by my side at the party, but I also wanted her in my bed. And with her still sitting on my lap, my wood was obvious. She wiggled her hips just slightly, not in a way that anyone else would notice, and then murmured a satisfied sound in my ear. What passed between the two of us was for our eyes and ears only, and I loved that.

I whispered, "Do you even know what you do to me, Kasia?"

She whispered back, "Are you staying with me tonight?"

"How bad do you want it?"

"*So* bad."

"I'll satisfy that itch if you promise you'll at least talk to your parents about coming to the party."

She threw her head back, exasperated. "You win." Getting up to leave, she grabbed her bag and then leaned down to poke my chest. "And it's Mama and Tata, got it?"

* * *

KASIA

He didn't realize what he was asking of me. It wasn't just that I wouldn't be there for the pre-holiday festivities, it was so much more. Arriving late was tantamount to declaring that I no longer viewed spending time with the family as a priority. And it was also the whole idea of dating an outsider—it would shake them up. Patryk was practically family. And even if my parents hadn't known Patryk since he was a baby, he would have been familiar simply because of our shared heritage. Dylan, on the other hand, was about as foreign to my clan as could be. He wasn't one of us.

I would be in for it. Not just from my parents but from my brothers, too. I did want to go with Dylan, though. I wanted to see who he was at home, with his childhood friends. And I was just finding it harder and harder to be away from him. I was hooked. I'd complain to Dylan that he was keeping me from my work, kicking him out or going back to my room alone some nights, but I'd smile when I felt him crawl into bed late and hold me close on those nights.

Dylan needed me as much as I needed him. I loved him. There was no question about it.

One ring, two rings, three. I had a pit in my stomach waiting for one of them to pick up.

"Hello?"

"Hi, Tata."

"Oh, moja kochanie (my sweetheart). How is school this week?"

"It's good. My business project has been coming along and I have a friend who's been helping me change some things on my website. It looks better. Have Tomasz show you."

"I will. This friend, she knows more of computers than you? Hard to believe."

"My friend is a he, and yes, he's pretty smart, Tata."

"I see," he said. My father was now out of his comfort zone. He didn't talk boys with me. "Mama is here, Kasia. I'll see you next week."

"Hello, anielica (angel). I can't wait to see you! Michal is bringing home a girl for Thanksgiving dinner. Did you know about that?"

"No!" She and I were like two gossiping hens together. "Who is she?"

There was pride in her voice when she said, "Another attorney from his firm. Not one about to make junior partner like *him*, but obviously a smart young woman."

I couldn't help but giggle. My parents were so proud of us that it was borderline ridiculous.

"Do you know her name?" I asked, even though I knew that was probably my parents' first question for Michal. Translation: was she Polish?

"Sophia DeLuca."

"Pretty name, Sophia. I can't wait to meet her. I wonder what she looks like."

"Michal is handsome, so I'm sure she's not zywkly (plain)."

"Mama, you think your boys are perfect!"

"They are." She was back to business. "I'm starting my shopping tomorrow. What day are you home, Tuesday?"

Here we go.

"I wanted to ask you something. Remember I was telling you about that boy, Dylan?"

I'd hardly shared anything about him, which was very unlike me. I usually told my mother everything.

"The boy from Connecticut?"

"Yes. I've been dating him for two months." That was a half-truth. We'd been friends for over two months but it was less than one month that we were *officially* together. Two months just sounded better, I thought. "Anyway, he has a big party the night before Thanksgiving at his house, and he wants me to meet everyone. I would be home first thing Thursday morning, very early."

"He wants you to meet his parents?" She sounded intrigued.

Another lie. "Yes, Mama."

"I'm surprised you haven't spoken more about him. Is he special to you?"

I felt warm all over as I answered, "Yes, he's special."

She sounded a little wounded when she asked, "When will Tata and I meet him?"

"Soon, but not this week. His family leaves and goes to Martha's Vineyard on Thanksgiving Day. If it will be too hard on you with all the cooking, I won't go."

"Don't be silly. Agata and Natalina will be here to help me. I want you to go."

"Are you sure? Will Tata be ok with it?"

"I'll handle him. But we meet him soon, yes?"

"Yes, Mama. Kocham cie (I love you)."

I practically sprinted over to Dylan's place Sunday night once I got off the phone. I guess I wanted to go to his party even more than I'd let on to myself.

Walking into his frat house, I realized that I no longer felt uneasy.

I was with Dylan, and that granted me the respect and protection of every brother in the house. I still wondered which ones had seen me in the flesh, but no one here ever mentioned it or made me feel the slightest bit uncomfortable.

Trish was sitting next to Brian, his arm around her as they watched a movie, while Christian and Melanie were snuggling on the other couch. They were also watching the movie, but Melanie's hand was behind her, latched onto who knows what part of Christian's body. She was totally into public displays of, ahem, affection.

Melanie. Let's just say I was not a fan. She had this odd and unsettling habit of looking me up and down every time I was in her presence. Sometimes she'd zero in on something and then smirk in a way that told me that my hair, my outfit or my shoes were not up to snuff, and then there were other times when she smiled in a way that creeped me out.

She did a slow perusal from my feet up to my face, as usual, and then smiled. "Here to see lover boy?"

I didn't make much of an effort with her. "Is that what we're calling him nowadays?" I turned my attention to Trish and Brian. "Is he upstairs?"

Brian answered, "He's at the gym but he should be back soon. Stay and hang out."

Christian propped himself up on his elbow when I sat next to Trish. "So what's Thanksgiving like at the Mazur house?"

I liked Christian, despite the stories I'd heard. He was always warm and welcoming. I smiled when I answered, envisioning my small, crowded kitchen during the holidays. "Lots of people and *tons* of food. My mother makes the full turkey dinner in addition to every traditional Polish dish you can think of."

"Sounds nice."

"It is, Christian. What are your plans?" He was from California so it wasn't a given that he was heading home.

Melanie piped up possessively. "We'll be at Dylan's, of course, and then we're spending Thanksgiving at my family's country house in Katonah."

"You're going to Dylan's party?"

"We go *every* year. Katonah is like, twenty minutes from New Canaan. Dylan and I are practically neighbors."

She might as well have just added, "Duh." Guess I wasn't up on the driving distance between two of the most exclusive zip codes on the east coast—my bad. Was she trying to make me feel like an outsider? Absolutely, I determined after she said, "I'm sure this party will be interesting for you, Kasia." She lifted one hand to her mouth as if she was holding in a laugh. "You *are* coming, right?"

Christian shot her an annoyed look and then gave me a reassuring smile. "It's a good time. I hope you can go, Dylan's counting on it."

I regretted asking for my mother's permission. Being in my kitchen, peeling potatoes while gossiping with my mom and two aunts? I was now homesick for that. Even being teased unmercifully by my brothers seemed like fun compared to enduring a night with New Canaan's up and coming set.

Thanks to Melanie, I was now anticipating walking into a lion's den rather than a casual party. I envisioned Vineyard Vines clad boys, their hair all cut in that effortlessly stylish shag, sipping whiskey just like their rich daddies. I saw the girls decked out in Alexander McQueen and Chanel for, yes, a house party. I imagined girls hanging all over Dylan because let's face it, he'd probably shagged a high percentage of them. I imagined a sea of people who were wealthy beyond measure and condescending.

It would be like high school all over again.

It's not like I ever felt inferior to those people, but there was a clear line drawn in the sand. I was not one of them. I was by no means poor, although I'm sure that's how they saw me. My parents did arrive in this country penniless, after all. And while the privileged set would always look down on our kind, I felt immense pride in what my parents had achieved through sacrifice and hard work alone.

Even though they could now afford to splurge a little, they wouldn't. Hard work and moderation was our way. Self-indulgent decadence wasn't in our genes. It wouldn't matter if my family had several million in the bank—I was not dropping Benjamins at Prada like those girls did without a second thought.

Just when I'd had enough and was about to bail, Dylan walked in with Justin. Shorts and a sweat-soaked tee clinging to his body in November—the boy had an internal furnace. I smiled at the sight of him and then snuck a glance at Melanie. She was practically salivating and being obvious about it, too.

"What a nice surprise." With a smile that could light up the night sky, he held out his hand and gestured towards the stairs with his head. "Come on."

I pushed off the couch, barely able to contain my own goofy smile. He always looked so happy to see me and his good vibes were infectious. It almost made me forget entirely about Melanie until her sharp tongue drew me back in. "Dylan, is CeCe coming to the party?"

I don't think Christian intended for anyone else to hear, but I definitely heard him snap, "Now you're just being a bitch, Mel."

Dylan ignored her and took my hand as he led me upstairs. He was uneasy when he asked, "Do you know what that was about?"

"I think Melanie's trying to mess with my head."

He was quiet in response, and didn't say anything as he stripped out of his sweaty clothes. His body was perfection, but I was no longer in the mood for a romp. Melanie had soured the mood.

"I'll be right out," he said as he grabbed a towel and went to shower.

"Dylan, what's this party going to be like?"

His smile fell as he came out of the bathroom. He looked to the ceiling, let out a breath and then looked to me. "What did Melanie say?"

"Maybe she thinks she's doing me a favor. You know, her version of a public service." The added eye roll making it clear that I despised Melanie, but I'm sure Dylan already got that. "She was just making it crystal clear that you'll be in your element, while little old me, from the outer-borough slums of New York City, won't fit in." He smiled, knowing I was joking to a certain extent, but I couldn't even fake a smile in return. "Not that I care, Dylan, I don't. I just want to be sure that if I do bother to come, I won't be subjected to a bunch of stuck-up debutantes trying to seduce you in front of me."

"What's going on in that brain of yours, Kasia Mazur?" He shook his head as he whipped off his towel and bounced onto the bed hovering over me. "I *loathe* stuck-up debutantes. Kocham tylko ciebie."

He butchered the pronunciation, but hearing that he *loved only me*, well, it had me melting underneath him into his touch. "You speak Polish now?"

"I look up corny stuff to say sometimes. I like it when I hear you slip a word in here and there. It's sexy."

"Polish? French is sexy, Italian is sexy...Polish is not the most melodic language."

He laid soft kisses on me in between words as he got me out of my clothes. "When you speak Polish, Kasia, it sounds like a fucking string quartet with a choir of angels singing back-up."

An hour later, after distracting me in the best possible way, Dylan gave me a playful spank on my behind. "It's Sunday. We're leaving school Tuesday. Did you speak to them yet?"

"I'm coming home with you."

He turned me to face him. He never gave me a reason to doubt his feelings for me, and now, with a smile spanning the width of his face, I knew he really did want me there beside him. "You're not fucking with me, are you?"

"I said I'm coming!" I pushed at his chest. "I had to lie, Dylan, and I hate lying. I said I was meeting your family."

"So what? Good cover."

"It's more than that. My family…They expect me to bring you home, to get—"

"Their approval. I understand. Just wondering, do you think they *will* approve of me? The way you describe your dad, and Mike, Alex and Tom…They sound like this big brick wall looking to stand between us."

"No, it's not like that. Once they get to know you, they'll love you." As I said the words I didn't really believe them. "It's just that you're different from what they're used to."

"Different from Patryk?"

"Yes."

Just the fact that Dylan automatically referred to my brothers by their American monikers, not as Michal, Aleksander and Tomasz, separated him from my world.

I was trying to envision Dylan in my rowdy house on Thanksgiving. Everyone speaking Polish, calling out to one another over the noisy racket, kids running all over the place, the unusual foods, the red cheeks once the shots of vodka started up—okay, Dylan would be on board for that. But overall, I think he would feel more at home on Mars. And I didn't know how my family would react to Dylan. My parents were gracious, they would make him feel at home, but would they be put off by his obvious wealth?

I could already envision my father staring out at Dylan's brand new BMW parked at the curb, disgusted. He would be thinking it's a car for pretty boys who don't know how to put in a hard day's work. Granted, my brothers were made up of one lawyer, one investment banker and one very sought-after landscape architect. But although Alex, the landscaper, was the only one who actually made a living working with his hands, the other two were no strangers to manual labor. My father's investment properties were often in need of repair, and my brothers had been helping out since they were in grade school. Compare that to Dylan's upbringing—I doubt he'd ever been called upon to change his own light bulb.

I cringed imagining everything that would inevitably go wrong when I brought Dylan home. I shouldn't have bothered with this elaborate lie. Now there would be no getting out of it—Dylan would have to meet the Mazur clan, and soon.

"You're going to have to come at Christmas. It will be taken as an insult, as disrespectful if you don't."

He looked less than thrilled. "I'll be there." Then he pulled me to lay on top of him, smiling as he caressed my bum. "I'll do anything to be with you, Kasia."

Dylan and his friend Ben were running around getting everything ready. I walked the main street of New Canaan as they did most of the heavy lifting, my thoughts drifting back to last night. Dylan and I spent the night home alone together and it was heaven.

Perched on the edge of the hot tub in our underwear, we ate giant bowls of sugary cereal for dinner and we talked for hours.

When the moment felt right, I told him that I loved him. His contented look told me he'd been waiting for those words. He whispered, "I love you, too," before we curled up together and slept in his childhood bed.

When a woman who resembled my mother passed by on the sidewalk, I was snapped back to the present. I felt a little guilty. My brothers would be stopping by just about now, helping my mom here and there, moving tables for my dad, all of them congregating in the kitchen. I would be missed.

I popped into an upscale gourmet shop and got a jar of some fig preserve that my mom loved to spread on crackers with goat cheese. I also picked up some pretty linen napkins that were outrageously expensive but special. I inherited my fascination with fabrics, patterns and textures from her. Mother would appreciate them.

Making my way down the long driveway leading back to Dylan's house, I got a chance to take it all in again. It was a spread right out of

Town and Country. The house was enormous, considering only three people lived here, and the grounds were so beautifully land-scaped that I was tempted to snap a picture for Alex. The garage door even opened automatically, as it detected a recognized vehicle approaching. The inside of the garage revealed, in addition to the brand spanking new Land Rover I was driving, no less than three other shiny vehicles that would suit any need: sporty convertible, stately sedan, and a pick-up truck for those days the family was feeling outdoorsy. My brothers would gag at the shiny, pristine finish on the truck.

Dylan and Ben pulled up alongside me as I sat parked in the car, gawking. I lowered my window in response to his gesture and then he asked, "What are you doing, pretty girl?"

I shook my head. "Your house is huge. You could fit like, five of my houses into this one."

Ben cracked up. "I'm with you, Kasia. This is downright ostenta-tious…Flashy, dare I say." He was baiting Dylan with the uppity accent.

"Bite me," Dylan retorted.

I liked Ben. He was talkative, silly and he immediately felt like an old friend. And I was grateful to have at least one extra person to hang out with tonight.

"Come on, Kasia, time to get to work."

"Are you going to make me move furniture?"

He gave my ass a playful spank when I got out of the car. "No, we'll do all that. You're in charge of moving anything you think looks breakable. We'll lock those things in a room off to the side."

I thought I was getting off easy, but there had to be over a hundred fragile, pricey looking knick-knacks to remove before the room met with Dylan's approval.

Ben took off then and Dylan led me upstairs to get ready. He followed me into his en-suite bathroom and stripped down, his eyes fixed on me as I stepped into his shower. His shower, by the way, looked like something you'd find in a five-star resort, with multiple jets, a marble bench and a full glass enclosure. I smiled when he came up behind me and ran his hands over my breasts, down my hips and then pulled me in even closer. His voice was rough and gravelly. "Do you know how many times I've thought about this."

I teased, "Thought about me visiting you at home?"

He chuckled low. "Yeah, having you visit." He tilted his hips forward. "But I've imagined you right *here*...Your hands braced against the tiles, water dripping down your tight body as I fuck you hard from behind." He moved his hand between my legs. "You want that too, I can feel it."

I was wet and swollen with need just from his words. The oxygen I was breathing made my lungs tingle and my head swim. I moved my hands up and placed them against the shower wall as I pushed my bottom back towards him. I looked over my shoulder, barely able to keep my eyelids open. I was lost.

"That's it, Kasia." He kept fucking me with his fingers as he rubbed his length against the seam of my bottom. "Feel how hard you make me?" He rolled on a condom and eased into me slowly, gripping the fleshy curve of my hips with both hands and grinding into me. He moved his head close to mine. "I wish you could see this. I wish you could see how hot you are, how beautiful your ass looks bent over for me, see the way your tits bounce when I fuck you."

No man had ever spoken dirty to me, and I was surprised by how much it turned me on. I think I would have collapsed from heart failure if Patryk ever laid this act on me, but Dylan made me feel like a sexual, sensual being. He made me more sure of myself when it came to sex.

He was taking his time, rolling his hips with every thrust, pausing to run his hands over me. It was sweet and good and mind-blowing, but I needed it now. "Harder, Dylan. I'm almost there. C'mon, do it."

My words sent him over the edge. I had to brace myself as his fingers dug into my hips and he pounded into me over and over. A feeling was coming over me that shook my entire body. Dylan held me up as I gasped his name, and a moment later he was grunting a string of half-formed curses, his body twitching as he came down from the high.

His breathing was ragged as he held me close to him, his body still bent over mine. "Kasia, that..." He rested his chin on my shoulder. "You're wrecking me, baby. That was the best sex of my life."

I turned, wrapped my arms around his neck and kissed him deep before I agreed, "Me too." I laughed as I said, "I don't think I've ever said a word during sex. I felt embarrassed at first, but I kind of like it when you talk to me that way."

"Please don't ever stop. Hearing your voice drove me fucking wild." He then set about washing my hair and soaping every inch of my body. He turned me to face him again. "You are perfect for me in every way. Do you know that?"

I smiled back at him. "You don't know the whole me, Dylan. I'm a package deal and you haven't met the Mazurs yet."

He took my face in his hands. "Hey, I'm sorry. I know you're missing being at home right now."

"I'm ok."

"I'll make it up to you at Christmas, I promise."

I was looking forward to that and dreading it at the same time.

Dylan kept me close and held my hand for the first hour of the party. He must have introduced me to fifty different people but I didn't remember one single name.

Everyone was nice enough, but I did sort of feel like I was crashing a party full of long lost pals. I wasn't one to wallow, though, so I mingled as best I could. As the rooms filled to capacity—*Was his entire graduating class here?*—I gave up and plopped onto a sofa in the den nursing a beer. I didn't want to be a drag, but I wasn't having anything close to a good time. I'd already spoken to Christian twice while Melanie patently ignored me, and the last time I saw Ben he was sandwiched between two girls. I walked through the kitchen to see Dylan doing shots with a few guys and slipped past them.

Just when I started to wonder if anyone would notice if I snuck upstairs and went to sleep, I felt a tap on my shoulder.

"Kasia?"

"Oh my God...Darcy? What are you doing here?"

I'm sure I looked and sounded like a nomad who'd just found water in the middle of the dessert. She did too.

"I can't believe it's you! Tom, my boyfriend, is good friends with the guy throwing this party."

"Get out! Dylan talks about Tom all the time."

She nodded with a knowing smile. "So *you're* dating Dylan. Tom is absolutely dying to meet you. He can't believe Dylan has actually fallen for a girl. Also, Ben rode to the party with us tonight and said, I quote, 'Dylan is whipped and she...is...hot.'"

Darcy mixed up two vodka cranberries and we snuck back to the den where we sat and talked for nearly half an hour non-stop. Darcy was a good friend to me in high school. She was as wealthy as everyone else at our posh prep school but totally down to earth. Darcy was just one of those truly good people who liked you for who you were, not for your name or your net worth.

Dylan found us and sat on the arm of the couch next to me. "You doing all right, Kasia? I feel bad I'm not by your side."

"I'm fine, I don't need a babysitter. Anyway, I found a long-lost friend of my own. Darcy Donovan, this is my boyfriend, Dylan Cole."

"Nice to meet you, Darcy. Long-lost friend? From where?"

Darcy answered, "We went to high school together. Kasia was like the coolest, most talented girl I'd ever met."

"That's how I'd describe her," Dylan said as he leaned down and kissed my temple.

"And I feel like I already know you, Dylan. Tom seriously talks about you nonstop."

Dylan's eyes went wide. "Holy shit, you're *that* Darcy? This night's getting better and better. Where is he?"

"He went to get me a beer a long time ago and I lost him. It's packed in here. You must have been Joe Popular in high school."

"More like the only schmuck who'd let this many people into his house."

With that, a borderline distraught, mighty tasty looking guy wedged his way through a group of people with his hands full. "What the hell, Darcy...I've been looking all over for you!"

Darcy smiled. "You were worried about me?"

Then Dylan bounced up off the couch, hugged his friend, made introductions and we all fell into easy conversation. The boys went back to mingling then. I'm sure they were relieved that us girls had each other to talk to. Darcy and I moved to the kitchen, had a few more drinks and caught up on everything.

"You can't imagine how happy I am that you're here tonight, Darcy. You've crossed my mind so many times in the past couple of years."

"Same. And just think, maybe next year we'll all be in New York together. Wouldn't that be great?"

Melanie, the one person who was always sure to ruin my good mood, slithered over. "Who's your friend, Kasia?"

I'm sure if Darcy was plain, Melanie would have been content to keep ignoring me, but Darcy was close to otherworldly, always had been. She drew everyone's attention.

"Melanie, this is Darcy." I'm sure Darcy caught my tone because she didn't reciprocate Melanie's overly enthusiastic greeting.

"You're Tom's girlfriend, right? We all *adore* Tom. Half of the girls here probably want to kill you." She laughed. "The other half wants to kill Kasia."

Darcy rolled her eyes. "Never knew you New Canaan girls were such a violent bunch."

Melanie kept at it, trying to make a new friend. "Are you spending Thanksgiving with Tom's family?"

"Nope, heading home tomorrow and then Tom's spending the tail end of the weekend with my family."

"Nice," she chirped. "Is Dylan coming to your house over the break, Kasia?"

Melanie always hit the bulls-eye she was aiming for. I forced a smile. "No, not this time."

She cocked her head to the side, feigning a look that said: *I never would have said anything if I'd known.*

When she walked away after fawning a goodbye and—gag—a promise to meet up with Darcy the next time she was at Tom's, Darcy whispered, "Now *that* is a class-A bitch."

"You have no idea. She's like Brooke Carter and Samantha Paulson rolled into one." Darcy winced at the mention of the two nastiest, most stuck-up girls from our graduating class.

"Do you have to interact with her a lot?"

"She dates one of Dylan's frat brothers, so the answer is yes. Pretty sure she has a thing for Dylan, too. She creeps me out."

"I have one of those to deal with, too. It's not fun."

Before Tom and Darcy left, they convinced me to take the ride back to New York with them instead of the car Dylan had arranged for me. I hugged my friend, so thankful to have reconnected with her tonight, and I hugged Tom. I liked him immediately for the way he treated Darcy. It was obvious that he adored her.

Dylan didn't stir when the alarm blared or when I lifted his heavy limbs off me so I could get out of the bed. I bailed on the party and went upstairs when Darcy left at around two, but the party raged on until I heard the last stragglers slurring out their goodbyes after five. I even showered and blew my hair dry with the bathroom door open—nothing was waking Dylan. He smelled like a gin mill.

I poked him on the shoulder when I was dressed and ready. "Happy Thanksgiving, Dylan. I'm heading home."

"Mmkay," he mumbled.

Nice.

Coming down the stairs, I took in the mess of dirty glasses clustered on every surface and the beer pong table collapsed in a corner. My boots made a nasty, wet suction kind of sound against the sticky floor with each step I took. I was worried for Dylan's sake. I didn't see how his parents could be ok with this. I started to clear off the center island in the kitchen but barely made a dent when the horn sounded a minute later.

"Kasia, glad to see you survived!" Tom looked bright-eyed and sober, the polar opposite of Dylan at this very moment.

"I snuck upstairs as soon as you two left. But I feel bad leaving now. The house looks destroyed."

He caught my anxious expression in the rearview mirror. "Don't worry, he's got an entire crew showing up here by noon. He pays them an insane amount of money to work on the holiday. It won't look like there's been a party here by five o'clock tonight. Not that the Coles would mind, they condone the nonsense, but like I said, the house will be immaculate."

"So Kasia, what have your brothers been up to?"

"Really, Darcy?" Tom teased as he looked back to me. "Darcy was just telling me about your family. I think she used the word *strapping* to describe your three brothers."

Darcy giggled. "I was telling him about the first time I walked into your house and they were all there. I almost fainted."

"It's ok, Tom, I feel the same way about her brothers." We both burst out laughing then.

He was a good sport, driving me into Brooklyn. And I was grateful, but my discomfort grew with each mile that brought us closer to my house. I felt downright queasy when we pulled up and my dad, Michal and Tomasz were standing outside, the three of them about to unload folding chairs off my dad's flatbed. They would already be judging Dylan harshly when they saw that Darcy's boyfriend, not mine, had taken care to make sure I got home safely.

Darcy exchanged surprised hellos with everyone, while Tom shook hands and introduced himself to my dad and brothers before jumping right in to help them to unload the truck.

I wasn't surprised when a few comments were dropped that morning. Darcy's boyfriend seemed like a "solid, good man," according to my dad. Michal not so discreetly inquired about where Tom lived. And when told he was from Connecticut also, the ensuing silence spoke volumes. Yep, Tom lived in Connecticut but managed to escort his girlfriend home, whereas I was left on my own.

Was I reading too deep into everything? Possibly, but I knew my family's view on the world, on what was right and what was wrong. Maybe I was just feeling the sting because deep down, there was a part of me that viewed Dylan's attitude towards this entire weekend as less than honorable. I'd dropped several hints. If he was really serious about impressing my parents, which he should have been, he would have made an effort to get here sometime this weekend, as Tom was doing for Darcy. *Stop over-thinking this,* I scolded myself.

Alex spied me scowling as I set the table. "Are you ok, Sloneczko?" His pet name for me, Sunshine, usually made me smile, but I wasn't feeling it.

"I don't think any of you are going to approve of my boyfriend. Unless I'm with Patryk, no one will be satisfied," I snapped.

He put his hands up defensively. "Hold up, Kasia. What are you talking about?"

I shook my head. "I just feel like...Sometimes I feel like if I don't bring home a nice Polish boy, then Tata—all of you for that matter— won't be happy."

"Come on, that's bullshit. I've never brought home a Polish girl and neither has Tomasz. Michal's girlfriend is Italian. As long as the guy treats you like gold, which he better," his eyes turned from warning to reassuring, "that's all that matters to us. Where do you get your crazy ideas?"

"I'm sorry, Alex."

He rubbed my head, mussing my hair affectionately. "I'm sure I'll like him, Kasia."

My mother joined us and fussed over my beautiful new table linens. That finally lightened my mood.

Thanksgiving was one of my favorite holidays, second only to Christmas. My mother's two younger sisters, Agata and Natalina, came with their families, packing the house to capacity. Since there were several years between my mom and my aunts, they always seemed more like cool older sisters to me. Now they were in their early thirties, with young children of their own whom I absolutely adored.

My niece, Veronica, was standing behind me on a chair braiding my hair into knots, while her five-year-old sister Olivia was painting my nails a nice shade of army green. If her hands were steadier I would have thought it looked great in a nineties grunge kind of way, so I made a mental note to try that color out at my next mani-pedi. The door opened, letting in a blast of chilly air, and I turned to see my brother Michal holding a strikingly beautiful woman's hand. The expression on his face was something entirely new. He was in *love*. This was the real deal. I tried to get up but was being held hostage in my chair.

She laughed when I nearly toppled. "Stay! You must be Kasia. I'm Sophia. I'm so happy to finally meet you."

I immediately knew this girl was going to be my sister someday. Isn't that crazy? I smiled back at her and then scolded the girls. "Up, right now. Come on, let's go meet Sophia." I hugged Sophia when I got close and then the girls introduced themselves as she crouched down to their level.

"Olivia and Veronica? I've heard all about you two!"

She reached into her bag and pulled out two little beautifully wrapped boxes, one for each of them. They squealed with delight as they each unwrapped a set of sparkly hair clips.

"You've made some friends for life," I told her as we made our way into the kitchen with Michal leading the way. He laid the boxes of dessert on the counter, and the pride in his voice was freaking adorable when he said, "Mama, this is Sophia."

My mother wiped her hands on her apron and took Sophia into a warm hug. "It's so nice to meet you. Michal speaks so highly of you."

Sophia blushed and looked back at Michal, happy and relieved. After she met all the aunts, Michal took her into meet Tata, the uncles and the rest of the cousins. When she was out of earshot I said to my mother, "They're getting married, Mama, I can feel it."

She raised her eyebrows. "You think so?"

"He's totally into her and she seems really sweet."

"Yes, she's lovely."

The verdict was in, and everyone loved Sophia. Michal looked like the happiest man on earth, and that's all any of us really cared about. Maybe when my family saw how much I loved Dylan they would feel the same way about him.

Or maybe not.

* * *

DYLAN

I was in dire need of some aspirins and a Bloody Mary. My mouth felt like it was coated in cotton and my head was throbbing. It took me a minute to focus on the clock, and when I saw that it was already noon I forced myself out of bed. My dad had a private plane booked for me at the executive airport. I had to get a move on.

Someone was banging on the door. The cleaning crew—right, I'd forgotten. Stumbling downstairs, I took in the scene. They definitely had their work cut out for them.

Once I was sitting on the plane, drink in hand, my thoughts drifted to Kasia, specifically back to our X-rated shower. Mmm… loved that girl. I shot off a quick text:

Happy Thanksgiving. Was ride down ok? Miss u already.

Kasia wasn't the kind of girl who was glued to her phone, so I wasn't even expecting a response.

Thank God she met up with Darcy last night. Making the rounds with me early on, I noticed Kasia's forced smile, knew she was trying her best but not having a good time. She was a good sport, though, and she was confident—never made me feel as if she needed me by her side like a crutch. But when I spotted her on the couch laughing with Darcy, it was a relief to see her having fun. What a perfect coincidence that one of my good friends was dating a friend of Kasia's.

I always had fun reconnecting with my friends from home. A lot of liquor was consumed last night and we had a lot of laughs. But my mood darkened when I thought back to the mostly one-sided conversation I had with Melanie late-night, when just a few of us were left standing.

"Where's miss prim and proper?"

"Stop being a bitch, Melanie, it doesn't suit you."

"You really think this is going to last? She's not like us, and last I checked, vanilla is not your favorite flavor."

"Being with her is anything but vanilla."

"You keep telling yourself that, Dylan. Right now you're probably pushing her to go further, oh so slowly." She kept teasing, every word laced with sarcasm. "You're being gentle and encouraging, and it's exciting for sweet little Kasia." When I turned to leave, she gripped my wrist. "It's exciting for her *now*, but I can guarantee you that her hard line is nowhere near ours. She'll never be able to give you everything you need."

That last line played over and over in my head. I didn't know whether or not it was true. I didn't want it to be. I loved Kasia, loved her with everything I had. I wanted this to be different, I wanted it to last. For her, I wanted to be a better man.

Thanksgiving was a formal affair at the Cole residence. All of the men wore jackets and ties, and the women were Vineyard casual but elegant—they weren't getting messy in the kitchen after all. Even the children were expected to remain neat and spotless, dressed like miniature versions of their parents. My cousin, Anna, stood out like a sore thumb for that reason.

Coming up behind her, I lifted her off her feet and spun her around. She was a tiny thing. Today, for this special occasion, she was dressed in snug fatigue-printed cargo pants, an obscenely tight black crop top that exposed a healthy strip of midriff, and black lace-up combat boots. I smiled thinking that Kasia would like her style. Anna's newest additions were the five piercings snaking up one earlobe and the change in hair color to black.

"Next time purple, ok?"

"Purple what, you freak?" She laughed as I set her back down.

"Hair. Next experiment should be purple hair."

"Don't tease me 'cause I'll do it."

"You think you're scaring me, Anna?"

She smiled. "I'm glad you're finally here. Some of your parents' snooty pals are looking at me as if I might be plotting a terrorist attack."

"I'm surprised Margot didn't convince you to change into a nice Burberry ensemble."

She waved me off. "Your mom is so cool. She never gets on my case."

It was true. Margot Cole came off as an uppity bitch to a lot of people—I've watched her reduce grown men and women to specks with no more than a condescending glance—but Anna was the daughter she never had, and my mother loved her as much as she loved me. My Uncle Todd was an ass, as was his ex-wife, and they'd screwed up pretty much everything when it came to Anna. My mother's mission was to make it up to her in any way she could. And I liked watching my mom with Anna. She accepted Anna's deviation from the perfectly cultivated façade that just about everyone in our social circle strove to maintain.

"So, have you given any thought to next year?"

She rolled her eyes. "I'm going to college. I'm not a total anarchist."

"Mom wants you at an all-girls school."

She knew I was screwing with her. "Not happening. If she mentions it I'll act like the idea of a lesbian affair is appealing."

"You're going to give her a heart attack eventually."

"No I won't. Seriously, she's pleased. She knows I'm set on Boston."

"Good. It would have been great if you were there this year, then Tom and Ben would still be on campus to look out for you as a freshman."

"God, Dylan, you're such a douche. Why do you think I need someone looking out for me?"

"Every girl does."

"I *have* a boyfriend."

"Yeah? You're still with Jonathan? He's ok with all that?" I gestured to the piercings and hair. "He just seems a little, uh, conventional, you know?"

"He's ok with it, but between you and me, I'm going back to blond next week. I'm not feeling this anymore."

I wrapped my arm around her shoulder as I led her into the kitchen. "You're the same old Anna to me, no matter what."

"I love you, Dylan. I hope you know that."

"Love you too."

Dinner was no different than any other year, with family, a few of my parents' close friends, and as usual, two or three couples who joined us because they were business associates and maybe had no family nearby.

I had to do the rounds. Lots of hand shaking, back-slapping, bullshitting about lacrosse, my classes, my impending graduation and starting up at the firm come summer. Then on to my mother and the ladies, politely answering inane questions about school and whatever other nonsense they wanted to know.

Dad's younger sister Colette was my favorite aunt. I actually *talked* to her. When she asked what was new, she wasn't making idle small talk.

"What's new? Well, I have a serious girlfriend."

She looked stunned. "For real?"

"Her name is Kasia Mazur. She's a senior at UV with me. She's from New York."

"Kasia, that's a different name. I like it, sounds very, um, exotic."

Exotic is a synonym for peculiar or ghastly, in case you were wondering.

"Her parents are Polish."

"Oh."

She didn't say anything negative, she never would, but it was there, that barely perceptible nuance of judgment.

"What, you think Vince and Margot won't approve, won't think that's up to standards?"

"Don't be ridiculous, Dylan, we're not bigots."

I smirked. They were snobs, one and all. I was too, I guess, but I knew better now. "If anything, she's too good for me, Colette."

"Sounds like you're in love, nephew."

"Yep."

Crap, my mother heard the last two lines of that conversation and was on me like a vulture. Worse, she looked hurt. "In love, Dylan?"

"Mom, I've only been dating her for a month but it is kind of serious. Her name is Kasia. You're going to like her, she's great."

My mother composed herself quickly as the wives of my dad's two associates closed in. Thankfully, the conversation shifted back to the same monotonous crap as before—best island getaways, where everyone was summering, college admissions crap, blah, blah, blah.

I laughed to myself as Dina, one of the wives, lingered by me long after the others had moved into the main room. She acted as if she was *very* interested in my views on the benefits of majoring in finance over economics. Her kid was in kindergarten, so I knew the real reason she was asking me stupid questions and hanging on my every word. I was well acquainted with her type. Poor Dina went and married a filthy rich dude twenty or thirty years her senior so she could live on Park Avenue, but now—horrors!—he couldn't get it up and she wanted a young stud to scratch that itch. Two months ago I would have fixed her another martini, snuck her out back to the boathouse and fucked her senseless, but times have changed.

I politely ended our conversation. Not gonna lie and say that my eyes weren't glued to her hips and ass swaying back and forth as she crossed the room away from me. Yeah, I was watching. Shaking my head, I knew that despite being in love with Kasia, I was still somewhat tempted. That in the very least, I'd beat off to some fucked up fantasy later on tonight with Dina playing the starring role.

There were some messed up things about myself that I was reluctant to admit but knew to be true.

<h1 style="text-align:center">Chapter Four</h1>

KASIA

Finals were breathing down our necks and I was working nonstop on Sweet Betty Threads for my thesis class. I was presenting my final project next semester, but my grade for this marking period would be based on a business plan which required venture capital acquisition strategies, cost projections, manufacturing specifics and a complete marketing campaign. It was time-consuming work but it energized me. Dylan was great for bouncing ideas off of and I loved that about our relationship. There was a strong, *ahem*, physical attraction, but we had so much more than that.

Dylan was busy with classes and conditioning workouts. We might not see each other all day, but he stayed with me or I stayed with him just about every night. We were as close to one another as two people could be.

As the end of the semester drew closer, we hammered out our plans. Dylan was coming to my house Christmas Eve and leaving Christmas morning to spend the day with his family. He asked me to come to Palm Beach with his family for the New Year, but I declined.

Instead, I was going to meet his parents for dinner one night in the city before they all left for Florida. Dylan seemed excited about it, but the thought of meeting his parents made me uneasy and I'm not exactly sure why.

Dylan's finals were over a few days earlier than mine, but he waited around so that we could drive up together. We were in his car heading to Brooklyn by sunrise on Christmas Eve.

I squeezed his hand when we pulled up outside of my house. "Ready, Dylan?"

"Guess so, but I'm actually a little nervous. I used to be so sure of myself…You've ruined me."

"I love you and they'll love you."

My mother opened the door and hugged me tight before hugging Dylan. "It's so good to finally meet you."

I think my mother knew I was a little anxious so she fussed over Dylan, thanking him for the flowers and desserts he brought and making him feel at ease. I looked around, loving how everything looked at Christmas. I'm sure it was nothing like the grand, formal display at Dylan's, but this was home and I loved it here.

Tomasz and my father came in next, carrying wood for the fireplace. My dad hugged Dylan straight away, which probably freaked him out, and Tomasz and Dylan fell into conversation right away about sports. *So far, so good*.

By dinnertime my house was crammed with family. I was happy to see Sophia again and even happier to see the look on Michal's face every time he looked her way. Dylan made the rounds with me, effortlessly polite and well-mannered—that was in his blood—and my father nodded when he saw Dylan hold out a chair and help my elderly uncle into it.

"I think you've passed with flying colors. I saw my father give my mother the look behind your back."

"The look? They're gonna knock boots *now*, with a house full of guests?"

I slapped his back. "You jerk! The *we approve* look."

He pulled me into a nook under the stairs and held me with his hands resting on my lower back. "I like it here, Kasia." He pulled me closer and nipped my earlobe as he added, "I like the wodka also."

"The wódka, huh? I figured you would."

"Can I push my luck and see if your parents will let me abduct you tomorrow?"

"I don't know, Dylan."

Alex, a little tipsy himself, came upon us then. "No sneaking off under the stairs. My father likes you now but don't blow it."

Dylan laughed and led me back out to the living room. I loved watching him with my young nephews, and he was patient, feigning interest convincingly when Veronica prattled on and on about her first experience at a Broadway show. Later on, as the music got louder and the vodka was flowing, I saw Dylan talking to my father and then my father patting Dylan on the back before he walked back towards me.

"What was that about?"

"I asked if I could take you up to Connecticut tomorrow for Christmas dinner. I lied and told him my parents were leaving early and wouldn't be able to meet for dinner this week in the city as planned, and they really wanted to see you *again*. I'm smooth."

"Smooth and borderline drunk."

"No I'm not! C'mon, I want you to meet my family, too. And anyway," he crowed, "your dad already said yes."

We spent the next morning with my family, opening presents around the tree, sipping coffee and eating babka. I was fully at ease and so happy that Dylan had not only made it through last night, but now seemed like he was on his way to becoming a fully integrated member of the family. I loved my parents for their kindness, and appreciated the effort my brothers made to make Dylan feel at home.

My parents bought a gift for Dylan, and he looked downright

emotional as he unwrapped the cufflinks and my father said, "Those are for when you head out into the real world, Dylan."

He thanked them and then remembered that his gift for my parents was still in his trunk. He hopped up and went out to the car in his bare feet. When he came back in shivering, he had a few extra people with him. Dylan mouthed Patryk's name, his eyes asking me, *What the hell is he doing here?*

Cue the awkward introductions. Patryk's parents spoke English perfectly well but launched right into Polish, which I found rude. His mother greeted me politely but without the warmth and familiarity I was used to. I hugged his father, whom I adored, and then Patryk hugged me and kissed my cheek, lingering a beat too long, telling me I looked great in a low, husky voice. Oh my Lord, it was painful.

I pulled back and looked him in the eye. "My boyfriend is here, Patryk."

My mother called for me then, needing my help to make more coffee and to set out food for the guests. I felt terrible when I looked over to see Dylan sitting on the couch alone, just taking it all in.

When Patryk went to intercept me on my way back into the living room, I stopped him by shaking my head. I didn't want to rub anything in Patryk's face, he was a good person, but I also didn't want Dylan to feel uncomfortable. "Come," I said as I led him over. "Dylan, this is Patryk, and Patryk, I'd like you to meet Dylan."

I felt sick.

Dylan was probably wondering why an ex and his family would come over Christmas morning unannounced, but it really wasn't unusual to just pop in on one another around here. We were a tight-knit community.

Pat's mom had no doubt gotten word through the grapevine that I was bringing someone home and she wanted to see for herself. Or maybe it was Patryk who wanted to size up the boy who'd taken his place. At any rate, I wasn't feeling very sympathetic after half an hour of listening to Patryk speak only Polish to my parents and brothers. Tomasz was clueless, but at one point I saw Michal raise his eyebrows at Patryk and then made a point of responding to him in English. Alex also made a concerted effort to include Dylan in the conversation. When they showed no sign of clearing out, I told Dylan I was going upstairs to get showered and changed so that we could leave.

"Are you ok?"

"I'm fine, Kasia, insanely jealous but fine."

When I came downstairs with my overnight bag, I felt terribly guilty. Patryk was looking at me with nothing but loss and sadness. Dylan was getting dressed in one of my brothers' rooms, thankfully, so I had a minute to speak with him alone.

"You look beautiful."

"Patryk, I don't know what to say."

"When I heard you were bringing a guy home I just...I lost it. I knew if you were bringing someone here it was serious. But I need you to know that I still love you, still want you...I want a life with you."

"I care about you, but—"

He shook his head to stop me from saying the words. "Please don't...Don't make it worse."

Dylan came back in with his bag, but when he saw us talking he quickly grabbed my parents' present from under the tree and walked into the kitchen, leaving us alone again.

"Do you love him?"

"Yes."

He swallowed and nodded. Walking out the front door, he said, "Can you tell my parents that I'll meet them at the Baranskis?"

"I will."

Dylan and I said our goodbyes to everyone, and I finally let out the breath I'd been holding when I sank into his front seat. Dylan squeezed my hand. "That was rough, huh? Are you all right?"

"I just...I don't like to be the cause of anyone's pain."

"He still loves you, that's obvious."

"But I love you...And now he knows that."

We drove in silence for a few minutes before he spoke again. "I don't blame him. If I lost you I'd keep fighting to get you back, too."

As we got closer to Connecticut, this morning's Patryk drama faded from my mind as I mentally prepared for my first meeting with Dylan's parents. "Do you think I'm dressed all right?"

"You never ask for my opinion on your fashion choices, so you must be nervous or something. Please don't be. I love you, they'll love you, and you look gorgeous."

Pulling into the garage, Dylan looked to me, eyes wide. "I almost forgot about Anna. Listen, my cousin tends to be a bit out there with the phases she goes through. She's had a rough time the past couple of years and she can be a little...She's a nice kid, but God only knows what she'll be wearing, saying or doing today. Just want to warn you."

"Ok," I said, perplexed.

I looked down at my outfit as Dylan led us through the front door. I'd settled on a cashmere sweater dress with suede boots. I didn't add any of my typical funky touches for fear of looking uncultured in front of this crew.

His father greeted us. The resemblance to Dylan was so strong, it was like being given a preview of what Dylan would look like in thirty years. I knew some pretty crazy things about his dad, but I put it all out of my mind and found him to be kind, albeit somewhat formal. My first impression of his mother was the same. She was sizing me up, and asked a lot of questions about my family, my schooling and my future plans. I didn't mind, though. It was clear she adored her Dylan, so the twenty questions routine was fine.

The house was full of family by the time we arrived, and Dylan held my hand as he introduced me to every last relative. When I saw a fair-haired beauty coming down the stairs, my first thought was that I'd love to dress her. I was lost in that thought, envisioning the way I would tailor a dress to her petite frame and debating which shades would best compliment her coloring, so Dylan startled me when he called out to her, "Anna Banana, where you been hiding?"

Without thinking I blurted out, "That's Anna?"

This girl was the polar opposite of what Dylan had described. She was golden-haired, fresh-faced, and dressed like she just waltzed out of the Boden catalogue.

"Ha! I bet Dylan told you I'd have a nose piercing and a shaved head."

"No, not at all," I recovered, shaking my head. "I'm Kasia. It's nice to meet you."

"Anna. Nice to meet you, too. I like your boots."

"Thanks."

Dylan stood between us and hooked elbows as he led us into the dining room. "We have been summoned to dinner, ladies."

"If the seat next to my dad is open, *please*, you have to take it, Dylan."

He looked to me apologetically before he answered, "I will, don't worry."

Dylan did wind up sitting next to his uncle, so Anna and I took the two empty seats on either side of Mrs. Cole, who sat at one head of their ridiculously long table.

Anna and I hit it off well. I told her I'd been staring at her as she walked down the stairs because I had a vision of a dress I wanted to make for her. You could tell she was a fellow fashion lover, as she excitedly yelled to Dylan across the table that he had to take her down to New York this week so I could do a fitting. Over soup, salad, several small appetizer rounds that I learned a new word for, *amuse-bouche*, then dinner and desert, Anna told me about her boyfriend, her plans for college, and her decision to live with Dylan's parents until she finished high school. Anna was bubbly and talkative, but there was an obvious underlying sadness in her eyes.

Mrs. Cole reached over to take Anna's hand every so often. She was hard to figure out, and I couldn't get a read on what she thought of me, but the love and support she showed Anna made me like her on the spot.

* * *

DYLAN

She didn't get the Margot Cole seal of approval, not that I gave a flying fuck.

I was asked no less than five times by different members of my "not bigoted" family what kind of name Mazur was. If you weren't named Paine, Prescott, Astor or some other name that sounded like your relatives sailed over on the Mayflower, you were suspect. That's just how they were.

At one point I heard my uncle ask Kasia what her father did for a living. He was such an uncouth douchebag. And even though Kasia could have legitimately answered real estate investment, I think she purposely said, "He has a few small rowhouses in Brooklyn. He's the landlord," just to make them all squirm.

Uncle Todd, who wouldn't have a pot to piss in without my father, was legit stunned. "You mean he collects the rent?"

"Yes," Kasia chirped. "Collects the rent, fixes leaky faucets, paints, makes sure the trash is out for collection every week."

Kasia was being a wiseass, throwing the garbageman bit in for shock value, and I nearly laughed out loud when I saw my mother's eyebrows lift, fighting against the fillers that paralyzed her facial muscles.

Try as she might to come off as democratic, my mother was Old Money, a snob since the moment she took her first breath. Old Money barely tolerated New Money, and Old Money flat out disdained No Money.

My parents came from similar families and had known each other for most of their lives. They were almost pre-destined to be together, as if my grandparents had conspired to marry them off. Margot and Vince weren't that obvious, but I knew my mother had a few front runners in mind for me, girls chosen carefully from within our social set.

When Kasia was off speaking to Anna and my Aunt Colette, my mother sidled up to me. "She's very beautiful, Dylan."

"She is, and she's a good person, Mom. She's smart and very talented. She already has her own business up and running."

The fact that I was ticking off Kasia's good qualities one by one, practically begging for my mother's approval—it ate at me. Why the fuck was I bothering?

"You're young, Dylan."

"What's that supposed to mean?"

"Nothing…Just that feelings ebb and flow at your age."

"If she was Cecilia Tate would you be feeding me this line of crap?"

"Dylan, I won't have you speaking to me this way!" Her voice smoothed, suddenly laced with concern. "I just know from experience…When people are from different worlds it can be hard to make it last."

"God, do you realize how ridiculous you sound? You're acting like I brought home a mail-order bride who doesn't speak a word of English."

I felt like reminding her that her *perfect* marriage to her blue-blooded man wasn't so perfect after all. And was *making it last* so great when your husband was banging a string of girls half your age? But I wisely kept my mouth shut on that topic.

"I'm sorry, Dylan. I didn't mean to upset you."

"I don't want to upset you either, but I think you should be a little more open-minded. That girl," I gestured towards where Kasia was standing, "is worth ten times more than any of the coked-up debutantes you want to push on me."

"Is it really necessary to be so crude?"

When I didn't answer, she tried again to placate me. The last thing my mother wanted was a scene. Margot Cole needed everything to appear as if it was *just fabulous* all the time.

"You seem to think she's wonderful, so given the chance to get to know her, I'm sure your father and I will come to feel the same way about her."

I knocked my drink back in one gulp. "Mother, your opinion means less than zero."

* * *

KASIA

I was happy to be back in New York the next day with Dylan. Christmas dinner was very nice and I was pretty sure I'd made a good impression on his family, but I don't suppose you could ever feel one hundred percent at ease in that "meet the parents" situation.

We spent the day doing errands in the city. He followed me around like a trooper for hours as I drifted in and out of stores on 38th and 39th Streets, where entire shops were dedicated to selling trims, buttons, beads, zippers, lace and thread. This was my Mecca.

As we walked uptown, Dylan insisted on stopping at a box office and picking up tickets for me to take Veronica and Olivia to one of the new over the top Disney-inspired Broadway shows over the break. I thought it was too extravagant but he insisted. I called Natalina to check with her first, and then I made sure to tell the girls that this was a present from Dylan. They squealed so loudly into the phone I thought Dylan might have burst an eardrum, and then Veronica told him she loved him. They were easy to please.

Walking through the city holding Dylan's hand, I couldn't help but imagine what our future might be like. "You know, we could do this all the time next year."

He teased, "You mean I can follow you around the Garment District and carry your bags? You're too good to me, Kasia." He laughed when I hit his chest, but then he stopped, grabbed my hand and held it over his heart. "I was actually just thinking the same thing. Next year we'll be here together. Our life starts together."

We ended the day having dinner with Darcy. Tom was away with his family and Darcy was leaving with hers in a few days. Dylan would be leaving tomorrow, too. When Darcy asked who else was going, he answered, "My cousin Anna is coming along, but you know how Palm Beach is, you can't walk a block without tripping over someone you know."

Darcy shrugged. "My family doesn't vacation there but half of our high school did, right Kasia?"

"Did they?"

"Sure. The Paulsons practically own half of Worth Avenue. The Yearlings, the Baxters...They all spend their holidays there."

"Samantha Paulson? You went to school with Samantha Paulson?"

"You know her, Dylan?"

I felt a tension headache coming on at mere mention of her name. She was haughty, conceited and borderline mean. Over the years, she'd thrown more than a few condescending remarks my way.

"Yeah, love her, she's a great girl. I've known her since we were little kids."

Darcy practically spat out her wine. "We cannot be referring to the same girl."

Dylan looked a little wounded on Samantha's behalf. "What? Our mothers are close friends. You two don't like her?"

I kept quiet but Darcy felt no such need. "Samantha was, by *far*, the meanest, most stuck-up girl in our school. I cannot believe you just used the words 'great girl' to describe her. Razor-toothed piranha is more like it. Am I right, Kasia?"

"Yeah, she wasn't particularly kind back then."

Dylan still looked doubtful. "Wow, I'm surprised."

Darcy was definitely feeling her wine. "I can't wait until *Samantha* hears who you're dating, Dylan. She'll be burning mad. Back when we were at Prep, there was this guy she used to chase after like a bloodhound. It was embarrassing. She'd throw herself at him but he wanted nothing to do with her. *He* only had eyes for Kasia. Half the boys in school had eyes for Kasia," she added, laughing.

"That's *so* not true, Darcy!"

She waved me off. "Samantha was always envious of you."

Thankfully the conversation drifted into other terrain, but I now had a pit in my stomach. Those were the kind of people Dylan's family socialized with? Spent their summers and holidays with? Those were the kind of people they enjoyed, that Dylan thought were *great*? I was so glad I'd turned down that invite to Palm Beach.

I was missing Dylan over the rest of the break, but I was busy with family and work. I babysat for Agata's little boys and I had Veronica and Olivia with me nearly every other day.

I let them call Dylan to thank him after the matinee let out, stopping them after ten minutes of constant chatter during which I'm sure he didn't get a word in edgewise. And when I finally got on the phone, he sounded beat tired.

"You sound like you're wiped out."

"Yeah, partying is like an Olympic sport down here. Every night there's something. I just woke up."

"Really?" I checked my watch. "It's five o'clock, as in five o'clock in the evening."

"Is it? Ugh, I have to get ready for dinner. There's like some young society fundraising event for the Fresh Air Fund tonight."

"Oh, the burden of being young, fabulous and absurdly wealthy in Palm Beach."

I said it as a joke, but I was more than a little nauseated. It wasn't hard to envision that scene. In my mind, boys in tuxedos and girls like Samantha Paulson in evening attire were living it up, happy to be back in one another's company. No more slumming it among the general population of college co-eds they were forced to intermingle with on a daily basis. The lowly service staff walked about with hor d'oeuvres on silver trays, while the guys sipped aged whiskey and the girls knocked back flutes of champagne. Ok, maybe I was being slightly ridiculous, but there was one overriding truth that hurt me soul deep: I would be a fish out of water in that world—in Dylan's world.

"Don't be mean, Kasia. You're supposed to be here suffering through this with me."

"Doesn't sound like you're suffering."

It was a struggle to hear him over the din in the noisy Theater District restaurant to begin with, and then Olivia went and spilled her Shirley Temple and began to wail.

"It's all right, Olivia. I've gotta go."

I did have to tend to Olivia, but hanging up on Dylan felt better than good.

* * *

DYLAN

I had a headache again, and the last thing I wanted to do was to get into it with Kasia.

She sounded hurt and pissy, and that damn near killed me.

If you knew what was going on down here you'd be a whole lot more than hurt, baby. You'd be kicking my sorry ass to the curb.

I'd fallen right back into the scene here, surrounded by my oldest friends and having fun. Every night there was a dinner, a fundraiser or a casual get-together at someone's place. It was like summer camp with lots of booze and cocaine.

I'd been here a week, and although I did miss Kasia, thinking of her made me feel guilty and that was a drag.

God, she would absolutely hate it here. She wouldn't feel comfortable with this crowd, with *my* people, and deep down it bothered me. Melanie dropped a few remarks to that effect, driving the point home whenever she got the chance.

Yes, the Pierce clan was here, and their estate was the site of more than one casual get-together for the younger generation. Melanie's parties were the most decadent. Christian was back in California, not that it mattered. He fully condoned her shenanigans and I'm sure he was having his own fun on the West Coast.

The night before I woke up to Kasia's evening phone call, I'd been at Melanie's. She always threw pool parties because she liked the environment to be as clothes-free as possible, and that night was no exception.

The second I sat down, she plopped herself onto my lap wearing a skimpy bikini bottom and purred, "Are you enjoying the holiday, Dylan?"

"Yeah, it's good to see everyone."

She wrapped her arms around my neck. "I know. It's so good to get away from everyone on campus sometimes, isn't it? And Dylan," she moved in closer, purposely pressing her tits into my face as she lowered her voice, "what happens here stays here, you know?"

"I've got to get up," I said, patting her hip. I looked around. "Anyone need a drink?"

When about six people answered me, a girl I vaguely knew volunteered to help me. I was just glad to get away from Melanie. I made a mental note to steer clear of her for the rest of the night.

By three in the morning I should have had the sense to leave, but that's not how these things usually play out.

Melanie always had a stash of blow on hand, and my friend James convinced me to do a line with him. He didn't have to twist my arm.

Just about every party guest was full of energy thanks to Mel's vast supply of pharmaceuticals.

She texted me soon after, asking me to come upstairs—some bullshit about needing my help with an emergency. I answered back something like, *not tonight*, and she wrote back that she was absolutely not interested in *that*. Believe me, I knew better, but I went upstairs anyway.

I could hear her from the end of the hallway. "Say my name when you do that." I followed the voices when I heard some guy grunting out Melanie's name. What was she up to? I opened the door and crept in. Her suite was set up so that you could stand in one part of the room and look into where the bed was while staying relatively out of sight.

Melanie was in bed with Tripp, boyfriend of her good childhood friend, Delia. Melanie shot me a smile that he couldn't see. She wanted me to watch and I can't say that I even gave it a second thought. I leaned against the wall, mesmerized as Melanie ordered Tripp around, giving him step-by-step detailed instructions on what to do to her. I won't get into all the details, but Melanie had a sick body, she could dirty talk like a pro, and she put on one of the best quality porn productions imaginable.

About ten minutes in, I felt a naked body behind mine, her hands reaching around and down to stroke me, undoing my board shorts in the process. I didn't even turn around to see who it was. I knew it was Cecilia.

Walking away was not even remotely possible at that point. I was too turned on from watching Melanie and I was high. I *had* to get off. I turned around and picked Cecilia up, and she had her legs wrapped tight around my waist a moment later. I nearly slapped her hand away, insulted when she went to roll a condom down my length. *A condom, are you fucking kidding me?* But thank the Lord at least *she* had some sense because two seconds later I had Cecilia up against the wall, fucking her rough and fast, just the way she liked it.

And that was that.

I woke up in bed with Cecilia on one side of me and Melanie on the other. I was a little fuzzy on the details but knew things had gotten a little wild. There were more lines, Tripp did Cecilia, I did Melanie, I did Cecilia again while she and Melanie were getting it on. I think that's when Tripp took off.

At around noon, I peeled myself out of bed. The girls were still comatose. I put my shorts back on and took a dive in the pool. My head was aching as I drove back to our place.

No one so much as blinked when I walked back into our house reeking of booze and looking all sorts of disheveled. Mother was just happy I was having fun. Happier still, probably, that I was having fun with *our kind*.

I felt like a dirty fucking dog. It's not like Kasia would ever find out. As much of a bitch as Melanie could be, I knew she'd never tell Kasia what happened. Melanie, Christian and I had an honor code of sorts between us that went unspoken. The entire situation, though, was fucked up and I was disgusted with myself.

How do I go back to being the loving, devoted boyfriend now?

* * *

KASIA

Seeing someone's bedroom for the first time, a person you know well, is a trippy experience.

Maybe I'm just using the word trippy because it was Valerie's bedroom.

Their home reminded me of that part of downtown New York where the brownstones have a federal feel and the cobblestones still haven't been paved over. Stately and historic are words that come to mind. The interiors were upscale, pristine and traditional as well.

That's why stepping over the threshold into Val's room was like entering an alternate universe.

First you're assaulted by a giant poster of The Exorcist. *It was filmed right down the block, I have to pay homage!* Then there's a giant print of a blindingly beautiful sunset by Edvard Munch. *The Scream is just so obvious, you know?* No, I didn't even know who the artist was until you told me. *Munch has so many great works, and his name just makes me laugh.* Yep, I could venture a good guess as to what Val associated with the name Munch. Each wall was painted a different color, and books were stacked and displayed on every surface. I picked up one with an especially creepy cover, then saw that most of her books were of the *It*, *Carrie* and *Pet Cemetery* variety. *Stephen King is God.* Who knew?

I love people who march to the beat of their own drummer, and that was Val in a nutshell.

She reached into her nightstand and took a half-smoked joint out of an antique silver box.

"Your parents won't mind?"

She shook her head as she took her first drag. Pausing to hold it in, Val offered me a toke and smiled when I waved her off. She laid back on her pillows as she exhaled the smoke, then licked two fingertips and pinched it off before closing it back away in her drawer.

Gesturing towards her door, she said, "Those two light up morning, noon and night."

Her father was high up in the diplomatic corps, so that was, ah, interesting.

"I hope you had a better experience with Dylan's parents than I did with Cooper's. Cooper's mother is definitely not a fan of mine."

"Did you smoke in *their* house?"

"No, I was weed-free! Wait, I shared one joint with Coop at the top of the slopes one afternoon but that was it. And his parents weren't around at the time. And I had to sleep in a room on the main floor, so I had virtually no access to Coop the entire shitty week."

"So what was with his mother?"

"I don't know. Maybe it's a 'no one's good enough for my baby boy thing' or something. I'd like to say I don't care but it's really bothering me. I like Cooper, a lot."

"Maybe you read her wrong?"

"It's possible, but my gut tells me no." She flashed me a wicked smile. "I should get pregnant. Serve that bitch right. She'd be stuck with me forever!"

We cracked up at the thought of it.

"How was Meet the Coles? I have to say, I was happily surprised when you sent me that text Christmas morning. I'm still not one hundred percent in his corner, but I have to admit that Dylan seems to be mucho, mucho into you."

I rolled my eyes at her half-hearted words of support. "Dylan's parents seem nice. I really didn't spend a whole lot of quality time with them. When Dylan was at my house it was more...intimate. He spent a lot of time talking to my parents and my brothers. At his house there was family and business associates and...I don't know...It was way more formal. I didn't give it much thought before now, but honestly, I couldn't tell you what his mother or father thought of me."

"Do you know what Cooper's mom gave me for Christmas? A set of bath soaps. Like old-fashioned ones that smell like lily of the valley mixed with an old lady's vagina."

"Val!"

"She totally re-gifted them, I know it. To think I spent a fucking hour looking for those gorgeous cashmere scarves for Mr. and Mrs. Stanton."

"My parents gave Dylan a set of engraved cufflinks. I was so embarrassed. I mean, who the hell even wears cufflinks anymore? But Dylan seemed really touched by the gesture."

"Your parents are so great, Kasia. Maybe I should just marry Tomasz instead."

"I would *love* to have you for a sister-in-law."

"Yeah, right." She flipped me the bird. "I'd corrupt your brother and you know it. So, what did Dylan's parents get you?"

"Nothing." It didn't even strike me as odd until Val asked. In response to her surprised look, I waved it off like it was no big deal. "To be fair, they weren't expecting me on Christmas Day. We originally planned to meet for dinner in the city one night later in the week."

"So his mother *was* under the impression that she would be seeing you at some point during that week?"

"Yes, but maybe she was planning on shopping for me after Christmas."

"Totally." Val nodded her head, laughing. "Mrs. Cole *needs* that day after Christmas discount, right?"

I laughed with her when I said, "Maybe she doesn't like me, Val," but deep down, the realization stung.

Bernadette and Trish both flew into D.C. the next day. We went to dinner with Val's parents and then stayed up late into the night catching up with one another. I told the girls about the awkward meeting between Dylan, Patryk and his parents. They knew Pat, and they all felt heartbroken for him. I was still having a hard time shaking it off. A few times over break I contemplated calling him, but after talking it over with my mother and Alex, I decided not to. Keeping up the relationship in any way would just make it harder for Patryk in the long run.

Trish was itching to head straight to the frat house to see Brian when we got back to campus, but not me.

I couldn't put my finger on it. I spoke to Dylan every day, he said the sweetest things to me and told me he loved me, but something had shifted.

He flew back to school from Florida, so it had been more than two weeks since we'd been face to face. Absence makes the heart grow fonder? Not quite. Something was most definitely off.

He texted while I was unpacking:

Where r u? Thought u'd come over w/Trish
Nope, I'm not coming to you.
Unpacking. Need to get some things done here.
He wrote right back:
Can I come over?
I was still feeling bitchy and distant, but answered:
Sure.

"Hi, baby." He nestled into my hair when he pulled me in for a hug. "I missed you so much. I should have flown back earlier. That last week dragged."

"I missed you, too."

He set me back down and rested his hands on my shoulders. "Is something wrong?"

I wasn't good at faking. I felt stiff and incapable of smiling. "I don't know, is there? Everything feels different."

"Whoa, where is this coming from?"

I still couldn't look at him for some reason. "I don't know. Maybe it's nothing, maybe it's just me."

"Did anything happen with Patryk? Did you see him again over break?"

I shook my head. "He has nothing to do with this, Dylan. I haven't seen him since Christmas Day."

He sat on my bed. "Then what's going on?"

"I haven't been able to shake this bad feeling. Ever since that night I spoke to you after I saw the play with the girls, I've been feeling like something is off between us."

"I was missing you the *entire* time I was away, Kasia. I even decided last week that I wasn't going on any more family vacations unless you could be there with me. Jesus, tell me we're all right. You're scaring me."

Was it all in my head? Was I insecure? Maybe, for as much as I acted like those girls from high school didn't affect me, maybe I did feel threatened by them. If that's what *this* was, then it was all on me. Dylan had certainly never made me feel less-than.

"We're ok." I nodded and forced a smile that I didn't feel. "Do you want to take a run? I need to clear my head."

"I'd love to but I've got practice in an hour. Can we go to dinner tonight?"

"Definitely."

"Good." He stood up and hugged me close. "I love you, Kasia, so much."

* * *

DYLAN

Shit, is she psychic?

I could feel the breath rush out of me and could only assume I turned a ghostly shade of pale when Kasia mentioned that awful phone call.

For a split second I thought maybe someone had told her, but there was no way that was the case. If Kasia knew even half of what I'd done down in Palm Beach, she would have been throwing shit at me instead of hugging me when I walked into her room today.

The fact that she knew me well enough to sense that something was wrong filled me with fucking sorrow. Kasia was the best thing that had ever happened to me, and I'd done something that would end it all. And for what? Nothing but a cheap fuck with some girls who've seen more cock than a couple of low-class call girls.

After Kasia pretty much hung up on me that night, I rolled over and went back to sleep instead of going out. I didn't have it in me. To say that Mother was not pleased would be a gross understatement. This was one of *her* charities. She was on the board and ran their biggest fundraiser in New York every spring. I played it off like I was sick, and in truth, I was. Self-recrimination and remorse ate away at my gut like acid, burning me from the inside out.

Melanie texted me later that night:

Do not tell me ur feeling guilty baby…u know im not telling anyone…plz come 2nite

I ignored her at first but then answered:

Not feeling good…ntng 2 do w last nite

Melanie referring to me as "baby" had me running to the bathroom to puke my guts out again.

I took Kasia to Donatella's, the Italian place we went to that first night. It was wishful thinking, an attempt on my part to turn back time and start all over again. We shared a bottle of wine and I held her hand across the table. We talked, skirting around the things that were awkward, the things that might hurt. By the time we polished off dessert, it felt better, like she was more relaxed.

Like she didn't suspect a thing.

That's how it had to be.

Over the next few weeks we fell back into our routine. I tended to stay with Kasia more than she stayed at the house with me. That's how I wanted it. It's not like Melanie was dropping subtle digs or innuendos. In fact, it was the opposite. She was nicer to Kasia than she had been before. When Kasia asked Melanie how Palm Beach was soon after our return, she answered simply and without a note of sarcasm, "It was good. You should come next time."

Still, I didn't want to spend any more time around Melanie or Christian than I needed to. I wanted to tone that part of my life down, if not abandon it altogether. I even toned it down with Kasia. I was more than content with vanilla sex, didn't push anything even remotely out of bounds. I didn't need to. Sex with Kasia was mind-blowing just because I loved her. Loving someone, fucking a woman who had my heart? What they say is true: the biggest risks yield the best returns.

Chapter Five

DYLAN

Parties were picking up around campus with senior year now more than half-way over, and our house was at the center of it.

I abdicated my role as head party planner to Justin, but I couldn't completely walk away. Kasia was typically here for our shindigs, but tonight Bernadette, Trish and Kasia were heading to Cooper's frat because Val complained they were never at Tau's parties. I would have tagged along with them, but Justin was giving me shit about being at another frat when we were hosting an event ourselves. He had a point.

Our place was jammed, as usual. The music, the people, the atmosphere—it was all good but I wasn't feeling it. I texted Kasia a few times but got no response. I liked that her nose wasn't glued to her phone screen like a lot of other people I knew, but the girl infuriated me when I had a pressing need to see her and she was absent-mindedly off-grid.

I settled on Trish.

How's the party?

At least someone had their phone. She answered:

Packed...is Bri behaving?

Trish had nothing to worry about on that front; my friend was crazy about her. I typed out:

Of course he is. K dsnt have her phone again. She ok?

She answered:

Yep...dancing up a storm.

"I'm outta here, Justin. You good?"

"Really, Cole? You can't even spend one night with your brothers without her?"

Melanie gave Justin a playful knock on the shoulder. "Leave him alone. He's in love."

Justin walked away, clearly annoyed.

"Exactly why are you being so nice?"

"You act like I don't care about you, Dylan. I do."

"The shit that went down in Florida? I don't want to lose what I have with her. I can't be that person anymore."

"I think you can try to bury that side of yourself, but you'll never change." Her eyes were sympathetic. "I don't think that's a bad thing. I think most people are repressed and we're the honest ones."

"You think I won't be able to stick it out with her?"

"No, I didn't say that. I think you'll be like most married people...You'll lie." She laid her hand on the center of my chest. "C'mon, Dylan, the world we live in? The world *you* live in? In a few months you'll be running a multi-billion dollar, multi-national corporation alongside your father. You'll be one of the most powerful men in this country one day. With that kind of power comes certain appetites and you know it."

My father: powerful, a commander of people. A man who gets pretty much whatever he wants whenever he wants it. Was I destined to be that guy? I mulled that over as I walked to Sigma Tau.

I spotted her as soon as I walked in. Kasia and Bernadette were dancing together, and while it wasn't even close to girl-on-girl action, I let my imagination go wherever it was so inclined to wander.

Making my way through the crowd, I focused on her body. The way her hips swayed in time to the music, the way her tits bounced just a little bit with every movement, the way her hair spilled half-way down her back—I wanted to fuck. I positioned myself behind my girl, and the moment she put her arms up in the air I moved in and pulled her hips close to mine.

"Get off me!"

I was doubled over from the elbow she shot to my ribs, but laughing. "Shit, Kasia."

When she turned and saw it was me, she yelled over the music, "What's the matter with you?"

I drew her back to me, pulled her in close to speak directly into her ear. "Do you know how hot you look dancing right now? How many guys have tried to hit on you tonight?"

She pulled back and glared at me. "Is that what you were doing, Dylan? Were you testing me? Curious to see if I'd let some random guy grind on me?"

She pushed against me with both hands, with enough force that I actually stumbled back. Steadying myself, I caught sight of her storming out the door.

"What the fuck?"

She spun to face me. "Have I ever given you any reason to doubt me? To think I'm into anyone else?"

"No! Why are you so angry?"

She came closer and stared me down. "Because my life is an open book. You know everything." Now her finger was in my chest and I was shitting a brick. "Did you sleep with Melanie?"

"Where is this coming from?"

"That's not an answer. It's a yes or no question, Dylan."

Maybe if I'd had more time to think I would have spun some

bullshit, but what Melanie said to me earlier about living a lie was still gnawing at me. "Yeah, I did. She's someone from my past."

"When was the last time?"

Now the lie was spoken without thinking. "Before you. It was before you, ok?"

She looked down at the ground. "I overheard some people talking about her tonight." I kept my mouth shut, waited to see where this conversation was going, always careful not to incriminate myself. "They were talking about what she liked in, um, bed. You know, comparing notes on her and laughing because her kinks could basically scare your average guy away. They were saying she liked two guys at once, or two girls and a guy." Now the pain in her eyes was obvious. "Your name was mentioned."

"I don't know what to say."

She was on the verge of tears. "Do you *need* that? I mean it. Do you need someone like her?"

"No! Damn, that was just...I don't know how to explain it."

She shook her head. "I'm not angry about *that*, ok? It was before you were with me. It's just that sometimes..." Kasia looked away for a moment before turning back to face me. "I just need to think, ok? Go home. I need to be by myself tonight."

"Kasia, please."

"I mean it...I need to be alone."

* * *

KASIA

He confirmed what I already knew to be true.

The image of him with Melanie made me burn with jealousy, but what really hurt was knowing he did things with her that were probably way out of my comfort zone—things he wouldn't ask of me.

I avoided his house for weeks because I didn't trust myself to be in the same room as Melanie. But Dylan was persistent, he wouldn't let me shut him out. He showed up the night after we fought and climbed into my bed without speaking a word. The next morning when I woke, he was looking down at me with dark circles underneath his weary eyes.

"Don't leave me, Kasia, please."

I didn't want to leave him. I loved him but I didn't trust in what we had. Down the road I didn't want to be the clueless wife with the lying husband, two people acting as if life is just fantastic while everything is a farce. I felt terrible alluding to his parents like that, knowing it would cause him pain, but I couldn't keep it all bottled up inside and go on acting as if I was happy.

"You think *I* want to be like them? When I'm with you, it makes me better. Maybe it's because you don't need me, you know? You'll be fine without me, but I *won't* be fine without you. If I end up with some society princess, I'll die. I'll become my father."

We made our way back to each other that month, but it was still raw and I was unsettled. I knew Dylan wanted to be with me and I wanted to be with him, but I kept asking myself who I was willing to be for him. How far was I willing to go?

* * *

DYLAN

She was back in my room for the first time in what felt like forever. I reassured myself that we were good, that everything was back to normal.

Kasia was reading on my bed and I was working on some financial data for my senior project. She got up to get a highlighter from my desk and opened the draw, fishing around, reaching her hand to the back. And fuck me, she pulled out a bag that had about an eight-ball's worth of coke in it.

"Study aid?"

"It's been in there forever. I haven't done anything…Wait I have smoked a few times, but I haven't done anything harder in months."

She looked back to the bag. "How does it make you feel?"

Please don't ask me this.

I didn't want reminders of the guy I was when Kasia wasn't around. She was innocent. Pretty sure alcohol was the only vice she'd ever dabbled in, and never once had I seen her wasted.

"Uh, I don't know…It's like you're more awake, energized, buzzing, chatty."

"Sounds like fun."

"I guess, but once you start it can be hard to rein yourself in. Before you know it you can consume a lot of it in one night and things can get out of hand."

"Does it lower your inhibitions?"

"Definitely."

"Can I try it just once, with you?"

"No." The answer came out like a bark, fast and definitive.

"Why?"

"It's not for you, Kasia. You don't want to try that shit." She put the bag back in the drawer and closed it. "Hey," I pulled her onto my lap, "I think I know where your head is at, and I don't want you thinking that doing or trying new *things* is something I need. Do you understand? I'm crazy about you."

She clearly did not understand.

Kasia led me upstairs Saturday night after we put in a few hours at our house party. She was cutting loose, and I remember laughing as I watched her knock back a shot with her girlfriends. I was ready to bail on the party at that point, so I was glad she was feeling the same. Once we were in my room she turned to lock the door. "You're mine now," she teased.

She wasn't drunk but had a good buzz going as she maneuvered me towards the bed. She pushed me back when my calves met the mattress, then set about performing an epic striptease as I sat there salivating like a damn dog. When she was down to nothing but satin and lace, she leaned over and set about undressing me. I breathed in that scent that was one hundred percent Kasia—the headiest, most potent drug known to man.

Shaking my head, I told her, "Sometimes I can't believe you're mine."

She bit her bottom lip as she undid the front clasp of her bra and moved onto the bed so that she was straddling my hips. "Tell me what you want."

"I just want you, baby…Just want to be inside of you."

"No, tell me what you *really* want," she whispered as she pressed herself down and circled her hips.

When I didn't answer, she popped back up and made her way to my desk, shaking her hips in a way that rendered me stupid. She fished the package out of my drawer and held it up flashing her best puppy dog eyes. "Let me try just a little…It'll be ok."

"No."

But she wasn't giving up that easy. "What are you afraid of, Dylan?"

"I don't want you to regret anything."

"If I'm with you then I won't regret anything."

I was pretty sure we were both going to regret it, but she was into it and I was tempted. There was always that part of me that wanted to push and go further.

"Just one line, and we're never doing this again. I mean it, Kasia."

She smiled at me, triumphant. And then we both did a skimpy line that was less than half of what I normally did.

Long story short, before the night was over she did another two lines, I did at least three more, and we didn't get to sleep until after five. And yeah, we, uh, did some things. I'm thinking we made so much noise that every brother in the house heard us.

Regrets…Coming right up, folks!

It was the first time I woke up next to Kasia and thought to myself, *She doesn't look so good.* Instead of the sweet-faced angel I was used to, Kasia's hair was a knotted mess and her mouth was hanging open—and not in that sexy parted lips kind of way.

I nudged her. "Hey baby, you all right?"

I felt like crap, too. Not just because my head was pounding from the night's activities and lack of sleep, but because we crossed some lines last night—lines I knew Kasia would never have crossed sober. My fault entirely.

She made a half-groan, half-coughing sound. "Oh, my head."

I went to the bathroom and got her some aspirins and a glass of water. "Take these and drink the entire glass."

When she opened her eyes they were red-rimmed and glassy. I wanted to hit the rewind button.

We both went back to sleep and I didn't wake again until I heard her in the shower. I padded in after her, took a leak and then sat down on the seat as I waited for her to finish. She came out and wrapped herself in a towel. Her eyes didn't meet mine.

"I'm really sorry. I shouldn't have let you do that last night. I feel like shit."

"I practically begged you, Dylan. You have nothing to be sorry about."

I couldn't help the cheerless laugh that slipped out. "I feel like I dragged you over to the dark side. I don't feel good about what we did." Her expression was pained and embarrassed. "That's never happening again." She sat on my lap but then shifted and winced. "Fuck, are you sore?"

"A little but I'm fine." With my free hand I pinched the bridge of my nose when what I really wanted to do was punch myself in the face. She moved my hand away gently. "Hey, don't do that. I'm not some naïve young girl. I went in with my eyes wide open last night. I'm just sorry that I'm not the type of person who can do those things and then feel good about it the next day." When I went to interrupt her she held her hand up to silence me. "You hold back with me. Last night you didn't hold back and I *know* you liked what we did."

"But I love it when it's us and we're together how we always are. Just that, nothing more. You satisfy me. I don't need it to be crazy or risky. What we did last night? I can't say that it wasn't hot or that I didn't enjoy myself, but I regret the drugs, I do. And I regret it because I know that deep down, that's not who you are."

"You know that I trust you completely, don't you, Dylan?"

I nodded, so grateful, wrapping my arms around her and resting my head against her chest. "I trust you with my life, baby."

Kasia dressed in comfy sweats and a long-sleeved tee from the drawer full of clothes she kept at my place. She rolled her clothes from last night into a ball and then set about stripping the bed and tossing everything into a big laundry bag. The room smelled like sex. I watched as she made the bed with the spare sheets, smoothed fresh pillowcases on the pillows, then arranged the comforter so perfectly that it looked like a hotel bed by the time she was done.

"Let's do something mindless. Let's go see a movie, get some dinner and then crash early at your place, all right?"

Her smile was weak. "Yeah, that sounds good."

"I'll be right back up."

I wanted to get a read on the situation, needed to know if we'd put on a show last night. I walked past a few guys playing video games on the couch—no smirks, no knowing smiles, no nothing. In the kitchen, Brian was at the sink washing out shot glasses while the beginnings of a Sunday sauce were simmering on the stovetop. He was surprisingly domestic. "What's up, Bri?"

"Nothing besides a splitting headache. I think I passed out at around three." Brian had the room next to mine, and while the walls weren't paper-thin, they weren't solid concrete either. If he didn't hear anything then we were probably good.

But then I ran smack into Melanie half-way up the stairs, and that feeling of relief evaporated on contact. She looked like the cat that got the damn cream. "Good morning, hottie. Seems like I may have underestimated your little knish."

"My *what*?"

"She's Polish, isn't she? Polish people eat knish and the words sort of rhyme...Don't you get it?" I rolled my eyes. "I wasn't purposely eavesdropping or anything, Dylan, but what I did manage to hear was pretty hot."

"You don't know what you're talking about. And by the way, picturing you with your ear up against my door is a little disturbing."

She threw her head back and laughed. "Oh, so you can *watch* me but I can't even listen in? No fair!" She moved in close enough for her tits to brush against my chest. "Just sayin'...I'm game if she is."

Melanie fucking scared me, I'll admit it. She was calculating, depraved, and had the emotional range of a shark.

"Steer clear, Mel. She's not like that."

As I pushed past her, she called after me, "I'm not so sure. Maybe she's one of us after all."

I was relieved to just hold her that night, nothing more. My arm was wrapped around her in the movie theater. We held hands throughout dinner and talked about anything other than last night. Kasia and I crawled into bed together afterwards, neither one of us looking to remove even the sweats we wore, and then I held her tight until she drifted off to sleep.

Chapter Six

KASIA

Spring was officially here. People were laying out on the quad in between classes, volleyball nets were set up, ping pong tables were moved outside, and barbecues were fired up with beers flowing at practically all times. This wasn't a slacker school, to get in you had to be a student, but school was winding down for us now and the atmosphere was decidedly festive.

Dylan and I were more than good. For better or worse, neither one of us brought up the topic of that night again. It's not that I was ashamed—I didn't feel judged by him at all—but I was confused about it still. There was a part of me that was so turned on by what we did, but I also felt like I wouldn't be able to face myself in the mirror if it happened again.

And the whole idea of graduation was messing with my head. It's something to celebrate, yes, but it's also something to grieve.

I was down about parting ways with three girls who were now like sisters to me. Val was heading to a creative writing program at Emory, Trish was moving home to Wisconsin where Brian would be close by working in Chicago, and Bernadette was starting her new job in San Francisco. I was heading back to New York. In a few weeks we'd be distant points on the map.

And while Dylan would be in New York with me, moving home meant the loss of our current cozy living arrangement.

While I dreamed of my own apartment in Manhattan, I knew I wouldn't be able to afford anything on that island for quite some time. But I was planning on talking to my father about one of his properties in Williamsburg that had a commercial space on the ground level and apartments that were rented upstairs. It was an old locksmith's shop now, but I dreamed of turning it into a retail store where I could focus on selling my pieces while having a true studio space upstairs to do more custom work. To convince him, I'd have to play the game. So I would do what every respectable, unmarried, young girl should do: live with Mama and Tata.

Dylan already had an apartment purchased for him on the Upper West Side in a luxury, full service building with a terrace overlooking the park. My stomach would knot whenever he'd talk about life after graduation. He just assumed I'd be spending nights at his apartment.

We slept together practically every night now, so next year was going to be a major adjustment. The Mazurs' daughter would not be anyone's dziwka, or whore. They weren't completely old school, but some things were non-negotiable. I'd get away with it occasionally, maybe if my parents thought a group of us were staying in Manhattan after a party or if they believed his parents would be there with us, but sleeping over was not going to be a regular thing.

I started plotting with my eye on the building at North Sixth and Bedford. It was a great area with lots of foot traffic near the waterfront in Williamsburg. I could already envision the design of the commercial space, so I was hoping and praying that I could convince my father to let me lease it for a steal. The icing on that cake would be if he let me keep one of the small apartments upstairs for myself, as an office and occasional crash pad when I was working late.

I was probably pushing it, but a girl could dream, right?

* * *

DYLAN

I played along but I was just going through the motions. I was ready to start the next phase of my life. I was ready to go.

We finished the lacrosse season, making it to the playoffs. My fellow senior Kappa brothers and I voted in our new President and Executive Council members, passing the baton on to the next generation of assholes. My senior project earned me an A and made dear old Dad proud, as it was a full-fledged business plan for an expansion he'd been mulling over.

Yawn, yawn, yawn.

The only part of my life that I wasn't trudging through was time spent with Kasia. She was the love of my life. I imagined waking up beside her ten, twenty years from now, and couldn't imagine that I'd feel any less in love with her decades from now than I did today.

Nothing lit me up the way she did.

Melanie came up behind me as I straightened my tie in the mirror. "Mmm...Don't you look delicious." I smiled taking in her dress, a bright red number with a high slit that showcased her assets to full effect.

I'll admit she looked hot, but I appreciated Kasia's sense of style more. My girl was sexy in an understated way. I didn't need to see Kasia's tits pushing up past the top of her dress. I knew what was underneath the fabric, knew every beautiful curve by heart.

"You look great, Mel."

"Good enough to eat?" She poked me, smiling. "I'm joking, of course." She sashayed past me, purposely shaking her fine ass, and went to join Christian, who'd heard the entire exchange and was smirking.

Tonight's formal kicked off Senior Week, a week of parties and activities that culminated with Graduation Day. A few days ago Christian asked if we wanted to ride with him and Melanie, but that was a hard no for so many reasons. I was relieved to see them off before Brian and I jumped in the limo together to get the girls.

When Kasia opened the door, I threw my head back and took in a deep breath before I smiled down at her again. She was so beautiful. "Turn around," I ordered as I circled my index finger towards her. I purred, doing my best fashionista impersonation, "The dress is divine. Who *are* you wearing, Ms. Mazur?"

She curtsied. "Funny you should ask. It's an *original* Kasia Mazur, available exclusively at Sweet Betty Threads dot-com."

"Baby, really, the dress is insane. Hugs those beautiful curves and it looks like it came off a runway. *You* look like you came off a runway. You're stunning."

"And you, Dylan, you look good enough to eat!" I bristled for a second at her choice of words, similar to Melanie's, but recovered before she noticed. She air-kissed me. "Don't want to ruin my make-up this early," she said as looked at me apologetically.

"No offense taken. Later on I'm gonna kiss, lick and bite every last speck of lipstick off you."

She winked and swatted my ass. "I can't wait."

That night was one to remember. I was smug in the knowledge that practically every heterosexual man in the venue had checked out my woman because she looked spectacular. I held her close when we danced and thought to myself that I could die a happy man if she was in my life. Sounds pretty corny but I was in a sentimental frame of mind these days.

I checked my phone while Kasia was freshening up in the bathroom and saw multiple messages from Ben. I had to reread them a few times until the shock wore off. I told Kasia to go back in without me so I could make a call.

"I see you got the messages."

"Holy crap, Ben."

"Yeah, it's bad. I just got back from his house. His parents were there. He was holding the baby and everything. It freaked me out."

"Does Darcy know?"

"Yeah, she knew from day one. But they're toast...Tom's pretty much fucked that up."

"Shit." I was speechless. How could he be so stupid and careless? I fucked around twice as much as Tom did but I'd *never* give some random girl an opportunity to trap me. Girls would always be begging for skin on skin, telling me they were on the pill. I never believed them and always protected myself. Besides my health, there was just way too much money at stake.

"What's he going to do? Does the girl want money?"

When Ben told me the girl was dead, I was stunned and a little guilty because my initial reaction was somewhat shallow. But then I just felt the weight of the responsibility that was now on my good friend, the poor bastard. I decided to hold off on telling Kasia. There was nothing she could really do for Darcy. I'm sure the girl was devastated.

When I did speak to Tom the next day, his voice was cracking as he relayed the basics. He told me he was keeping James and would care for him with his parents' help. When I asked about Darcy, Tom made his intentions clear and I found myself agreeing with his decision to cut ties. I would feel the same way, have the same sense of responsibility to make sure Kasia lived her life rather than be saddled with a baby that wasn't hers. I told Tom I'd see him the following week and reassured him that everything would work out, even though the words felt empty.

. . .

Senior Week flew by at warp speed, as the best times in your life often do. I made a mental note that two weeks alcohol-free was in order after leaving here. My blood type was practically Jack Daniels leading up to Graduation Day.

There were a few brothers I'd be seeing regularly after graduation. I would be in Chicago occasionally, so I'd be seeing Brian, and Justin would be working on Wall Street at the same firm as one of my lacrosse teammates. Christian had a job lined up in D.C. and was planning to enroll in law school there next year, so he wouldn't be too far away either. Melanie informed me she would be splitting her time between D.C. and Manhattan, to which I replied, "That's nice." I wasn't looking to spend much, if any time with her.

But Graduation Day would be the last time I'd be seeing most of these people. There would be class reunions, weddings and occasional get-togethers, but I was about to be a very busy man, so I recognized that this was truly goodbye.

For the most part I was ok with that. I preferred to keep my circle small. From a young age I realized my wealth attracted all the wrong sorts of people. I'd have enough ass kissers working for me, I certainly didn't need any groupies in my private life.

All of my closest friends were heading to the Vineyard for July Fourth. Every year I threw a bash at our summer place while my parents spent two weeks in Europe. In years past it's lasted for several days with people crashing all over the property, but this year was going to be different. Yep, this year my parents were staying put and the party was doubling as my graduation celebration.

When I started grumbling about having a graduation party, Mother assured me that the adults would only be there during the day for a barbecue and would clear out by seven or eight. It would be a mix of school friends, a select group of high school friends and some family friends. I was tempted to omit the last group, the Palm Beach crew, but that would not go over well with Margot or Vince. If the next in line to the throne from the Paulson, Eastman and Tate clans weren't invited, I'd have some 'splaining to do. It was going to be interesting, and not in a good way.

At least Kasia would have some of her own friends there for moral support. Still, I couldn't help but envision worst-case scenarios, such as disastrous run-ins with Cecilia Tate, Melanie's bitch of a mother, or my own mommy dearest, Margot Cole. I made a mental note to threaten my mother before the party.

Kasia and I weren't seated close to one another, but I knew from her smile that she heard me holler as she made her way across the stage. I made a bee-line for her right after the ceremony, coming up behind her and taking her by surprise when I lifted her up and spun her around. There was something unexpectedly special about this day and I guess I was feeling emotional.

I whispered that I loved her and then heard several men clearing their throats loudly behind us. Kasia blushed and her brothers all laughed when we turned to face them.

Kasia told me that graduations, even from grammar school, were considered big events in her family. College graduations were monumental, with the entire family traveling. Kasia admitted she was relieved that the university limited the number of tickets to the ceremony, otherwise her aunts, uncles, nieces and nephews would have tagged along as well. Maybe it's because I wasn't used to it, but I got off on being surrounded by her big, noisy clan.

Right as Mr. and Mrs. Mazur were taking turns hugging me and Kasia tight, I felt a hand tapping my shoulder. I turned to see my mother smiling at me with my father by her side. When Mother embraced me, it felt vastly different. Kasia's parents squeezed when they hugged, while my mother held you delicately, almost at a distance in comparison. I decided right then and there that I preferred the tight squeeze version better.

"Mom, Dad...I'd like you to meet Kasia's family."

I chuckled to myself as Mr. Mazur crushed both of my parents like he was doing a reverse Heimlich maneuver, followed by Mrs. Mazur, who always gave a quick back rub with her hugs. No doubt my parents felt sexually assaulted by the time they were through. But Margot and Vince, always composed, recovered quickly. My mother complimented Kasia, referring to her as their *lovely daughter*, which earned her points. And then I think she was actually taken off guard by the picture the group of them made together, laughing when she commented that she's never seen such a good-looking family. I had to agree. Kasia and her mother looked like beautiful sisters, Mike's girlfriend, Sophia, looked like Penelope Cruz, and her brothers were not ugly, as evidenced by the lingering glances they were getting from every girl who passed by.

Before Graduation Day, Kasia and I discussed whether or not we would go out together with our families or separately. Kasia was all for separate, and although I wouldn't admit it to her at the time, I was relieved. I think both of us were envisioning a cacophony of Polish speaking people and the horrified expressions of my haughty parents. So we made plans to meet up later in the day after our families went back to their respective hotels. All of our friends were meeting up for our one last night on campus. But now, standing in the midst of this happy group, I wished that we were going out together. The idea of the three of us sitting down to a quiet lunch at some uppity Michelin star-rated restaurant seemed lonely.

"Mom, maybe we should just eat with the Mazurs. They're going to a casual place, so I'm sure adding three more onto the reservation isn't a big deal."

Her smile stayed fixed in place when her eyes cut to me. "That's not possible. We're dining with the Pierces."

"Since when?"

"Didn't I mention it?"

No, Margot, you didn't.

Kasia squeezed my hand just as I was about to launch into an argument with my mother, then smiled to let me know it was all right.

And although I stewed like a pissed off ten-year-old on the drive over to Le Escargot—or whatever the name of that constipated haute cuisine restaurant was—lunch with my parents wasn't as bad as I'd anticipated.

Christian and his parents joined our group, so that gave me a little buffer, and for better or worse, Melanie was a friend of mine, albeit in a jaded, twisted sort of way. She was loyal, and although their relationship was unorthodox, I knew she loved my friend Christian and wanted the best for him. I also had to give her credit for being more cordial towards Kasia once she knew I was serious about her. Melanie had considerably dialed back the bitchy.

My parents and Melanie's go way back, and although my mother was very fond of Melanie, she was definitely not on the list of eligible bachelorettes for yours truly. Mother wasn't much for gossip, but I'd overheard a few comments over the years. Enough to know my mother thought Melanie had "unfortunately" taken after her father Reginald, a known philanderer and all around dirty dog. So at the very least, I was safe from my mother's matchmaking efforts.

When Melanie told everyone she was doing an internship at some society scene magazine—unpaid and de rigueur for rich, directionless young socialites—Margot assured her she was going to have a *fabulous* year. I think my mother may have done something similar when she was our age, so Melanie was now on a comparable career trajectory. She would work for next to nothing at a meaningless job, marry a fella as rich as she was, pop out a kid or two, take up tennis, and then organize fundraising efforts for "suitable" charities.

When the ladies began to speak in hushed tones that everyone at the table could hear, my ears perked up. Apparently Tom's situation was the talk of my hometown. Mom heard about Tom's situation from her tennis partner, which meant every mother and father in New Canaan was now using my bestic as a cautionary tale.

Melanie gasped out a "poor Tom" at the same time her mother quipped, "Will these boys *ever* learn?" Christian's mother looked to Melanie before taking a healthy sip of her martini, diplomatic in her silence. And while Vince generally didn't comment on such trivial things, he made a point of looking at me directly when he said, "That's a wake-up call for all of you young men."

Was he kidding me with that bullshit? Was he insinuating that Kasia might be looking to trap me? I felt like telling him to heed his own advice and make sure he didn't knock up any of the hot young secretaries he repeatedly hired, despite their questionable organizational skills. I loved the man, but what a fucking hypocrite.

* * *

KASIA

Although I wanted to spend the day with Dylan, I was more than happy to part ways with his parents after the ceremony.

The brief meeting between our families went well, I thought, but I just didn't get the warm and fuzzies from either one of them. I was happy to enjoy the day with my family instead, one hundred percent relaxed.

I knew the Coles and Pierces were dining at the one upscale, ridiculously expensive restaurant near campus. My family could afford that kind of meal but it wasn't our scene, so I made reservations at a casual barbecue joint instead. Sitting at a picnic table, drinking beer, eating messy ribs and laughing out loud was more my family's style than a subdued four-course luncheon that probably kicked off with a gag-o-licious bowl of ice cold vichyssoise.

During lunch I began to lay the groundwork for the proposal I was going to hit my dad with in the very near future. Sophia gave me a great opening when she started talking about student loans, voicing her concern over the number of today's students graduating underneath mounds of debt.

The Mazurs didn't do debt.

I was very proud of my parents. They came to this country young, scraping by until they were able to purchase their first multiple-family dwelling, and then bought more properties only when they had the means to do so. Their philosophy was simple: you only purchased what you could afford in cash and you never lived beyond your means. We didn't own flashy cars or high-end designer clothes. And although we all went to prestigious universities, our tuitions were covered by scholarships. If not for grants and scholarships, I would have received a city or New York state college education, and that would have been just fine because it was quality *and* affordable. My parents weren't impressed by showy opulence. They were impressed by hard-working people who made their own luck.

So I used the topic to my advantage, adding that I was not only graduating without debt but considerably richer than I started out freshman year.

"Has the business made you a few dollars?"

"About eight thousand dollars, Michal. I've saved nearly everything I've made from making dresses privately and from the sales on the website."

Aleksander slapped his hand on the table, laughing. "Are you serious? That's fantastic! You did that while you were a full-time student? Imagine how you'll be able to grow the business now that you can devote all of your time to it?" He rubbed his hands together. "I mean it, Kasia. I've seen the website and you have the start of something big. Consider me your first official investor."

"Really?"

"Absolutely. And I wouldn't front you seed money if I didn't think I'd make it back tenfold."

"Another entrepreneur in the family," my father chirped happily.

"Do you think so, Tata? I really want to do this. I think I can make a good living from my business."

"If you are determined, you can do anything."

I didn't push him any further. I was just laying the foundation for now.

Chapter Seven

KASIA

Unlike some of my friends who were dreading the move back home, I was looking forward to life in New York.

My family was close, and I never dreamed of a future that would take me far from them. And I was becoming fond of the person who, in my mind, would soon become its newest member. There was no doubt that Michal was in for the long haul with this girl. Sophia and I talked and laughed over lunch, made plans to hang out and shop as soon as I was back in New York, and she invited me and Dylan to come out with them to see her brother's band play. I knew this girl would be my sister someday and the thought of it made me truly happy.

Being back in New York would also give me the chance to reconnect with Darcy. We spoke the night before her senior formal, right after Tom bailed on her. She was all *I'll be ok*, but I knew she was suffering. She called me back the next day crying so hard she could hardly get her words out, and warned me I was going to have to keep her occupied twenty-four-seven until she got over him. I wanted to be there for her.

I was definitely going to be busy with family and social obligations, but I had to stay focused on scoping out the potential retail space and convincing my father to get behind me on the venture. I knew it was a big ask. The lease would have to be way below market value and then there was the issue of renovations. If it looked the same as the last time I saw it, I'd have to take Aleksander up on his offer for seed money, and lots of it.

Busy was good, as it kept me from missing Dylan day and night. His father was putting him to work right away, the two of them jetting off on a business trip to China and Malaysia. He'd be gone for the first two weeks of June, and that would just be the start of it. Dylan would be putting in long hours as he worked to establish himself in the New York offices. I wouldn't be seeing much of him until July Fourth weekend, and since his parents were going away with us, I wasn't looking forward to it like a true vacation.

We drove home together the day after graduation, and I was tearful as we said our goodbyes after he had dinner with my family. We hadn't spent more than several hours apart during the past few months, so two weeks seemed like an awfully long time.

"I'm going to miss you, Kasia."

"It's a good thing I'll be busy or else I'd be going crazy missing you."

"When are you going to ask your father?"

"I'm waiting for the right time. Tomorrow I'm going there with Aleksander so he can give me his opinion about renovation costs and everything. Then I'll have a better idea."

"You know where I stand."

"Don't, Dylan. You know I appreciate the offer but I can't accept. This is mine and I have to do it on my own."

He feigned a hurt expression but then smiled. "I know."

Dylan offered to help me secure a space in the Meatpacking

District right underneath the High Line. It was premium commercial real estate and so ridiculously out of my league. The trendiest upscale designers had retail stores there. I was twenty-two, and my business—well, to even call it an actual business was a stretch. Dylan had the means and connections to make it happen, but I was adamantly against the idea. I firmly believed in that old saying: *Don't mix business with pleasure.* Besides, I was too young to be tied to anyone, financially or otherwise.

The difference was around twelve hours between New York and wherever he was in Asia on any given day, so it was convenient, I guess, but we were on opposite ends of the clock.

"Why do you always get the mornings and I get the nights? Are you checking to make sure I'm home at night, Dylan?"

He had a wicked gleam in his eyes. "I do like to make sure you're home safe in Greenpoint with no roaming eyes on you. If I thought you were shaking your ass in some club I'd go out of my mind."

"Fair warning, I will be shaking my ass later on tonight, but I'll be with Michal and Sophia so you have nothing to worry about. What about you? Am I supposed to be on board with you out at night surrounded by hot, eager young businesswomen?"

"No chance of that. More like crinkly old Asian dudes pushing sake on me, then waking up hungover for endless hours of meetings."

"You expect me to believe that?"

I made a joke of it, but there was always a nagging voice in the back of my head that questioned whether or not Dylan was capable of monogamy.

He reached his hand out to touch the screen. "I can't wait to see you. You have no idea how much I miss you."

I put my palm up to meet his. "I miss you too."

"Just think, by this time next week we'll be christening my new apartment, room by room."

I cringed when my parents came to mind. "Yeah, we're going to have to talk about that. I don't think Mama and Tata will be condoning sleep overs."

He waved me off. "Don't worry. I'll spin some bullshit to make it happen. I have your parents eating out of my hand right now. A late concert one night, trouble getting car service another...I have it all planned out."

I smiled at his confidence. He really didn't know what he was up against. "If you say so, Dylan."

"I say so, and what I say goes. First my new king-sized bed...I'm a traditionalist after all. Then the shower...Remember how much we like the shower?" I was getting warm all over listening to his sexy voice. "Then the nice, cool granite countertops in the kitchen." He tapped his chin, plotting it all out. "Oh yeah, then the sofa. I want you bent over the sofa looking back with those fuck me eyes."

"Jeez, let me lower the volume on this thing. If my parents hear this conversation they'll never let me see you again." I let out a frustrated sigh. "I can't believe you're sending me out on the town like this...All hot, wet and unsatisfied."

"Hey, hey now! I don't like that kind of talk."

"Just kidding. I love you, I miss you, I want you...And on that note, I hear Michal downstairs. I have to go."

"Be safe, baby."

* * *

DYLAN

Vince was all business on this business trip. There were no assistants booked to accompany him—shocker—and there were no wild, late night outings with clients. Aw, dear old Dad felt the need to make a good impression on me.

He shouldn't have bothered. Way back when I used to feel hurt on my mother's behalf, but no more. My father loved her, respected her and relied on her in many ways. Mother had razor-sharp instincts and her networking skills had netted my father a number of good contacts over the years. They had a good partnership, and maybe that was enough.

Maybe it was good enough for them.

Did my mother know about his extracurricular activities? And if she did, was she turning a blind eye to it all? Kasia would never accept that kind of relationship and I didn't want that for us. More than anything, I wanted to be with her an no one else. I wanted to be content and happy in that life.

Chicago came out of left field. My father waited until after I popped a benzo and settled in for the long flight home before tilting his tablet in my direction to reveal my schedule for the next couple of months.

When I questioned him, he scoffed, "It's not a relocation. I need you there to oversee operations. You knew you'd be traveling."

Already feeling the effects of the sleeping pill, I offered up a half-hearted protest. "Knew I'd be traveling...Didn't know I'd be spending half my life in Chicago."

"Is it going to be a problem?"

That's Vince Cole-speak for *end of discussion*.

"No, Dad, of course not."

Two weeks out of every month. Six months out of the year trying to keep up some bullshit version of a long-distance relationship.

I was tempted to accidentally knock the last few sips of my gin and tonic onto his lap, but drifting off to sleep, I began to see the potential upside. Her parents would have to let her come out to visit me at least one weekend a month. Yep, Chicago could be our little vacation together away from her overprotective parents.

I'd make it work.

I had to.

I was glad I got back on a Friday because I was still a little jet lagged and was looking forward to sleeping half the day away on Saturday.

I groaned, dragging ass on my way to the restaurant. Now that Kasia was back in her parents' clutches, I'd have to get her back home to Brooklyn tonight. And Mr. Mazur would judge me harshly, comparing me to Saint Patryk if she rolled up in a damn car service.

She was a sight for sore eyes standing on the corner of Columbus and Seventy-Second, frown and all.

"I'm cancelling our reservation. You look like you could face plant on the sidewalk right now."

"Is it that obvious? I felt fine this morning but now I feel exhausted."

Tapping into her phone with one hand, she looped her free arm through mine. "Come on. Let's go back to your apartment and get you into bed."

"No, I'll rally. Besides, I have to get you back to Brooklyn later. I don't want to be on your dad's shit list from day one."

She smiled and waggled her eyebrows. "My parents are away. Michal gave them a trip to the North Fork wineries for their anniversary." She laughed, shaking her head. "I guarantee you they're going to hate it, but the silver lining to that cloud is that I can sleep over."

"What did you tell them?"

"Just that I didn't want to come back home late and then stay in the house all alone."

"They went for it?" She nodded. "I'll make it up to you. Tomorrow night I'll take you out on the town, anywhere you want."

"Dylan, I don't care about that. I'd much rather curl up next to you tonight than spend three hours in a restaurant."

Everyone always talks about gratitude. All the self-help books, all those talk show hosts—they tell you to be grateful for the little things in life. Sounds like sappy bullshit but I think they're onto something.

I was damn grateful when I dropped my keys on the table and Kasia fixed me a glass of cold water, gesturing for me to drink up. I was grateful when she led me into the bathroom and undressed me as I practically sagged against the vanity. I was grateful for the clouds of steam, for the hot water beating down on my skin, and for the gentle loving hands that washed my hair, washed my body, then wrapped me in a towel and led me to bed.

I fell asleep before the takeout was delivered, and when I woke up the next morning I was home. My bed, my girl in my arms—all was right in the world.

The clock read eleven-thirty, and a solid sixteen hour sleep was exactly what the doctor had ordered. I moved in, my entire body now fully awake, and Kasia wiggled her ass back even closer in response.

I'll never forget her voice, sweet and drowsy when she said, "Mmm, I've missed this."

My hands moved then, exploring every inch of her as if I needed to learn the curves of her body again. "You feel so good, Kasia." I rolled onto her and held both hands above her head in one of mine. "Have you been good while I've been away?"

She shook her head, licking her lips. "I've been very, very bad. How are you going to punish me?"

We could never get past a line or two of role-playing before busting out laughing, and today was no exception. We spent the entire day in bed together, leaving only to heat up the leftovers from last night, which we ate in bed.

"My plan was to christen every single room. We've got our work cut out for us."

"I'd say that after today *this* room is thoroughly christened. My body is actually sore, like I've been at the gym for hours kind-of sore."

I teased, "Am I *so* big that I've hurt you?"

She went to get up from the bed and shrugged. "I've had bigger."

"What?" I grabbed her around the waist and dragged her naked body back to the bed with her laughing uncontrollably. "You better take that back," I threatened as I tickled her into spasms.

"Stop it, Dylan!"

"Take it back, Kasia."

"No!" She was nearly unable to breathe when she gave in. "Okay, okay! Just stop, please."

"Now am I, or am I not the biggest you've ever had?"

"Ugh, I don't want to stroke that inflated ego of yours. You already think you're a sex god or something."

Wounded, I denied it. "I do not. I just need to know, Kasia."

She rolled out from under me and pushed me back onto the mattress, moving to straddle me. Golden waves fell just past her breasts, the promise of sex from the tight nipples that peeked out in between. She looked like some living work of art staring down at me.

She knotted her brows and stuck out her lower lip, but there was a smile creeping through that phony pout. "I'll admit that this," she said as she inched her body back and stroked her hand slowly up and down my hard length, "is the biggest," she licked her lips slowly, driving me crazy, "and most talented cock I've ever had the pleasure to know."

What followed was the best blow job of my life.

So it was torture driving her back out to Brooklyn later that night. It was Saturday night, but Kasia's parents were home and she had a family baby shower or something the next morning. She didn't think it was worth pushing her parents to ask for another night. Besides the traffic, I just hated sleeping without her. I was used to her soft body next to mine and to that sweet smell that was uniquely Kasia. My apartment was too quiet and empty when I got back.

I decided to turn in early but my phone rang sometime around midnight. It was Melanie. I could hear from the music and chatter in the background that she was at a party.

"Hey, you're back!"

"Yeah, got back a couple of days ago."

Why did I even pick up? Even talking to her felt wrong now, but that was my issue. I was going to have to learn how to manage this. Our families were close. It wasn't like I could totally cut ties with her.

Bored and aggravated, I asked, "How's life as a college graduate?"

"Hold on," she said as she moved someplace quieter. "Um, it's been busy. I moved into my new place. Your mother was here last week with my mother giving me decorating tips. It was comical."

"Sounds like fun."

"Loads."

She sounded uncharacteristically glum. "You all right? Are you missing Christian?"

"Yeah, I am. I thought having my own apartment in the big city would be the absolute best, but these past two weeks have been lonely, you know? I'm at a party with people I barely know tonight, Christian's in California, the few girls I'd actually call real friends are traipsing around Europe or God knows where, and I'm working at a place where everyone treats me like a goddamn imbecile."

"You're *not* an imbecile. It's an adjustment. You just have to give it some time, Mel."

"Yeah, but in the meantime it just blows." She drew in a shaky breath. "Hey, I know you have to be careful with Kasia and everything, but do you think we could hang out one night after work? Christian can't come back out east for another two weeks."

"He's making my party, right?"

"That's when he's flying back. He wouldn't miss it."

"Good, and yeah, Melanie, we'll hook up one night this week." She actually sounded like she needed a friend.

I drove out to Brooklyn Sunday night with the sole purpose of telling Kasia about my conversation with Melanie. I was trying to avoid any missteps, trying my best to be as open and honest as humanly possible. We sat drinking cappuccinos in a corner café near her house, and as expected, Kasia rolled her eyes when I told her how depressed Melanie sounded.

"Do you mind if I meet up with her for a little while after work on Thursday?"

"We're supposed to go see Sophia's brother play on Thursday."

"Oh...I'll call Mel and change it to another night."

"Don't bother." Leaning over to stroke my cheek, she forced a smile. "And I'm not saying that to be a bitch, although I can't say I'm buying the whole damsel in distress act. I'll take Darcy with me on Thursday. Sophia's brother is pretty cute and he plays guitar. Maybe he'll take her mind off of Tom."

"Uh, I don't want to be responsible for setting Darcy up with some other guy."

She frowned. "I know, and anyway I was half-joking. She's not even close to looking for a rebound guy, so don't worry. I hate seeing her so heartbroken."

"Yeah, Tom really fucked up a good thing." I took her hand in mine. "That's why I wanted to tell you and make sure it's all right before I made plans with Melanie. I don't want any secrets screwing things up for us, ok? And if you're uncomfortable with it, then just say the word and I won't go. I mean it."

"I'm not like that. I'd never say no. But don't ever expect the two of us to be friends. Melanie is *your* friend, she's no friend of mine."

"How's that supposed to make me feel?"

"How's it supposed to make *you* feel?" She was wide-eyed. "Are you kidding? I'm *trying* not to feel insecure about you wanting to spend time with her. It's enough that I'll tolerate you hanging out with," she lowered her voice to a whisper and leaned in close, "someone you've fucked. Remember," she mocked, "you've had *sex* with the girl? Don't ask me for more than that. Don't ask me to pretend that she's a nice person, or that she isn't an absolute bitch to me when you're not around. Sorry, but I'm not fake. You want to console your friend, be her shoulder to cry on? Go ahead. I had no choice...I *had* to interact with her when we were at school, but that's over and done with now. I choose *not* to spend time with people I dislike."

She was on fire. What had been a casual chat a minute ago was now a full-on bitch fest. "Kasia, I won't go."

She threw her head back, exasperated. "How did we get here?" A moment later she said, "You want me to tell you that I'm fine with it? I'm fine with it." Shaking her head, she said, "God, I was so happy yesterday, so happy to finally see you again. Now I feel so... frustrated."

"Shit, I wish I never started this."

"But you did." She stood up then and gestured for us to leave. "I'm all right. Now if you don't go I'll feel like some pathetic, jealous witch. You're going and let's just change the subject, ok? I'm done talking about this."

I raked my hands over my face. I was angry at myself and annoyed by her reaction. But what did I expect? If she told me she wanted to go out with some guy who'd seen her spread out in all her naked glory, I certainly wouldn't be patting her on the head and telling her to go have a good time.

I held the door open for her and whispered, "Kasia, I love you."

"I don't need to be reassured. Listen, I appreciate that you came *all* the way out here to tell me, to be up front about it. I do. But can we just call it a night? I have a busy day tomorrow. I'm meeting my brother at six-thirty before he goes to work."

"Is it about the store?"

She nodded, cheerless. "We checked it out last week. It looks promising but he wants to see it again before I speak to my father about it. He wants to have a firm estimate of the renovation costs."

I was trying to be upbeat, to end the night on a good note. "That's good, right?"

"It is."

Her smile was weak and her tone told me that she was done. She wanted me to leave.

"Ok, I'm gonna head back." I took her hands in mine. "I *am* sorry, baby, I was just trying to—"

"I know. I trust you. We're good."

"Can I see you tomorrow night after work?"

"Dylan, you can't drive out here every night. I'm ok, really. I need to get some work done and you have to put in some long hours at the office, so let's just plan on seeing each other Friday night, ok?"

We'd just spent two weeks apart and she was already telling me she needed space.

* * *

KASIA

The anger was simmering so close to the surface I felt as if I could explode. That girl was poison. I thought after graduation I was done with Melanie, but she kept popping up like a bad penny, or herpes.

I hid out in my bedroom after I got home, disappointed and angry with Dylan and with myself, too. His ridiculous request came out of left field. I had no time to think it through, to prepare a response that would give the impression of being sure in my own skin and undaunted. Nope, I came off like a jealous, spiteful girl who didn't possess a self-assured bone in her body.

We spoke on the phone every day, and I acted as if Sunday night's conversation never happened. I told him all about the potential store site, the conversations with my father, and Alex's thoughts about renovation costs. I went on and on, while silently praying Dylan wouldn't bring the sore topic up again. He didn't. Thursday afternoon he called to ask where the band was playing, and asked if he could meet me there later that night. I was striving for casual when I answered, "You have plans tonight, Dylan, and so do I. I'll see you tomorrow."

Being with Darcy took my mind off of Melanie. If Darcy could plaster a smile on her face and be social, the least I could do was show her a good time. We actually wound up dancing, drinking a little too much and having a great night. The band was really good, and Sophia's brother was not only drop-dead gorgeous but totally into Darcy. I may or may not have spied her making out with him in a dark corner late-night. But Darcy told me the next day she basically cried on the guy's shoulder in between kisses and the two parted as friends.

Dylan called me a few times over the course of the night, but I didn't answer. I finally shot off a short text after the third missed call, something along the lines of: *Can't talk, too loud here*. My inner passive aggressive bitch held off on writing: *You need someone to talk to, Dylan? Talk to your girl, Melanie. That's who you chose to spend your night with*. Yeah, our date tomorrow night was going to be *so* much fun.

I woke up early Friday morning and took a long run. Left my ear buds at home because I needed to think, needed to clear my head. I kept saying I wasn't jealous, but I *was* acting like an easily threatened girl who lacked so much as a shred of self-confidence. So I decided to suck it up, to ask Dylan how everything went and then move on. Really move on, not just say I was moving on. I'd let that girl ruin my week, ruin the time I had with Dylan after being apart for so long.

I wanted Dylan to be honorable and honest, but I'd just given him an entire week's worth of reasons not to be.

* * *

DYLAN

The entire week was spent kissing up to Kasia. I called her twice a day, she didn't call me once. I listened patiently as she went on and on about her life, as if I didn't have a shitload going on in my own. I wanted to clear the air, but got the distinct impression that the topic was off limits. So the elephant stayed permanently situated in the room, and by Thursday afternoon I was pissed off.

I was mad at myself, wishing I could go back in time to that phone call and tell Melanie I couldn't hang out with her. And I was angry with Kasia. I told her the truth, was only looking to console a friend, and this is how she reacts? Dealing with the distant and cold version of her this week was screwing with my head. I was desperate for her to just get over it, for things to go back to the way they were, because shit, I missed her. And forget about Melanie. I was in no mood to see her. The girl had managed yet again—without even knowing it this time—to cause problems between me and Kasia.

And while my girlfriend was pretty much ignoring me, Mel was blowing up my phone, firing texts off left and right to plan our get together.

Since this was supposed to be me cheering up my lonely, forlorn friend, I figured it would just be the two of us meeting for drinks at Bemelmans. Instead, I walked into the lounge where Melanie was holding court with no less than ten of our friends. I scanned the group and noticed Cecilia first, then Samantha Paulson, Avery Manning, Charlie Price, James Bradford, and Delia and Tripp, among others. The scene was nothing short of a Palm Beach reunion.

Awesome.

Melanie floated across the room in her four inch stilettos and wrapped her arms around my neck. "Dylan, I've missed you!"

"What's all this?"

"I know. It's great, isn't it? The other night you made me feel so much better. I was in a funk and I needed to snap out of it. What better way to do that than to throw a party, right?"

"I'm glad you're feeling better, Mel."

"I am," she tapped my nose playfully, "and it's all thanks to you."

Melanie hooked our arms together and led me into the center of the group. I said my hellos and caught up with everyone, but I had a pit in my stomach.

Socializing among this set without Kasia felt wrong, deceitful even. Avery drove the point home when she teased, "I keep hearing about this girlfriend of yours, Dylan, but I've never met her. Is she some kind of recluse, or are you afraid we can't play nice?"

Melanie spoke loud enough so that everyone could hear. "Some of you must know Kasia. She's from New York, after all, and I know she went to Prep on what, Dylan, scholarship or something?"

My words came out terse and clipped. "Yes. She had a scholarship to Prep and also to Virginia, a full academic ride."

I thought that would shut her up, but I was wrong. Melanie—all of these people for that matter—didn't give a crap about your accomplishments. They only cared about your family ties and your net worth.

Melanie chirped, "Samantha, didn't you go to Prep? You *must* know Kasia."

"Kasia..." She did her best to look lost in thought before the light bulb miraculously went on. Eyes wide, she said, "Oh, I think I do know her...Blonde hair, Polish immigrant?"

I couldn't help but laugh. "Yeah Samantha, that's her."

Polish immigrant. What a fucking twat. I thought back to that night at dinner with Darcy and Kasia. Samantha had me fooled, but not those two.

She backtracked in an effort to make nice. "I do remember her, Dylan. She was quiet, though. She didn't really make an effort to get to know any of us, so I can't say we were good friends."

Charlie joined us. "I remember Kasia Mazur from Prep. She *was* quiet, but really nice and fucking brilliant at math. She used to ruin the curve in AP Calculus." He laughed before adding, "I hated her and drooled over her at the same time. What's she up to now?"

"She's great. She's living in Brooklyn, getting ready to expand a business she started in college."

Samantha looked as if she'd just sucked on a lemon, while

Melanie looked positively gleeful knowing she'd succeeded in making Samantha miserable. I just didn't get these girls.

Cecilia rested her hand on my arm and asked what kind of business it was. She seemed genuinely interested, especially when I mentioned that Kasia designed and custom-made her clothing line. Cecilia told me she "couldn't wait" to meet Kasia, while I sent up a silent prayer that the two would never cross paths.

Cecilia Tate shared a playpen with me, was at every one of my birthday parties, and our families vacationed together. Our mothers met on their very first day of college, and from that moment on they were best friends.

Cecilia was pretty, nicer than the girls she spent time with, and she actually had a brain in her head. She was an equestrian who used to compete at a pretty high level before easing out of that life in college.

With college and everything, we didn't cross paths as often anymore, so running into her last winter in Palm Beach was a blast from our sordid past. I always got the impression that while Cecilia participated in some wild nights, she wasn't really one of us. She was besties with Melanie but they weren't cut from the same dark cloth. I always had a soft spot for Cecilia, but being around her now was another reminder of how my two worlds just didn't seem to fit together. How could I ever bring Kasia around this crew? Cecilia reminded me of the impending collision when I heard her and some of the others chatting happily about the upcoming *weekend* in the Vineyard.

Weekend? Fuck me.

In years past, most of the people gathered here tonight crashed at my house after the party for a day or two, or several. Cecilia, Melanie, Samantha—it would be a fucking disaster if any of them slept over while Kasia was there. I literally began to sweat just thinking about it. It couldn't happen. I made a mental note to call my mother tomorrow and have her arrange another rental house nearby to catch this overflow.

I noticed Tripp and Delia with Melanie over by the bar, and wondered how he managed to pull off the loyal boyfriend act while in the company of Melanie, the girl I'd watched him do unspeakable things to merely months ago. But Tripp and I had learned the rules to this game from seasoned pros long ago, and now had it mastered. We crafted believable lies, knew to act arrogant in the face of an accusation, and above all else we knew to deny, deny, deny. It was done with impunity—men like us didn't care if we were ultimately found guilty or exonerated.

Melanie shot me a knowing wink and that's when I was done.

I called Kasia again but still no answer. Third time. I had one last drink with James and Charlie and then grabbed my suit jacket off the back of a barstool.

She was at my side in an instant. "Don't tell me you're bailing on us already. I haven't had a chance to spend any time with you."

"Mel, the only reason I agreed to come tonight was because I thought you needed a friend." I gestured around the room. "You've got plenty of people to entertain you here."

"Don't be a little bitch, Dylan. Is this how it's going to be now? You're dropping everyone? It's just you and Kasia? How fucking boring."

"Don't."

"I like *her*, Dylan. You saw how hard I tried last semester. It's Kasia! *She* acts like she's too good for *me*!" Melanie said that last line as if it was the most absurd notion.

"Kasia knows we've been together. She's just not looking to be besties with anyone I've slept with. You can understand that."

She stepped back, wide-eyed. "You told her about us?"

"Kasia found out on her own and she was cool about it."

Melanie was now looking at me as if I was deranged. "Does she know about New Years?"

"You think I'm stupid?"

She relaxed then. "Well, you know you have nothing to worry about. Tripp certainly isn't looking to publicize it," she gestured over to Tripp and Delia getting cozy in a corner, "and Cecilia would *never* do anything to hurt you. She lives and breathes for you."

I rolled my eyes at the overly dramatic remark. "Easy now."

"You *know* that's true. And you know she never does any of that crazy shit unless you're around, right? Cecilia has always wanted to be…I don't know…Whatever you need."

I felt guilty and restless, overwhelmed with the urge to just get the hell out of there. I leaned down and kissed Melanie's cheek. "I'm heading out. See you at the Vineyard."

She grabbed my hand as I turned to go. "All right, I'll see you then. And thanks, Dylan. It means a lot knowing you'd come just because I needed you."

I smiled back. I had a hard time being mad at her. We just went back too far and shared too many experiences that were beyond private. She knew shit about me and I knew shit about her that could bring down business empires, block one from running for public office, and prevent significant others from committing to the depraved individuals that we were—or had been, as I hoped was true in my case.

I checked my phone one last time as the cab sped crosstown through the park. Kasia had pretty much ignored my calls, texting back just once, offering up some bullshit about the band being loud.

I wasn't mad at Kasia. I got it now, even felt hurt on her behalf. I imagined her, the quiet scholarship kid, enduring that uppity prep school environment while putting up with bitches like Samantha Paulson. I wouldn't leave her side during the Vineyard weekend. I was hell bent on sending a message to all those society scions: Kasia was with me, she was all I wanted, and I was lucky to have her.

* * *

KASIA

I felt like crap all day, knowing I'd probably made him miserable last night. That was my intention at the time, but after the fact I got no pleasure from it. I wanted a do-over.

I texted Dylan subway directions to Bedford Avenue, but wasn't surprised when a sleek black town car pulled up on the corner of North Sixth in front of a building that needed some serious TLC.

"Hi," I whispered, too sheepish to meet his eyes.

He hugged me tight and whispered back, "Hi, yourself."

I sighed, relieved that he wasn't upset with me. "I'm sorry about last night...About this whole week."

"No," he held my shoulders taking a step back. "I know I would have been annoyed if you told me Patryk needed *you*, so I don't blame you. That won't be happening again. It's just that...It's awkward, Kasia, because our families are close. We're going to be crossing paths with that crew, there's no way around it. But when we do, I want it to be us, together."

"Was Melanie ok?"

"I do think she's lonely for Christian and feels kind of lost on her own, but typical Melanie, instead of meeting her for a drink, I showed up to a fucking soiree. I saw your pal, Samantha. And by the way, you and Darcy were right. She *is* a bitch."

"Samantha Paulson? "

"Yeah, Prep was well represented. Samantha was there and so was an admirer of yours, Charlie Price."

I smiled. "Wow, Charlie? He was so nice."

"He was praising your looks and your skill with numbers."

"I think he tried to cheat off me in calculus a few times."

"I bet he did. Anyway, it was nice to see some of them but I really wanted to be with you. I felt like shit when you wouldn't answer my calls."

"I'm sorry. I was so angry with you, with her, with myself…And I was wrong."

He took my hands in his, swinging them from side to side. "You're mine, Kasia, and I'm yours. Understand?" I nodded and he squeezed me tight. "Good."

Breaking apart, I gestured to the grate-covered storefront behind us. "So, what do you think of it?"

"This is it?" He was trying his best to look enthusiastic, but as his eyes took in the somewhat gritty surrounding streets, he couldn't hide his concern. "It's definitely got that, uh, urban vibe you're going for."

I undid the padlock and threw the grating up before battling with the nearly rotted-out locks on the front door. Some locksmith this guy had been. "Come on in."

The dust covered shelves, the creaky wide-plank wood floors, the antique lead windows—it was like an empty canvas for me. I was in nirvana every time I stepped inside this place because I could envision what it would become.

I pictured the Sweet Betty Threads logo brought to life on the storefront sign, the dresses that would hang on antique dress forms in the window, and the clean, open interior of the shop. I splurged on a chrome finished, retro-look computerized cash register long before my father even agreed to this deal.

When I turned back to Dylan, he was watching me and smiling. "You can already see what it's going to be, can't you?"

"Down to every last light fixture!"

He picked me up off the ground and hugged me tight. "It's going to be great." He looked out the front window. "And there's tons of foot traffic, you're right."

"I already had Darcy's brother and sister-in-law come out to take a look. Luke is a general contractor and Kate's an architect. Kate's drawing up some plans for me."

"Isn't your dad looking to do the work?"

"It's a little involved. There's some plumbing and electrical to be done, even though structurally speaking, it's sound. And there's the design factor, too. This can't be a gut and sheetrock job like my father would do." Looking up to the exposed wooden beams that I just loved, I added, "I want to keep the original details."

"If I can help you in any way, please let me."

I knew what he was implying, and although it was a loving gesture, I was adamant about doing this on my own.

"You're so sweet and I know you want to help me, but I have to do this the right way. Alex is investing in me for a small share of the business, and I'm using that start-up money for the renovations."

"Maybe *I* want to be an investor. Why can't I get in on the ground floor like Alex?"

I laced my fingers around his neck and drew him down for a kiss. "Business 101, Dylan...Don't mix love and money."

We went two doors down to a wine and tapas bar. It was a cozy place with low lighting and dark velvet banquets wrapped around small round tables. I practically sank into him when we sat down together. I was so relieved to be back to our normal.

After we ordered drinks and the waitress dropped menus, Dylan turned to me. "Let's never do that again. I don't want to ask if you're ok with something and then do it anyway when it's obvious that you're not. I was wrong to put you in that position. And please, don't shut me out and pretend nothing's wrong when there's a problem."

I let out a deep breath. "Agreed. I just felt like I couldn't talk to you about it. I always think of myself as this confident person, but there's something about Melanie. Maybe there's something about all the Melanie Pierce and Samantha Paulson types in the world that rattle me. Say what you want, but that's the type of girl you're used to and it's who you're conditioned to be with." I held my hand up to silence his protest so I could finish. "I don't need you to tell me I'm worthy, or that I'm better for you than they are. That insecurity I was feeling might not have been rational," I shrugged, "but it's what I felt."

He nodded his head looking down at our entwined hands. "I understand, but you need to know that you're everything to me. Everything."

We rode the train back to Greenpoint, and by the time we got to my house it was almost ten and my parents were turning in. They greeted Dylan with hugs and kisses, then left us on the couch watching a movie.

"I hate that we can't spend the night together," he whispered.

"I know. It's killing me, too."

He looked towards the stairs to make sure the coast was clear and then moved me onto his lap, situating me so that I straddled him. He kissed me deeply, slowly running his hands back and forth from my thighs up to the sensitive sides of my breasts. Against the base of my neck, he murmured, "I love how your body feels." I reached my hand down to stroke him over his pants and then shushed him when he let out a soft moan. "I'm sorry, Kasia, but I want you."

"Tomorrow. You have me all day tomorrow."

He sighed, moving me off his lap to sit beside him, wrapping an arm around me to pull me in close. He kissed my head, yawning when he said, "Tomorrow."

Dylan had been working twelve-hour-plus days, every day, so it was no wonder he fell asleep about fifteen minutes into the movie. I made him comfortable and then went up to my room, wishing he could curl up next to me. I told myself the same thing: *Tomorrow*.

There were no slackers in this house, so I was only half asleep, listening for my father early the next morning. When I heard him stirring at around six, I went out to the hallway, yawning and rubbing my eyes. "Tata, Dylan fell asleep on the couch so try not to wake him, ok? He's been working crazy long hours and he's exhausted."

He smiled at me and kissed my cheek. "Hard work is good for a young man, Kasia. It's good your Dylan is a hard worker."

My father was pleased not only by Dylan's work ethic, but by the respect he showed in keeping things G-rated while under my father's roof. I was, and would always be, his little Kasia.

Dylan woke at nine to the smell of coffee and freshly-baked cinnamon babka. My father was already back from an early run to the hardware store and a quick fix at one of his properties. He was writing numbers in his ledger while my mother and I sat at the table sharing the Saturday sections of the Times. Making his way into the kitchen, Dylan looked gorgeous, hair sticking up, wrinkled clothes and all.

"Good morning, everyone."

My mother smiled and said, "I hope you slept well. Next time you take Michal or Aleksander's old room. I can't believe Kasia left you on the couch!"

"Mama, I didn't want to wake him."

"I did sleep well, Mrs. Mazur. I actually feel great."

"So how is the job, Dylan?" my father asked as he handed him a cup of coffee.

"Thanks, Mr. Mazur. It's going well. I've always worked there on breaks, ever since I was in high school, so I'm acclimated there. Just a lot more responsibility now and a lot more travel."

"Like last month, you'll be in Asia mostly?"

"No, just once or twice a year. I'll actually be spending a lot of time in Chicago for the first two years. I have to talk to you about that, Kasia. My father wants me there part-time starting next month."

"Part-time?"

"Yeah," he looked disappointed, "about two weeks out of every month."

I was trying to mask my surprise. "Wow. I mean, I'll be really busy too, but that's a lot."

My father weighed in. "That's how it is. You do what you have to do when you're starting out. You sacrifice."

My heart sank. The long distance thing would be a challenge, if our recent little stints of time apart were any indication. The look Dylan gave me expressed his same concern. But then he smiled as he grabbed the babka from my hand and took a bite. "This is delicious," he said, finishing it off and licking the crumbs from his fingers. "Anyway, Kasia, you've never been to Chicago. We can think of it as an adventure."

My father's hand stopped mid-pour as he was refilling his cup. He didn't say a word, but I know he was more than a little irked by Dylan's assumption.

Mama and Tata were just going to have to deal because I was *not* going two weeks straight without seeing him every single month.

Chapter Eight

DYLAN

Despite my best efforts, Tom wouldn't budge. This was going to be my first July Fourth without him since I started throwing these parties.

Little James was babbling in the background like he was trying to get in on the conversation. "Is he talking?"

Tom laughed at my ignorance. "He's only five months old, asshole. He's just making sounds."

"Hey asshole, you better watch it or else his first word is going to be asshole."

I missed Tom, but guys don't say things like that to other guys. And I felt bad for my friend because his situation just sucked. He was trapped at home and hurting without her.

He held back for most of the conversation, but then caved and asked if I'd seen Darcy. When I told him no, but that Kasia and Darcy were spending a lot of time together, he asked if she was happy. I said I didn't know, even though Kasia regularly gave me updates that were of the *Darcy is miserable, Darcy is devastated* variety. Tom sounded miserable too. But since he was hell bent on cutting ties, I went ahead and reminded him of the many willing, attractive women that would be at my party looking to take his mind off his troubles. That didn't sell him, and I felt like a jackass for suggesting it.

Ben would be there, along with around fifteen or so other high school friends. A good number of my fellow alumni were coming, with Melanie, Christian, Justin, Brian, Trish, a few more frat brothers and teammates rounding out the group representing Virginia. My gut churned when I pictured CeCe, Samantha, Tripp and my other old friends sipping cocktails on my back deck right alongside their uptight parents. It would be great if I could just entirely omit that last group.

During the quick flight up Thursday morning, I started making plans. My parents weren't coming until the next day, so I was looking to making the most of my time alone with Kasia.

I wanted to give her the full experience, so we drove in from Chilmark and rented bikes in town to explore that side of the island. We rode most of that first day, stopping at the gingerbread cottages in Oak Bluffs, walking the shop-lined streets of Edgartown, and capping it off with beers and lobsters before heading back. I loved being the one to show her new places.

"This place is magical. I feel like I've stepped back in time."

"Magical...I guess I've always taken it for granted, but I liked seeing it through your eyes today."

She looked around the property when we came out onto the back deck. It was a view, with rolling green hills and the ocean just beyond. "Just look at it."

I wrapped my arms around her waist and rested my chin on her shoulder. "I'm so glad you're here with me. God, I've missed you."

"I miss you, too," she said as she turned in my arms and rested her head against my chest. After a moment she whispered, "I knew it would be different when we were living apart, especially now that I'm back with my parents." She paused, her voice cracking. "But it's so hard."

"Hey, no, don't cry. It *is* hard but it's temporary. And we're here now. I've got you all to myself."

She cracked a sad smile as she wiped at a stray tear. "You're right."

"Get in the hot tub. We need to soak those muscles of yours after riding all day. I'll grab us some beers."

I glanced back to watch as she shimmied out of her shorts and tested the water with her foot before lowering herself in slowly. Few girls looked as good in a bikini as Kasia did.

As I set about getting our drinks and some snacks, my thoughts were fixed on what she said. To go from spending every night with her loving body in my bed to stealing two or three hours together whenever we could *was* hard. It fucking blew. Worse still was being under the watchful eye of her parents. I sometimes felt like a man in the middle of the desert with no hope of finding water. Shaking it off, I reminded myself that tonight it was just the two of us in this big house. And it's not that I wasn't thinking about sex—I was—but holding her all night long and waking up together was foremost on my mind.

"Here you go, lovely Kasia. How does it feel?"

"Like heaven." Taking a few crackers and some of the cheese, she said, "Oh good, I'm starving." I still got turned on by the sight of her eating. "You know what I was just thinking?"

"I'm dying to know," I teased.

She splashed me and smiled. "These past few weeks you've been listening to me talk on and on about the store, the plans, the renovations—just everything. I haven't even asked how it's been for you. Do you feel a lot of pressure there? It's just, you're so young and you're expected to be the boss to men and women who are so much older than you."

"I've never thought about it like that because I'm above them. Wait, I sound like a dick. What I mean is that I've been being groomed for this since I was a kid. I expected to come in as management. It's like my father, the CEO, is my direct supervisor and I don't answer to anyone else. There's pressure, but I don't feel it in a bad way. It's a challenge and that's exciting."

She sipped her beer and then smiled as she set it down on the deck. "I guess that's why you don't mind all the long hours."

"The days do fly by."

"I'd like to see you in a business meeting someday. I bet it would be a total turn-on." With that, she reached back to undo her top.

"What are you doing?"

"Who, me? Nothing," she said as she made her way over and straddled me. She reached down beneath the water and undid the ties on the sides of her bikini bottom. "I think I lost my suit," she murmured between soft kisses.

"How many times can I fuck you tonight, Kasia?"

"Right now, then later on in the shower, and then again in your bed...Three times."

"I'm good with that."

"Take yours off," she whispered. "I want to feel you against me."

I slid my suit off and sat her back in my lap. I ran my hands up and down her back as she kissed me. This right here, was heaven.

"You know, we're gonna be all right."

"Huh?" she breathed, sounding as if she was drugged with desire.

I pulled back a few inches. "We're going to be ok with the distance. I won't let anything come between us."

"I just hate being away from you. Video chats are painful...No touching, no kissing."

"But then we'll be together like this, touching," I kissed her lips softly, "and kissing." I shifted, touching her breasts and then taking them in my mouth one by one as she arched her back so that she was pressing in closer to me.

The sun was setting, and before long we had only the moon to light our way. "Come." I led her out of the hot tub and was heading into the house when she tugged my hand back in the other direction. "Yeah? Outside?"

"There's no one around, right?"

"We're all alone."

She turned to face the deck railing and took my hands, placing one on her breast and leading one down between her legs. "Touch me, Dylan."

I appreciated moments like this one, when Kasia proved to me that life with her would be anything but bland and boring.

I took in her scent, priming her with my hand as I breathed in and scraped my teeth along the back of her neck. My girl was the sexiest creature on this earth. "You are so fucking hot, so wet for me. Your body, baby, it's perfect...So perfect for me."

Her words came out on a breathy exhale. "I need it now."

"You need me, Kasia?"

I had her moaning with my touch. "I need you, please," she pleaded. "Oh," she breathed as I eased into her. She braced her hands against the railing. "Fuck me good, Dylan. I need this."

Damn, I'd missed us. Everything we said and everything we did was just between us, just for us.

The realization hit after I came, hard and strong. "Uh, we're ok, right?"

She looked back to me, her breathing still ragged. "Of course I'm still on the pill."

"We've just never—"

"I know, we've never done it without. It felt pretty great, though, right? But not a good idea. We won't do that again."

She turned and wrapped her arms around my waist, and the feeling of her body pressed up against mine had me wanting her all over again.

"You always feel incredible, Kasia, but that was so damn good. I guess it's fine to go without. I mean, it's just you and me."

She gave me a kiss that was more like a peck before shaking her head. "Neither one of us would be ready to deal with the consequences, so it's best we don't take any chances. Now come on," she said as she led me back inside, "I was feeling pretty ballsy a few minutes ago, but all of a sudden I'm a little freaked out thinking someone could be watching us."

"If anyone was watching then they just got quite a show."

"It *was* pretty hot, right?" she asked.

"So hot that I want to do it again."

"Shower with me?"

I loved this girl.

We fell asleep together wrapped up in my fluffy down comforter after I'd hit my version of the trifecta.

* * *

KASIA

I sat up in bed with a start when I heard voices downstairs. What time was it? Shit, Dylan's parents were here already. I pulled the comforter up to cover my breasts and nudged him. "Hey, wake up." When he didn't stir I nudged him harder and whispered, "Did you bring my bag upstairs last night?"

He let out a groggy, "Wha?" before rolling over.

Looking around the room to realize I didn't even have a pair of underwear handy, I started to panic. "Dylan, your mom and dad are here and I have *no* clothes! Get. Up. Now."

He raked his hands over his face. "What the fuck are they doing here so early? They just ruined my plans for snuggling with you all morning."

With that, he rolled his body on top of mine, trapping me, and threw the comforter over us both so that we were covered head to toe. He was hard, which made me want to do him again and also made me laugh.

"That's funny, huh? You little tease. Now you're gonna get it and I don't care who hears us."

"Oh my God, Dylan, stop!" Picturing the mess we left downstairs, complete with my bikini and his boardshorts tossed aside next to the hot tub, I began to feel physically ill. "Our bathing suits…Your parents are going to know—" He tried to silence me with a kiss but I turned my head and pulled away. "Please, go downstairs, stash the suits and then bring up my luggage. I'm going to hop in the shower."

He groaned. "All right, I'm going." With his hand on the doorknob, he looked back at me and winked. "Don't worry, I'll tell them I slept in the guest room last night."

"Yeah, they'll believe that."

"That, sweet Kasia, is the difference between your parents and mine. Mine don't care."

I was beyond happy to see that my bag had materialized when I came out of the bathroom. I carefully laid my clothes out on the bed and then took a little extra time blow drying my hair. Maybe I was stalling, but I also wanted to look my best. Over my bathing suit (today I chose a one-piece) I wore one of my designs, a casual tunic dress in hot pink with a stitched white floral pattern.

I made my way downstairs, scolding myself as I fought against the feelings of self-doubt and anxiety that seemed to increase with each step I took. I couldn't help it. I'm sure Dylan didn't feel completely at ease around my parents either, but surely he got the vibe that they liked him. I didn't know where I stood with Margot and Vince Cole.

"There she is," Dylan called out happily when I joined them in the kitchen.

"Hello Kasia, it's good to see you again." Mr. Cole wasn't overly formal, but he wasn't warm either. He was somewhere in between.

Mrs. Cole crossed the room and took me into a light embrace before kissing me on both cheeks. Ugh, how European of her.

"Dear, it's so wonderful to see you."

"You too," I said as I looked from one to the other. "You have such a beautiful home. Thank you for having me."

"I do love it here. It's so relaxing, isn't it?" Mrs. Cole asked.

"It is. This is my first time on Martha's Vineyard. I think I've fallen in love with it already."

"Kasia was a good sport yesterday," Dylan said. "We must have ridden ten or twelve miles. We were all over the island."

"But we didn't hit the beaches yet. That's today's plan, right?" I looked to Dylan.

"Yep. We'll head to South Beach for a while and then back over towards Menemsha. And I've been craving fried clams, so we're stopping for those at some point."

Mrs. Cole broke in, her smile tight. "Please be back in time to head over to the Tates' later on. They've invited us for dinner."

Dylan shook his head and put his hand up. "Mom, I'm seeing all of those people tomorrow. We've already got our day planned."

"But I told them you and Kasia were joining us. They're expecting you."

I put my hand on his arm. "I don't mind, Dylan."

Resting his free hand on top of mine, he looked directly at his mother and said, "But I *do* mind, Kasia. I never get to see you and I have the day planned out for us."

Mr. Cole shrugged. "Margot, just tell Bunny and Paul they aren't coming. You should have asked Dylan first."

"I'll tell them," she said, managing to sound relaxed while the air in the room grew thick with tension. "I just hope Cecilia won't be too disappointed. She'll be alone, with no one for company but us boring old adults."

Dylan's tone was sharp. "She's not a toddler, Mother. I think she'll survive."

I was beginning to perspire, even though the central air in that house was seriously cranking.

His mother's expression brightened. "It's fine, really." Looking to me, she said, "Come, let me show you the garden. We can pick some herbs. I'm about to make a frittata."

By her abrupt change in attitude, I got the feeling Mrs. Cole didn't do confrontation. Honestly, I was grateful. Just being around his parents made me uneasy to begin with, forget about how I felt standing there while they were about to launch into an argument.

To say I wasn't looking forward to my personal tour of the grounds was an understatement.

Together, just me and Margot Cole.

Yay.

"Dylan is very possessive when it comes to you...Possessive of his time with you, dear. You must be very special to him."

"Mrs. Cole, I'd be happy to go to dinner with your friends tonight. I can try to convince him."

"Thank you, but that won't be necessary. And you should know, once one of the Cole men makes a decision, they are not easily deterred."

Donning a pair of gardening gloves, she smiled and then handed me a basket.

"Dylan tells me your brother is a landscaper."

"Yes, Aleksander. He's actually done a few properties up here for his New York-based clients."

"Fascinating."

I didn't know her well, haven't been in her presence enough times to paint an accurate picture, but when she said *fascinating*, it took me back to Christmas at the Coles. She had a habit of throwing out one-word declarations—*charming, interesting, delightful*—that didn't land with sincerity and left you questioning her meaning. *Was* she fascinated or thoroughly unimpressed?

"And your other brothers? There are four of you all together, is that correct?"

When she said the number four, she did so with raised eyebrows.

Maybe I was being overly sensitive, but I assumed she deemed this to be entirely *too* many children for one family.

"Yes, there are four of us. My brother Michal is an attorney and my brother Tomasz is an analyst at an investment bank." I made sure to pronounce my brothers' names using the full-on Polish accent. Just because.

"All very accomplished."

"Thank you. I'm proud of my brothers."

"And Dylan speaks so highly of you, Kasia. He finds your business acumen very impressive."

"That's yet to be seen, Mrs. Cole. I'm really just starting out."

I swallowed in the ensuing silence, the pressure of this little "get to know you" chat wearing on me.

She snapped some herbs from their stems and handed them to me. "You make Dylan very happy."

"I hope so."

She took my free hand in hers and smiled. "Let's head back. You can help me cook this thing since I have no idea what I'm doing in the kitchen."

I tried to take her friendly overture as a positive sign, but Mrs. Cole's smile was one of resignation, not true happiness. It was the same smile she gave to the guy who came to clean the pool later on that morning.

* * *

DYLAN

"Do you think it's a good idea to blow your mom off about tonight?"

"Are you seriously looking to spend the evening with *Bunny* and Paul Tate? Take it from someone who knows, it'll be boring as fuck."

"I can't believe a grown woman goes by the name Bunny. I can almost envision her sipping vodka tonics at the club after her tennis lesson."

I pinched her ass as we made our way towards the bike shed. "You're not far off the mark."

"Ouch!"

"My mother will live. I'm not wasting any of our time together fulfilling her social obligations."

"Hey, where's Anna?"

"She'll be here for the party. She had to spend the week with her mother. You know, visitation bullshit. She's driving up with Uncle Todd tomorrow."

"I guess the divorce was tough on Anna?"

"My Uncle Todd is an absolute dickhead, and Anna's mother... Don't even get me started on her. I still can't figure out how the two of them produced a quality individual like my cousin."

"Your mother is very good to her."

I nodded. "Anna brings out the best in her for some reason." As we went to roll the bikes out of the shed, I stopped for a moment and took her hand. "I love my mother. She's a good person, but she can be small-minded and harsh sometimes. I understand that about her."

She eyed me warily. "You sound like you're trying to prepare me for something. Maybe for her disapproval?"

"No, that's not what I'm saying." Damn, Kasia's ability to detect bullshit never failed. I looked away when I added, "I'm sure she adores you." Adore, love? Not now and maybe never, but Mother *would* come to accept Kasia. She didn't have much choice in the matter. "I'm just letting you know that she's not warm the way your mom and dad are. I mean, she's not a cold bitch or anything, but she might not make you, uh, feel the love. Know what I mean?"

She laughed. "Yeah, I get it."

It's not like I was looking to butt heads with my mother, but the Tates? There was no fucking way I was spending the evening sipping cocktails at Bearberry. Yup, Bunny referred to their home by name a name she bestowed upon it herself. There was even an understated wooden sign at the entrance to their driveway, weathered by design to look like it had been there battling the elements for a century instead of a decade.

I remember joking with Mom that instead of naming the estate after the seaside shrub with the cool name, Bunny should have named the place after the blue wildflowers that dotted their entire property. My mother didn't gossip as a rule, and she wasn't one to laugh behind her friends' backs, but she damn near cackled at that one. "Liverwort! Wouldn't that be just d-d-darling?" I smiled thinking back to that moment, my mother loose and carefree, thumbing her nose at all the pretentious bullshit. That's when I loved her most.

Yeah, my parents could have threatened to disown me and I still wouldn't have changed my plans. Being in close quarters with Cecilia Tate was not a good idea. I didn't need any reminders of that disastrous coke-fueled Grecian orgy in Palm Beach—the mere thought of it turned my stomach—but I was also hell-bent on avoiding her because there was more than a shred of truth to what Melanie had said. I knew Cecilia was into me, and I also knew our parents would consider it a fucking match made in heaven. *I hope Cecilia isn't too disappointed.* Fuck that. Never in a million years would I subject Kasia to an intimate dinner hosted by Bunny Tate, a woman who was jonesing to be my mother-in-law.

My mood lifted once we started pedaling towards South Beach. This was my stomping ground as a teenager—the place where I had my first taste of independence, my first beer and my first summer fling.

I ran into some locals who were friends way back when, so Kasia and I played in some volleyball games and had a beer with them before heading over to a more secluded beach on the island. And I don't know what it is, but there's something about being in the water that makes kissing so much hotter. I wished we had one more day alone in the house together. Kasia and I didn't get the chance to skinny dip in our pool, and it would have been the perfect night for it. As the sun set, Kasia and I ate fried clams at Larsen's, holding hands across the picnic table, totally and completely relaxed.

Then she broke into my bliss. "Where are you sleeping tonight?"

"In my bed with you, duh."

She winced. "I know your parents are way cooler than mine, but I don't think that's a good idea. They'll think I'm too bold," she smiled, "or that I'm easy."

I threw my head back, exasperated but laughing. "All right, I'll take a guestroom tonight. My parents aren't staying at the house the night of the party though, so it'll just be for one night."

"One night...That won't be so terrible, right?"

"Not if I take you home and have my way with you before they get back from Bunny's. C'mon, let's go."

"Ok, but I want you to call me Bunny when you," she gave me her best soap opera-seductress look, "make *love* to me."

"You're a whack job, Bunny." I put on my best orgasmic voice. "Oh, Bunny." I was chasing her back down the path towards the bikes while she was laughing in fits. "I'm gonna fuck you so hard, Bunny."

When my parents came in, Kasia and I were curled up on the couch together. I was watching the Yankee game while Kasia was out cold. Dad waved and went right upstairs but my mother lingered.

"How was dinner, Mom?"

"It was lovely. Cecilia was stuck with us, though, poor thing. She's very excited about the party tomorrow."

I was going for bored and disinterested when I replied, "That's nice," but I was borderline seething. I didn't want to hear that girl's name, especially not while Kasia was lying in my arms.

"Well, I'm heading to bed...Table deliveries, the caterers and the florist will be here early."

"Yeah, we'll be heading up soon. I'm staying in the guest bedroom next to yours."

"Why?"

"Kasia's family is pretty strict. She feels funny about staying with me while you're here."

Clearly amused, my mother said, "She didn't feel funny about leaving every stitch of her clothing strewn across the back deck yesterday."

"Mom, please." I hoped she realized the "please" was meant to convey a great deal. Please be good to her, please don't make her feel uncomfortable around all those snooty women tomorrow, and please, for my sake, love her.

My mother leaned down to kiss my cheek and then reached over to stroke Kasia's hair, telling me in her own way that she'd read me loud and clear. "She's such a beauty, Dylan."

"She is."

* * *

KASIA

I must have been wiped out from all the exercise because it was already ten when I rolled over to check my phone. I think I'd put more miles on a bike in the last two days than I had in all of my life. My muscles ached in a nice way as I made my way downstairs after showering.

The main floor was buzzing with activity. There were at least seven or eight people being directed by Mrs. Cole, who stood in the middle of it all, clipboard in hand and totally composed.

"Good morning."

"Ah, Kasia...I'm glad you had a good sleep."

Surveying the organized chaos, I offered, "Is there anything I can do to help?"

"No," she waved me off. "Take the morning and go get pampered in town." I was more than happy to be dismissed. "Our guests will be arriving at three."

Dylan sidled up to me. "Hey, I've been waiting for you to wake up. Take a ride into town with me? I want to pick up a new tie for later." He whispered when his mother's attention was diverted, "I have to get out of here. My mother is in social animal party planning mode."

He didn't have to twist my arm to spend a few hours in town. We split up so I could get a manicure and pedicure, and I wound up getting my hair blown out as well. Nothing crazy—I didn't want to look different, but I didn't want my hair to be a frizzy mess from the humidity and sea breeze either. A blow-out would ensure that my hair looked silky and smooth all day long, and for reasons I was trying my best to ignore, I felt the need to look spectacular today.

I came upon Dylan sitting outdoors at a coffee shop reading the financial section. He looked up from the paper and said, "Well, hello," as he did a slow perusal of my body.

"Did you get a tie?"

He held up a small bag. "Extra nerdy. It's got some pink whale print shit on it. Margot will be pleased."

"Really?" That surprised me. "Your mother has a great sense of style, Dylan."

"I know, but she always likes us dressing the part. On the Vineyard we aim for the casual, prepster vibe. Prepare yourself for a lot of bright pink, navy blue and kelly green. Although with the holiday, you may get some very obnoxious red, white and blue ensembles."

Walking back to the car, I commented, "Casual in my book does not entail collared shirt, tie, long pants or pricey slip-on moccasins."

He spun me to face him, and with a flair for drama, he sighed before saying, "As I feared, Kasia, it'll never work. We're simply from two different worlds." Then he backed me against the side of his truck and planted a raunchy kiss on me.

By the time we made it back, I had less than half an hour to get myself together before the guests arrived. I'd been working with linen a lot lately, and had sold a good number of the simple shift dress I was wearing today. Mine was orange linen cut a few inches above the knee but not quite mid-thigh. Custom fitted to my curves, the back had an exposed zipper to show the navy tape surrounding the zipper itself. It was classic, I thought, with a little edge. I slid on a pair of strappy navy blue sandals and some earrings, then inspected myself in the mirror. I knew I looked good, but was fighting off the butterflies in my stomach nonetheless. I threatened Trish in the hopes that she and Brian would arrive earlier than the rest, but it would be a long two or three hours before most of the younger crowd began trailing in. I had to brace myself for solo time with the up and comers, not to mention their stuck-up mummies and daddies.

There was a soft knock on the door before Dylan walked in. The satisfied smile on his face calmed me. "You look beautiful, Kasia. Come on, people are here already and I want to show you off."

So I met the infamous Bunny, Cecilia's mother, and the name was more than fitting. Her matronly frame was stuffed into a bright red and navy print dress, vodka tonic perched in her hand at all times, and she spoke about goings on at "the club" as if they were major world events. Her daughter seemed nice enough and definitely more interesting, as she told me about the master's in art history she was about to begin in the fall. I also met Melanie's mother, who reminded me of Cruella DeVille. She was all hard angles with sharp, pejorative eyes that raked me over from head to toe. Ugh, like mother like daughter. Dylan intercepted that exchange soon after Mrs. Pierce approached, and for that I was thankful.

He stayed close by for most of the afternoon, holding my hand as he introduced me to everyone as "my girlfriend." I didn't need him standing by my side like a sentinel, didn't need his protection, but I have to admit that I found it sweet.

"Dylan, would you let go of the girl for a moment? You're positively hogging her," Mrs. Cole teased as she led me over towards a group of women on the other side of the large deck.

"Kasia, I think you know a dear friend of ours," she said, smiling as we approached the group. One girl had her back to me, but I knew it was Samantha Paulson before she even turned around. "Samantha, you know Kasia from Prep, don't you?"

Eyes wide and super-pumped, her look was all: *Oh my God, it's been so long!* And Lord, her face looked as if it might just crack from the effort of holding that forced smile. James Lipton would never be asking this one where she'd honed her acting chops.

"Kasia, it's *so* good to see you! I was with Dylan a few weeks ago, out with our entire crowd, and he told me he was hanging out with you."

Dig number one: *our* entire crowd. Subtle, I'll give her that, but meant to ensure I understood that I was *not* one of them. Dig number two: hanging out with you. Translation: you will *never* be anything serious to him.

"Right, Dylan mentioned it. You look great, Samantha."

I guess when pushed I could be just as bitchy because she did *not* look great. Samantha was crammed into a dress that didn't fit, her make-up was too much for a daytime outdoor event, and the high-lights, which I'm sure cost a fortune, made her naturally warm brown hair look over-processed. The false eyelashes did nothing to brighten her cruel eyes, and the nose, the exact one purchased by several of the girls I went to high school with, didn't do much to improve her looks either. In fact, the way the surgeon made it turn up slightly at the tip accentuated the stuck-up vibe she gave off. But more than anything, it was her attitude that made her ugly.

"So, Dylan said you're living in Brooklyn."

"Yes, I'm back with my parents for now. What about you?"

"I just got a *fabulous* place in Tribeca. I need to be close to my job. The hours are murderous at the magazine."

"Isn't Melanie working for a magazine? Do you work together?"

The she-devil herself slithered right up behind me. "No way. Samantha and I are direct competitors. Love this dress, Kasia."

She slid her index finger up along the zipper, all the way from the base to the nape of my neck. Guess the rumors were true about her interest in both sexes. I took a step to the side. "Thanks, Melanie."

Cecilia walked over, and then it seemed our group had broken into young and old, with Mrs.Cole abandoning me to the wolves. Melanie looked to Cecilia. "CeCe, have you met Kasia?"

So Cecilia was CeCe. Interesting.

Looking to me, she smiled warmly. "Yes, we've met."

Samantha shot me a look that told me she was up to no good when she said, "CeCe, I haven't seen you since Palm Beach!" She grabbed her in a chokehold of an embrace, from which Cecilia nearly stumbled back. "That was just *the* best, craziest break *ever*. I needed a week to recover after I got back to school."

Melanie grinned in a self-satisfied way. "Yeah, it was pretty crazy."

Samantha looked to me then. "Next year, *if* you're still with Dylan, you have to come."

What. A. Bitch.

"Why on earth would she want to go there? Don't you have to, like, show your AARP card to gain admittance? Aunt Margot dragged me down there this past winter, but I already told her that I'm out on that trip next year."

Ah, Anna. Loved her dearly.

I turned and gave her a grateful hug. "I'm so happy you're finally here!"

She whispered, giggling, "You owe me one of these cute little dresses with the sexy zipper for that rescue."

"Done."

Melanie gasped, teasing, "Anna, is that you? Where's the belly ring and the mohawk?"

"Up yours, Melanie."

Melanie laughed in response, unaffected, while Samantha looked as if she was still trying to recover from Anna's blow. I'd had enough —simple conversation with this crew was more stressful than high stakes poker. I saw Trish coming in with Brian and dragged Anna away to introduce them.

As the party morphed from a staid gathering for the upper crust to college reunion mode, I began to relax. After Dylan's parents left, I went up to change out of my dress and into a bikini and shorts, like most of the girls were wearing. When Dylan spotted me, he walked away from some guy mid-conversation and pulled me in close, swaying to the music as he planted kisses along my neck.

"No mauling me in public, got it?"

"Mmm, it's hard not to...I'm hard," he whispered, laughing as he reluctantly broke away from me.

I looked over my shoulder to see if we'd made a spectacle, only to see Samantha, Cecilia and Melanie clustered together, eyes fixed on us. Samantha looked sour-pussed, Melanie was leering as if she was itching to join in, and Cecilia looked downright depressed. My Spidey senses told me there had been a hook-up between Cecilia and Dylan in the past, but I decided to take the high road. Dylan had a past. I knew that, and I was determined not to let it cloud my feelings about the present or the future.

Trish and a few other girls from school provided a good buffer against Samantha and the rest of them, but being with Trish made the absence of Val and Bernadette more difficult. We started out video chatting at least once a week, but Val wasn't in on the last two calls and she already bailed on a girls' getaway we were planning for the fall. I had the feeling that Trish and Bernadette would stay close, while Valerie would inevitably drift away. Val didn't attach. I guess I'd known it all along, but since she'd gone down to Atlanta to start workshop groups, it became painfully obvious. The last time I spoke to her she told me she was done with Cooper, the guy she all but worshipped not too long ago. Yep, Val was an out of sight, out of mind kinda girl.

At one point I surveyed the scene and determined that all in all, it was a great night. I met some new people, got to know a few of Dylan's high school friends better, our college friends made plans to visit us in New York, and Dylan and I made tentative plans to hook up with friends out west while Dylan was in Chicago. As for Dylan's *other* friends, I was happy to see the few friendly faces I knew from that crowd, like Charlie Price. I had a good laugh when he admitted to passing calculus thanks to my large handwriting. I also met Tripp and his girlfriend, Delia, liking them both, which had me thinking that maybe I could tolerate some of those get-togethers in the future.

Samantha ruined that feeling when she came over, totally interrupting a conversation in progress to squeal excitedly, "CeCe told me she's leaving for Chicago next month and your mom told me that's where you'll be based. That's great! I'm sure CeCe's *so* glad she won't be out there all alone."

What is your problem with me? Truly, why me? Why had this spiteful girl been hell bent on trying to hurt me since we were fourteen years old?

Dylan's body stiffened at her words, as did his hold on my hip. "I'm not based in Chicago, Samantha. I'll be in and out, and very busy while I'm there." He flashed Samantha a big smile and then looked to me. "I'll be begging Kasia to come out there and keep me company as often as possible."

She tried her best to look sincere, but I knew Samantha, knew she was incensed by his subtle rebuff. "Yes, I'm sure Kasia would jump at the chance to be with you."

She wasn't worth the spit required to form the words for a comeback.

When she skulked away, I laughed and raised my right hand in an oath. "I swear, I never did anything to piss that girl off in high school."

"They're all the same, Kasia. They have no talent, no drive. They'll work a meaningless job for a year or two at a society-page magazine that's only in print because of their parents' subscriptions. Even Cecilia, with that *impressive* master's degree in art history? She's just killing time. Maybe she'll do a short stint volunteering as a docent at the Met, or maybe if she's *really* ambitious, she'll get her parents to purchase her a gallery of her very own. And that gallery, by the way, will never turn a profit. Just by being the beautiful, smart, independent girl that you are, you make girls like Samantha seethe."

I vaguely remember making my way upstairs with Dylan at what had to be around four in the morning, and woke just a few hours later in dire need of water and some aspirin. I put on a bathing suit, certain that a quick dip in the pool would ease my headache. As I made my way downstairs, the smell of stale beer hit me. There were plastic cups on every surface—some empty, some full, some that had obviously been used as ashtrays. I couldn't help but start clearing the counters and tabletops.

"What are you *doing*?" a grating, reproachful voice called out. "There are people to take care of that. You're not the cleaning lady, are you?"

I burned at the condescending reference to the menial job many Polish immigrants took as they struggled to gain footing in this country. My own mother had cleaned houses for years to help put food on the table before my parents' business became profitable.

"Samantha, you haven't changed one bit, have you?"

"And that's supposed to mean what, exactly?"

"You're still a nasty, mean-spirited witch."

"Aw, poor Kasia. Did I hurt your feelings? If you're expecting a warm, happy reception from the people in our circle, you're a fool. Do you think his parents approve? Think Margot and Vince are pleased that Dylan's involved with someone like *you*? I can assure you, that's not the case."

"I don't care what anyone in your circle thinks of me. I certainly don't care what *you* think of me." With that, I went out onto the deck, and where she could definitely see me through the sliding glass doors, I slowly stripped down to my bikini and then raised my arms above my head leisurely as I tied my hair up in a band. Yes, it was immature and petty on my part, but I thought, *Let that cow get an eyeful*. I knew to girls like Samantha, you could never be too rich or too thin.

I dove in, and my headache eased as I swam the length of the pool underwater.

"Good morning," Charlie greeted me as I resurfaced. "I'll regret not asking you out while we were at Prep for the rest of my life."

He must have fallen asleep on one of the lounge chairs last night. Ugh, I'd inadvertently just given him a show.

"Well you missed your chance, dipshit, she's mine," Dylan called out before doing a cannon-ball into the pool.

There were several people passed out on loungers like Charlie had been. The rest were doubled and tripled up in guest bedrooms, of which I'm sure there were at least five or six. Only a handful of us were awake.

"Hey, good morning to you," I said, kissing him as he moved in closer. "The water just took my pounding headache away."

"Did you have fun last night?"

"Yeah, it was great. The earlier part of the day wasn't as painful as I thought it would be either."

"I'm glad. At one point I saw you surrounded by my mother's friends and their daughters. I was worried."

"I can hold my own," I said as I splashed him.

"That's it, Mazur, you're going down." With that, he sprung on me and pulled me under before slipping one hand underneath the fabric on my backside while tickling under my arm with the other.

"Stop!" I pleaded as I came up for air, barely able to breathe.

"Yeah stop, get a room, whatever," Charlie teased.

My eye caught Samantha standing in the doorway with Cecilia. Getting more familiar with that part of Dylan's world was something I could do without. I knew I'd never be able to let my guard down around those girls, and life was too short to waste energy on people who weren't worth it.

* * *

DYLAN

My goal was to make sure Kasia had a good time and I was pretty sure I'd succeeded. From my vantage point, she didn't seem intimidated by the other girls or slighted by any of my mother's friends, so I was relieved. As a group, they could be downright nasty, especially when they sensed that a good marriage prospect—me—might be in danger of being whisked away by a lowly commoner.

It's not that I cared whether or not they accepted Kasia—they could all fuck off as far as I was concerned—it was more that I wanted her to feel secure and comfortable in my world, with me.

As I jumped into the pool that next morning, I was thinking two things. First, I was gonna slap the shit out of Charlie Price if he didn't stop looking at Kasia like he wanted to fuck her, and second, I was excited that we had an entire day and night ahead of us before we had to head back to New York on Monday. Maybe we'd get to christen the pool later on tonight after all.

I was thankful that most people left early on Sunday, leaving just a few of us hanging out at the house. It was down to Ben and the new girl he was hanging out with, Trish, Brian, Melanie, Christian, Justin and his girl. She was based in New York now too, which gave me and Kasia another couple to hang out with.

Sunday night was mellow in comparison. Brian lit a fire in the pit, and we all sat around bullshitting, drinking beers at a considerably slower pace and smoking. As the joint made its way around the circle, I was surprised when Kasia took it from Melanie's outstretched hand, and even more surprised with the truly friendly way that Melanie asked Kasia if she wanted to give it a try. Melanie didn't tease or dare her, she just seemed truly curious to know if Kasia had ever tried it before. Mel instructed her not to inhale too deeply the first time, but of course Kasia did, and we all had a laugh with her when she choked on it. Although I was not looking for those two to be buddies—I still felt a little anxious when Melanie so much as spoke to her—I didn't want them to hate each other either. Melanie would always be in my life to some degree, and despite everything, she's someone I would probably always consider a friend.

The one and only hit we'd taken off the joint had hardly any effect on me or Kasia, and I was glad for it. I wasn't into being out of my mind when I was with her. I wanted to experience her, talk to her, hold her and remember every minute of it. That one crazy night still made me cringe whenever it came to mind.

We went upstairs as the group started to break up. Kasia went in to brush her teeth and then called to me from the bathroom. When I got in there she was perched up on the counter in her birthday suit. Her smile was shy as her feet swayed from side to side, legs crossed at the ankles. "Hi," she whispered.

I stood there for a few moments, taking in her beauty and her raw sexuality. This woman was mine—mine to love, mine to protect, mine to fuck, ravish and pleasure.

With one hand on each knee, I spread her out before me, watched the leaky head of my cock enter her, closed my eyes in pain and ecstasy when she gripped me like a vise, and damn near cried when I came.

We fell into bed, bone-tired and satisfied. The next morning I got to stay in bed late, Kasia curled up and nestled into my body. I watched her sleep, more content than I'd ever been. I thought to myself that people probably contemplated marriage just so they could experience this mind-blowing goodness on a daily basis.

. . .

"I'm sure I won't need to call," I answered when my father told me to get in touch with him if I ran into any obstacles.

My parents came to see us off. They were staying in the Vineyard for a few extra days before heading back and I was pleased about that. My father's willingness to take more vacation time now that I was at Cole Industries full-time was testament to his confidence in my abilities.

Once we were on the plane I pulled out my tablet to show Kasia my calendar for the rest of the summer. There would be ten days in Chicago at the end of July, a quick four day trip to Dublin mid-August, and then the last ten days of that month in Chicago again. I asked her about coming over to Dublin with me, being honest that I would probably only be free for dinners. She rubbed her hand along my thigh and smiled. "Dylan, I don't want you to be worried about this. I know you have a lot on your shoulders right now. Once in a while maybe I'll tag along, but I'm not looking to be your plus-one, all right?"

"Oh, I definitely know that." I looked at her, unable to hide the longing. "Sometimes I wish you needed me and had nothing to do but globe-trot with me."

"I'll never be that girl, existing just to follow you around. And be honest, you wouldn't like that either. I do plan to pop out to Chicago whenever it works for us, though."

"I think your parents are going to be ok with it."

"They're going to have to be."

I teased, wide-eyed, "Little Kasia is going to defy Mama and Tata?"

She landed a light punch to my arm. "I'll persuade them, not defy them."

"I'd be so lonely for you if you didn't come. Maybe it's just because these past few days have spoiled me, but ten days a month... It's a lot."

"I think," she made a pinched face and exaggerated the words, "CeCe would be *more* than happy to keep your bed warm."

My girl was perceptive, I'll give her that. "Well, I only want *you* to keep me warm."

"Be careful with her, Dylan."

I felt my throat constricting. "What do you mean?"

She looked out the window and quietly repeated, "Just be careful."

I lifted her hand and kissed it, loving her so deeply in that moment that it physically hurt.

I told myself that no one was a threat to us, that I wanted no one but her, just as a mocking voice in my head reminded me that I'd already cheated on Kasia. God help me, after just three months together I'd cheated on her. I'd gone six months since that night without so much as a passing desire to be with anyone else, but I fully understood that I was not the poster boy for monogamy.

Not even close.

Chapter Nine

KASIA

"I just came from my meeting with Luke and Kate. The plans look so good!"

"That's great. When can they get started? How soon will the permits be approved?"

"Do you know that I didn't even take that into account? I was under the impression they could start work right away. Me of all people, with what my father does for a living?"

"You're just excited. How long did they say?"

"Best case scenario, two months, worst case, five months."

Dylan nodded reassuringly. "The waiting period could turn out to be an advantage for you."

"How?"

"You've got to start thinking bigger. You need to hook up with a manufacturer for your designs. Say the word and the meetings will be set."

"I love you and I love that you want to do this for me, but—"

He put up his hand. "I know, I know."

It would be easy. It would be so easy to let him take me on as a project, a subsidiary, a whatever. But I had to do this on my own.

I worked the rest of the summer sewing, filling my orders from the website and working on new designs. Even with the limited number of orders coming in, it was a struggle to get the work done. It hardly felt like there were enough hours in the day. One night as Dylan and I were chatting on-line, he sighed, watching as I continued to work on a pleat. "You need an employee, Kasia."

"I'm not ready."

"You love your phrases, so let me put it to you in a way that you'll understand. You have to spend money to make money, expand or die…What other adage can I come up with here?"

"I know, I know. I feel like I'm working around the clock. I've been sleeping like four hours a night but I don't feel tired, I feel energized."

"But you can't just keep spinning your wheels. Someone needs to be managing the orders, doing the shipping, and doing the damn sewing so that you can create and market the brand."

"You're right."

"You know this is my selfish side talking, don't you? I'm away now, but when I get home I *need* my woman."

I dropped the fabric onto my bed and smiled. "I can't wait to be your woman when you get home, Dylan."

"Three more days and you're mine."

"I'm yours."

I spent Dylan's first stint in Chicago working furiously, taking only one day off to meet up with Darcy and her friends down at the beach. We had just two weeks together before he jetted off again for the entire second half of August. Once he left I put my head down and buried myself in work again.

We were both busy. I loved that he bounced ideas and dilemmas off me, eager for my feedback, and he was a great sounding board for me. On the days we were apart, we spoke on the phone for at least an hour every night. I struggled with the separation but believed we were ok. Despite the distance, we were close.

September brought him back to me. We fell back into a routine but I always knew it was temporary. I became very well acquainted with his calendar. This month I had fifteen days until he was gone again—a week in Stockholm, one day in New York and then another week in Chicago. I announced at dinner one night that I was flying out to see him. My parents weren't thrilled but they didn't protest. I think even Tata knew that keeping us apart, especially when Dylan was working so hard, was not right.

Dylan's place in Chicago was as posh as the one in New York. The doorman knew exactly who I was when I walked into the elegant lobby, and he personally took me upstairs and let me into Dylan's apartment. When I entered, the woman who tended to his housekeeping was leaving, instructing me that she'd left lunch for me on the counter and "dinner for you and Mr. Cole" in the refrigerator. To me it was a surreal type of luxury, but this was everyday life for my boyfriend.

We met up with Trish and Brian that weekend and it was great, albeit a little weird. They seemed different, so grown up and established. After we got home, Dylan told me Brian was planning to propose to Trish this Christmas. He wanted to know if I thought it was too soon. Truthfully, I wasn't sure. I told Dylan if they felt it was right then that's all that mattered, but I didn't say everything I was thinking out loud. For me, a serious commitment like that would be too much, too soon. If Dylan asked me to marry him right now? Just the thought of it frightened me.

Dylan sensed my unease and laughed to lighten the mood, but it did little to mask his confused and hurt expression. "Don't worry, I wasn't about to get down on one knee, but it's good to know that if I did you'd probably faint."

"Who wouldn't want to marry you, Cole?" I teased before I

leaned up to kiss him. "Margot and Vince would completely freak out, though, right?"

"Margot and Vince *would* blow a gasket if we got hitched at twenty-two, I guess." He was silent for a moment before asking, "When do you think you'd be ready?"

"It's not so much about age, like a specific number, as it is about being established. I want to be able to stand on my own two feet first. How about you?"

"I really haven't given it much thought until now. I've thought about the person but not the timeline." He took my wineglass and placed it on the table before easing me back onto the couch. "Don't panic like you just did, Kasia, but there's only one person I want to spend my life with."

When I smiled up at him, he kissed me tenderly and loved me in a way that made me think I could happily spend the rest of my life with this man.

In October I pushed my luck with my parents and tacked two extra days onto the weekend. I spent Monday checking out the shops in Ukranian Village and Oak Street, and then I met up with Darcy's college roommate, Caitlin. She was doing an MBA at Northwestern while running a retail site focusing on up and coming designers. The site was already generating some buzz and she wanted to feature a few of my pieces. I was beyond flattered. I admired Caitlin's passion and her confidence—the girl oozed calm, cool and collected. From the first day I met her, I had a strong sense that we'd be working together for years to come.

On Tuesday I popped by Dylan's office a little early. We were meeting for dinner and then I would be flying back first thing the next morning.

I was sad to go. Waking up together on Monday and Tuesday

this week had been dreamlike, like a peek into what the future could hold. Dylan up before the sun, dressed in his custom-made suit looking hot, kissing me as he went off to work. It felt very married and grown-up, and I liked it.

I took extra care dressing before I went to his office. If I was being one hundred percent honest, it was because I was feeling territorial. I wasn't part of his life out here. I wanted the people he worked with—the women—to know he was taken. Pathetic? Oh yeah.

I was happy to see a kindly, middle-aged woman sitting behind the desk outside of his personal office. Cole Industries' headquarters were impressive in New York and here in Chicago as well. The front desk receptionist led me into a foyer with staggeringly high ceilings and floor-to-ceiling length windows overlooking Michigan Avenue. I was taking it all in, momentarily distracted by the view before she brought me back down to earth. "Can I help you, dear?"

"Yes, I'm here to see Dylan Cole. I'm Kasia."

"He's in a meeting right now. Is he expecting you?"

I smiled apologetically. "Not exactly."

She gestured to a chair. "Sit tight for a minute. I think they're almost done but if it's more than five minutes, I'll let him know."

"I don't want to disrupt anything." She didn't respond, just smiled and went back to whatever task she was working on. After exactly five minutes, she picked up her telephone and said, "There is a Kasia here to see you, Mr. Cole."

Dylan came out soon after, smiling. "Hey, I was hoping you'd surprise me with a visit."

He held me and gave me a quick kiss before introducing me to his secretary, Mrs. Wilde. A moment later a woman followed, leaving his office with several leather-bound files in her arms. She was attractive. Her hair and make-up were impeccable, and she wore clothes that were professional but chosen to showcase her figure. The charcoal pencil skirt hugged her lower body, and her plum silk blouse had one button too many undone—just my opinion. She carried herself with a level of confidence that was borderline arrogant, and her look told me she was more than pleased that I was even bothering to size her up.

"I'd shake your hand, but as you can see my hands are full with what Mr. Cole lays on me. I'm Gwen."

I smiled, ignoring the reference to Dylan and "lay" in the same sentence. "I'm Kasia. It's nice to meet you, Gwen."

"It's great to finally meet you, too. He talks about you *all* the time." Then she looked to him and said, "If you'll excuse me, I'll get right to work on these, Mr. Cole."

"Thank you, Gwen," he said, nodding. Then he turned back to me, smiling. "Come on in."

I had to remind myself that conjuring up negative scenarios out of nowhere was immature, ridiculous and just downright tragic. I would not be jealous. I did decide, though, that while I liked Mrs. Wilde, I was not so crazy about Gwen.

DYLAN

Twelve times.

I thought when it got to double digits I'd stop counting, but no.

I'd just had Gwen in my office again.

I couldn't stop.

The first time we met in July, we didn't hit it off. I think she was under the false, albeit amusing impression that since I was young and new to this office, that she wasn't my subordinate, someone under my complete and utter control. We got that cleared up rather quickly.

She all but barged right into my office as I was sitting at my desk settling in that first morning. She thrust her hand into my personal space as she said in a matter-of-fact tone, "Gwen Ward. You'll be clearing room on your calendar for me during your visits. We'll be working closely for the next few months."

My initial thought was, *Who the fuck does she think she is?* I deliberately didn't take her outstretched hand. No, I wanted her to feel foolish. I stood to my full height instead, looking down on her when I asked, "*Who* are you?"

She visibly shrank, but to her credit it was barely perceptible. She lowered her hand and took a short step back, her tone changing to one that was decidedly more dutiful. "I'll be your direct liaison regarding labor union issues, Mr. Cole." I didn't respond. A moment later, she added, "I apologize for bursting in." She smiled. "I'm typically pretty forward."

I never let anyone believe they had the upper hand with me. If they thought my youth was a handicap, they were soon disabused of the notion.

I sat back down and took her in. Nice body, good face. "Have Mrs. Wilde set aside some time for you after lunch today so you can bring me up to speed."

"I will. Thank you, Mr. Cole."

That was another thing. I was "Mr. Cole" to all employees. Didn't matter if they were an intern working the mailroom or a senior executive pushing retirement age—I was their boss and was addressed as such.

I watched as she left the office, imagining Gwen with her skirt hiked up and bent over my desk, begging as she screamed, "Harder, Mr. Cole!" Then I laughed to myself and she was no sooner out of my mind as I set about reviewing my agenda for the day.

As promised, Gwen was working closely with me, as labor relations had been problematic. The most pressing issue was a potential strike at a Midwest plant that made hydraulic parts. One of our subsidiaries was the world's largest manufacturer of construction machinery, so if the union went ahead with the strike there would be broad reaching ramifications. I was a quick study, but her expertise in this area was indispensable.

I spent a minimum of two hours every day working alongside her during my first two trips to Chicago, and we were in regular contact when I was in New York or elsewhere. In September, after good faith efforts at bargaining were met with silence on the part of the union, a strike seemed imminent. On my first day back, Gwen, two other senior executives and I spent hours strategizing behind closed doors. It was exciting, my first real challenge. It was the first time when I was at the helm, not my father. I touched base with him, giving him updates regularly and getting some constructive feedback, but this was my baby.

Kasia and I spoke every night. It was helpful to bounce ideas around with her, too. I was happy on those rare nights when she listened intently, but with Kasia, conversations would never be one-sided. That wasn't necessarily a bad thing. I mean, I didn't want an empty relationship where my woman lived for only me and lapped up my every word mesmerized. But Kasia's ability to simply listen without sharing what was going on in Sweet Betty Threads Land was limited. I humored her of course, but business-wise and in terms of responsibility, it was like comparing colossal-sized apples to miniature oranges.

Gwen and I often worked after hours, so we got to know each other better. It was impossible not to when your evenings consisted of sharing takeout while poring over documents for hours on end. Like me, Gwen didn't seem to mind the long days.

She caught me off guard one night when she mentioned she was a newlywed. "You've only been married three months and your husband puts up with you never being home?"

"I work late, he works late," she said, shrugging her shoulders. "It works for us, I guess."

She went on to tell me about her husband's fledgling career in corporate law and his need to put in long days and weekends if he planned to advance.

"How about you, Mr. Cole? Do you have a wife or a girlfriend who has to put up with this?" she asked as she gestured towards the stacks of files that covered the desk.

"Yes, a girlfriend. She's back in New York."

Gwen gave my arm a playful punch and teased, "Does she have a name?"

I wasn't sure how I felt about her tone or the familiarity of the gesture, but I went along. "Kasia."

"Exotic name."

I stood up to get back to work and to indicate that the conversation was over. Gwen was my subordinate, and my relationship with Kasia wasn't something I was willing to discuss. Why? Because the very first day I'd met Gwen, I recognized the look in her eye. The same one Melanie had. The same one Christian had. The same one I had. The one that said: *Just say the word and I'm ready to go.*

"Your Kasia is quite the beauty."

It was the day after Kasia's unexpected visit to the office. I dropped her off at O'Hare before coming in late this morning, and I'd been in a bad fucking mood ever since. Gwen arrived for our standing four o'clock meeting, and after closing the door behind her, she came up close behind me, stroking her hand up the inside of my thigh as she whispered, "I missed you last night."

I was telling my dick to stand down but it wasn't obeying orders. "Gwen, you and I—"

"Are having fun and working off steam after these long, stressful days," she said as she pressed her body into mine and continued her exploration. "I'm attached, you're attached. Don't make it more than it is. I'm not. And besides," she chirped as she removed her hand abruptly and straightened herself, "she has no idea. Did you like the whole, *he talks about you all the time* bit? Meanwhile," she rolled her eyes, "nothing could be further from the truth. But I guess I don't say much about my husband either."

Chapter Ten

KASIA

The buildings department decided to impart the worst-case scenario, so it was mid-November when the permits were finally approved.

Luke came out to the site with Kate to review the plans with me again, but because of the delay they were now seriously overbooked. They were committed to renovating a boutique hotel in Soho, and asked if I'd be willing to have them oversee the project indirectly while one of their top guys served as project manager. I was disappointed, but at that point I really had no other choice. Finding someone else would take time and I didn't know squat about this sort of thing. My father and brothers could do some of the work, but since they had jobs of their own I could be delayed indefinitely. After Kate assured me that their guy was a true craftsman who did impeccable work, I agreed.

My father agreed to let me use the first-floor apartment as a workspace during the renovation, knowing it was best for me to be on-site to supervise the project.

That next Monday I arrived at the building on Bedford and

North Sixth Street before sunrise to start unloading my samples, machines and fabric rolls. As I struggled to heave my portable work table up the front steps, I fell, the table landing on top of me as my elbow scraped painfully against the stone steps. The table was lifted off me and pushed aside a split-second later, and then two broad, calloused hands were lifting me up as if I was feather-light.

"Are you all right?"

"I'm fine, just clumsy."

"No, you're bleeding. Wait, I have something in my truck."

The man opened the passenger side door to a pick-up that had seen its share of miles and hauling debris. He approached again with a first-aid kit and then looked to me for consent before he cleaned my elbow with a disinfectant wipe and put a bandage on for me.

"I'm Jake, by the way."

"I'm Kasia."

"Kasia Mazur?"

"The very one."

He smiled in a way that lit up his entire face. "Then I should call you Boss. I'm your new project manager."

"You're so young!"

As soon as the words left my mouth I was sorry. It was wrong to equate his youth with incompetence, and I had no reason to doubt him. He had, after all, just done a stellar job of administering medical care to me.

No harm done, I supposed, because he continued to smile when he said, "I have a baby face. I'm not as young as you think."

I smiled back. "I think you're about twenty-six. Am I close?"

"Better than close, you're psychic." He held up his right hand in a pledge. "But I assure you I know my way around a hammer and nails."

"I'm sure you do. Luke and Kate have been singing your praises."

I immediately compiled a list of all the single girls I knew. Jake was *good* looking. Tall with a brawny build, dark brown hair that was nearly black, and friendly bright blue eyes. Yum. I made a mental note to have Rene's roommate, Maureen, swing by after work one night. Maybe I could do a little matchmaking.

One upside to Dylan's long business trips was the friendships I now had time to develop with other women. I had plenty of free nights to meet for drinks, see concerts or just hang out. Darcy and I still managed to see each other a few times a month, but now that she and Tom were back together, she was gone nearly every weekend and a good chunk of her time was devoted to Tom's son, James. Through her, though, I'd met Rene, her roommate Maureen, and of course, Caitlin. Whenever Caitlin was in from Chicago I'd get together with all of the girls. They took me in as if I was one of their own.

After regaining my bearings, Jake helped me get the rest of my things into the apartment and then he set about visually inspecting the downstairs. I watched, noting that anyone who showed up ready to work before the sun rose was my kind of employee. Then I ducked out to grab two coffees from a shop on the corner, cream and sugar on the side for Jake.

"Thank you, Kasia." He paused, looking uncomfortable when he went on to ask, "Would you prefer I call you Ms. Mazur?"

"No," I said, unable to stifle a laugh. "Kasia is fine. So you take your coffee with cream, no sugar?"

"Yes. And you, in case I'm running out for some?"

"The same. So, um, I have the plans in my car—"

"I've reviewed them already. Today I'm going to get a good idea of the structural elements and lay out a plan with a timeline. Tomorrow we start gutting. Are you going to be using the apartment upstairs?"

I nodded. "I'll be using it as a temporary work space. I'd like to be here so that I can oversee the renovations and make decisions when you need my input."

"That'll be great. It cuts down on a lot of confusion and wasted time. I'd recommend that you don't work up there for the next five days, though. The noise and the dust may be too much. And wrap up your fabric samples...I'd hate for them to get damaged or ruined. I have some plastic sheeting in the truck. I'll grab it now."

"Thanks, Jake."

So far, so good. Seems like a hard-worker, thoughtful, and open to having my feedback on a regular basis.

Jake dropped off the plastic sheets and then disappeared back downstairs. I spent a few hours setting up the first floor apartment. I needed to clean the windows, replace light bulbs, hang blinds and just make the space inhabitable. I spent an hour alone just cleaning out the old, musty refrigerator. At noon I was literally inside the lower kitchen cabinets, wiping out every last speck of dust when Jake called out to me. Startled, I smacked my head as I tried to get out from under there.

"Sorry!" he said as he rushed over.

"Wow, I'm quite the spaz today," I said as I rubbed the back of my head.

"Damn, I just wanted to let you know I was done." He leaned over, inspecting my scalp. "There's no blood. Do you feel all right?" When I nodded, he asked, "Do you have a few minutes to go over my timeline for the work?"

"Of course."

Taking a look around, he said, "I'm impressed. This place looks one hundred percent better than it did a few hours ago."

"Yeah, I can't work or cook in a space that isn't spotless...My neurotic side."

He looked around again, concerned. "I'll have the guys come in and clean here after we finish gutting the downstairs. Believe it or not, the dust will travel up here."

There was something so kind and considerate about this guy. *I definitely have to set him up.* But then it occurred to me that he was more than likely already attached. Guys who looked and behaved like him didn't stay single for long.

"Please don't have the men waste any time up here, Jake. I can take care of it."

"I'll seal off the entrance," he said, looking to the door. "That'll help."

Jake opened his notebook on the counter and gestured for me to join him. He went over all the notes, explaining each phase of the project to me in detail. I noticed the timeline indicated he'd be wrapping up in ten weeks.

"That would bring us to mid-February. Should I really plan on mid-March?"

He looked confused. "If I say ten weeks, it's ten weeks." Shaking his head, he added, "I won't bullshit you, Kasia."

I don't know why I sucked in a breath at those words, it's not like he said anything offensive, but he immediately apologized, maybe thinking he'd been too forward with me. "I mean, I don't give out false dates just to make customers happy, to have you thinking I'll be done earlier. I know a lot of contractors do that."

"No, thank you. I appreciate that."

"Ok, I'll be going then. We start tomorrow at the crack of dawn." He smiled when he added, "And stop by as often as you like this week. I'll have a hard hat waiting for you."

I forced myself to nod politely and hold my smile in check. I didn't want to have too easy and friendly a relationship with Jake, right? I had to maintain some sort of client-worker thing with him. But he seemed like the kind of person I could easily become friends with. Walking the fabric rolls into the back bedroom one by one, I felt the need to give myself a warning: *Be careful, Kasia.*

"I have someone you need to call."

"And hello to you too, Caitlin. What's up?"

"Where are you? I can barely hear you."

"Hang on a sec." Making my way up the subway stairs, I tucked into the vestibule of an office building on Union Square. "Better now? I was just getting off the train."

"Sounds so romantic," she said wistfully. "I think New York is where I'm meant to be."

"Yes! We're all plotting to get you here after you finish school."

"School, schmool...I'm learning more on my own than I am listening to those stuffy professors, which is why I'm calling. I've gotten orders on your items, and as you asked, I posted a three week back-order date. You *need* to expand. People want items immediately, Kasia. With certain buyers the custom-made marketing strategy thing makes them feel like they're getting something exclusive, but most shoppers want it like, yesterday. I just texted you the number of a guy...Brian Fash. Meet with him. Other designers swear by him. He can help you set up your manufacturing operations."

"I know I need to do this, but I just hired two employees and I feel like—"

"Like you're jumping off a cliff. I know, been there. You're incorporated, though. You won't lose your shirt, your life savings...You're protected. You need to make the leap, Kasia. I'll be here with moral support, advice, anything you need."

"I'm calling him now. Thanks, Caitlin. Oh, I almost forgot! When are you in town? The contractor working on my store is awesome. I'm thinking of him for either you or Maureen."

"Do *not* introduce him to that bitch! I want first dibs." Caitlin was one of my new favorite people in the world. The girl just made me laugh. "Give me a full description."

"His name is Jake."

"Good, hot name."

"He's very good looking, he's kind, he's polite."

"How's he hung?"

"What? How the hell would I know?"

"You haven't taken so much as a glance in that general vicinity?"

"No!" My cheeks had to be bright red.

"Take it easy, girl. I always check out the goods. Face then junk, and in that order."

"You may be too much for him to handle. Maureen might get first crack at Jake after all."

"I'm staying with Rene and Caleb for New Years. Don't you go introducing him to Maureen before then!"

"I'll see," I teased, giggling. "I can't make any promises. I'll call you after I speak to Fash."

"Good luck, Kasia."

*　*　*

Jake and his crew had been at it for three weeks, and I was amazed by how much the space had been transformed in that short period of time. Luke and Kate came by twice to check in, but they really didn't need to be supervising Jake. You could tell he knew his stuff and he led his workers in a commanding but respectful manner. Luke and Kate were relieved that I was happy with his work because they were up to their ears in their own projects.

Everything seemed to be happening at warp speed. Dylan was a great support, albeit from afar, but he talked me down off the ledge a few times as my plans with Brian Fash progressed. I was officially on the verge of having my designs manufactured and marketed on a much larger scale.

The plan was to launch a spring/summer collection in late February, with a greater marketing presence on-line, and hopefully, the retail store up and running. I was working non-stop.

When Dylan suggested a short getaway over the Christmas break, I said no at first but he was persistent.

"Just three days. I know any longer than that would be too stressful. You *do* need to be there to supervise, but I don't want you to burn out. Three days of lying in the sun relaxing will recharge your batteries. And I need this, too. I miss you."

Lately the job took Dylan to Chicago more than half of every month, so we were seeing less and less of one another. We still spoke every day, but there were nights he got home so late that we cut our calls short. There were times when I really struggled with the distance, missing him so much that it hurt. And when I was being especially dramatic, I wondered if the day would ever come when we would be in the same place at the same time.

I kept telling myself this was temporary. Once I was established and things calmed down for him with this strike, life would return to a more normal pace. He believed that, too.

* * *

DYLAN

We clinked glasses in response to my father's toast, congratulating all of us on the hard work we were doing to fend off the strike.

Things had been tense over the past month, but we were making positive strides and it now looked as if the strike would be averted. The negotiations had garnered national attention in the financials, and I knew my father was pleased with the way I'd handled myself in the labor talks and in the interviews I'd granted with the press.

Tonight, six of us were out to dinner, a Christmas gathering for what my father referred to as his A-Team in Chicago. By now I knew these people very well, as I'd spent the majority of October, November and December in Chicago. It was like being thrown into a foxhole with strangers. Over the long days that extended into nights, you ended up learning about everyone's personal baggage: families, spouse troubles, whatever. The only person who didn't share was me. I was so busy that I really didn't have time to dwell on a daily basis about how Kasia and I were changing, but I would think about it when I listened to Mike, for example, talk about how his wife complained incessantly about the kids, or when Gwen and I were alone and she'd dismiss her husband as a clueless jerk.

"Why did you marry him?"

"I love him, Cole." She never once called me Dylan. "Or, I don't know…Maybe I just love our life? But he wants to change everything. Now that he's doing well at work, he won't let up and it's so irritating. He's always asking me when I'll be ready for the next step, you know?"

"Kids?"

"Kids, the suburbs, leaving work to be a full-time mommy."

"Are you ready for that?"

She looked at me as if I was high. "I will *never* want that. I'm not like other women, but I guess you've already figured that out." She made her way closer. "I want this," she said as she sat herself in my lap and loosened my tie. "I want power, control. I like who I am at work. I'm good at it."

I undid the buttons on her blouse. "You are, Gwen."

"It's not appreciated when you're a woman." She sighed and my mouth watered when I got a glimpse of her tits. "God, his mother is relentless, always asking about grandchildren. I'm either going to suppress everything I am, or I'm going to wind up divorcing him."

I didn't want to know all this, did I?

"How about you, Cole, do you want children?"

"Yes, without a doubt. But I guess it's easier for men, right? No one expects us to slow down, to quit doing what we love."

She was topless in my lap as she set about unbuckling my belt. The guilt didn't register anymore. Fucking her was part of my routine, no different than brushing my teeth. I gestured for her to get up and then led her over to the leather couch. I didn't even bother locking the door. Mrs. Wilde knew exactly what we were up to, and she wouldn't interrupt unless the building was on fire.

I had no feelings for Gwen beyond professional respect, and she never gave off the vibe that she was looking for anything more. The second she did, this would be over and she knew it. My life was boxed into neat little compartments. Kasia was running twenty-four-seven lately, too busy to make it out here. There had been only one quick trip in November, and that time she never even made it to the office. Keeping my two worlds separate didn't take much effort at all.

I was proud of Kasia and pleased she was taking the next steps to expand her business. I knew the kind of pressure it entailed and I was amazed by her ability to handle it. So yes, I was proud of her, but there was always that persistent, nagging desire for her time and for her support. I was second in line, could never get enough of either one.

We were equals.

That was great, and it wasn't.

Chapter Eleven

DYLAN

I was going to ask Mrs. Wilde to shop for Kasia's Christmas gift, but I didn't want her to develop an even lower opinion of me than I'm sure she already held. So the day before I was set to fly home, I ran out at lunch and hit the first jewelry store I came across on Michigan Avenue.

"Dylan?"

I looked up to see Cecilia Tate making her way towards me, heels clicking on the marble floor with two eager sales clerks trailing behind.

"Wow, Cecilia...It's good to see you."

"You too!"

When we hugged, I made the moment awkward when I jerked back on instinct. Her hair smelled like Kasia's, the same brand of shampoo she's used since the day we met. It's a smell I'd come to associate with happiness and comfort—the scent of Kasia and no one else.

I flashed her a bright smile and took her hand in an attempt to smooth things over. "How are you liking Chicago?"

She shrugged. "Ok, I guess. School is good. I've met a few people, but it's a little lonely to be honest. I find myself flying back east whenever I have the chance."

"I'm so swamped when I'm here…I barely get out of the office."

"I know," she said with her eyes downcast. "Melanie gives me updates."

"Are you heading down to Palm Beach for New Years?"

"Of course, aren't you?"

"Not this year. My parents are going but I'm taking a quick trip with Kasia before flying back out here."

"How is she?"

"She's great!" My voice sounded overly chipper, phony to my own ears. I toned it down when I added, "She's crazy busy. Her business is really starting to take off."

"I'm happy for her. She seems like a really good person."

I always liked that about Cecilia. She didn't have that bitchy, competitive thing going on like most of the other girls in her crowd.

"She is. She's terrific, CeCe, but it's tough. I mean, I barely get to see her anymore." That little extra bit of info just seemed to come out of nowhere.

"Do you have time for a quick drink? I mean, I have to find something for my mother first," she laughed, "but the Ritz-Carlton is right next door."

"Sure. I left shopping to the last minute, too. I have to get something for Kasia."

"I'm impressed that you didn't have your assistant just pick something out for her. I don't think my father has ever stepped foot into a store. He looks as surprised as Mother does when she opens his gifts."

With CeCe's help, I settled on a pair of diamond studs. Checking them out later on that night, I was kicking myself. Two giant sparkling rocks. Not Kasia's style—not even close. Even I thought they were ostentatious.

Kasia would see the gift for what it was. So different from last year, when I was excited to buy her present and shopped with thought and care. Now I was going for speed and efficiency, throwing money around in the hopes that it would make up for the lack of effort I was putting in.

Cecilia and I spent no more than an hour together afterwards, catching up over drinks that I capped at two. I made sure to zip my lip about Kasia for the rest of the afternoon. It wasn't like me to voice my fears like that. Cecilia didn't fish for information, though, and for that I was grateful.

When we were getting up to leave she said, "Thanks. It was nice spending time with an old friend. I have a date tonight and I'm already dreading it. That whole getting to know you routine is so tired. I like it better when people already know my story."

"Who's the lucky guy?" She rolled her eyes in response to the compliment. "What? Any guy would consider himself lucky to have you on his arm."

She lowered her eyes. "That's my problem, Dylan. I don't want just *any* guy, you know?"

Cecilia was making it so that a toddler could read between the lines. She was putting it out there but I wasn't about to bite. Sliding her coat up and over her shoulders, I kissed her cheek just as a brother would.

"It was really good to see you."

"You too, Dylan. Merry Christmas."

KASIA

What do you get the man who has everything?

There's nothing he needs so you have to get him something he wants.

I was circling the perimeter of the men's department in Bergdorf's, physically and emotionally spent, and nothing felt right. Dylan had more watches than he could loop around both arms from wrist to shoulder. He didn't need a wallet, an electronic gadget or cologne. I was near tears after wandering around aimlessly for close to an hour, struck with the realization that I just didn't know what Dylan wanted anymore.

As I sat on my bed that night, wrapping presents for my nieces, nephews, aunts, uncles, parents and brothers—yes, I'd managed to get meaningful gifts for everyone else in my life—I couldn't shake this bad feeling.

Dylan was on the last flight heading back to New York. He was meeting me at the store after work tomorrow and then coming home to have dinner with my family. No chance to be alone with him until the following day. Before ending our call the other night, the both of us exhausted, we made plans to spend the entire day holed up in his apartment. One day, that's all we had. Then Dylan would be spending Christmas Eve at my house and we'd both head up to Connecticut to have dinner with the Coles on Christmas Day.

I wrapped one last gift before calling it a night: two center orchestra seats to the American Ballet Theatre. I overheard Mrs. Cole mention once that she studied ballet as a child, so I was pretty sure she'd appreciate the gift. Why, oh why couldn't I come up with anything for Dylan? I was so damn frustrated I could scream.

The next day I was at my studio way before the workmen showed up. The list of things I had to do before Dylan arrived was a mile long, and this week wasn't going to be very productive between all the holiday parties and our quick island getaway to St. John.

I glanced up at the clock at six-forty-five when I heard a knock on the apartment door. I'd been at it for almost two hours.

"What time did you get here?" Jake asked as he let himself in and handed me a coffee.

"A little after five...Couldn't sleep." I breathed in the scent and smiled. "Thank you, I was just starting to get a caffeine craving. I'm so busy this week. I envy those people who start preparing for Christmas in October. I think they're onto something."

"You didn't finish your shopping yet?"

"I'm almost done. I just can't figure out what to get for my boyfriend." I shook my head, shut that train of thought right down. "I'll come up with something."

"It's hard to buy the most important person something because you want it to be special, meaningful." And at that, I damn near started to cry. Special, meaningful? I didn't have a clue. "Are you ok, Kasia?"

"Yeah." I straightened my posture and swiped at one wayward tear. "I'm just a little overwhelmed, overtired, over-something," I said, attempting a smile.

"You work harder than anyone I know. I admire you for that. Most girls your age aren't so driven."

Desperately in need of a topic change, I asked, "So, what are you doing for the holidays?"

He shrugged. "Family, quiet, nothing crazy. You?"

"Family, not quiet, very crazy."

"Sounds like fun."

"It is."

Jake looked like he wanted to say something more but then decided not to. "I hear the guys coming in. Holler if you need anything." With that, he turned and left.

I'd come to look forward to my little morning chats over coffee with Jake. Our conversations always flowed with an easy back and forth. And as the days and weeks passed, I came to know him better.

There's always more to a person once you scratch the surface, and that was certainly the case with Jake.

I now knew that Luke Donovan was mentoring Jake, and had been serving as his supervisor for the past two years so that he could complete the required hours and training to become a licensed independent contractor. Jake admired both Luke and Kate, so he was genuinely happy when I told him how they regularly praised the quality of his work. I also learned that Jake was taking night classes at NYU to complete his undergraduate degree in engineering. When he casually dropped that piece of information one morning, I'm sure the surprise registered on my face. How could he possibly have the time or energy to do both? He worked so hard during the day and most of the work he did was physical.

Sometimes I found myself watching him work. I might go downstairs thinking about how a fixture might look or where a display layout should be situated, but then my eyes and thoughts would fixate on the muscles rippling beneath Jake's shirt or to the sliver of skin on his torso that revealed itself when he lifted something overhead. The man's body was perfection, there was no doubt about that. I told myself that it didn't mean anything, it was just natural to look.

I did introduce Jake to Maureen, and tried my best not to be obvious about it. She thought he was great, but Jake didn't pay her anything more than a polite interest. When I asked if he wanted to grab a drink with us one night as he was finishing up, he smiled and declined. Maureen sulked over her wine for all of about twenty minutes before a cute guy from her job walked into the bar.

Jake never mentioned a significant other and I never asked him outright, but someone made him smile whenever she interrupted his long days with a call. Lucky girl, whoever she was.

. . .

Jake stopped talking mid-sentence and his expression changed. Before I could turn to see what was up, Dylan whispered in my ear, "Hey, beautiful," right before he wrapped his arms around my waist from behind and picked me clear up off the floor.

"Hi," I said, struggling to keep the confusion and irritation out of my voice. He was two hours early, and what was with the caveman act? I took a deep breath in an effort to compose myself, but still felt awkward and embarrassed gesturing between the two of them. "Um, this is my contractor, Jake. And Jake, this is my boyfriend, Dylan."

Dylan was standing tall and sporting a smug expression when he extended his hand. Jake shook it without smiling and then turned away, getting right back to work.

"Come upstairs with me for a minute."

"It looks great in here, baby. It's really coming along."

"Yeah, I'll give you the full tour later on. Let's get out of their way while they work."

When he closed the door to the studio I couldn't help but turn on him. "What *was* that? You practically felt me up in front of the workmen."

"What are you talking about?"

"Don't you think that was a little ridiculous?"

"Sorry," he said, shrugging in a way that told me he wasn't the least bit sorry. "Couldn't help it. I don't like the way that guy looks at you."

"Who?"

He studied me with one eyebrow cocked, as if he was trying to decide whether I was being naïve or dishonest. "The way *Jake* looks at you." When I ignored him, he came closer and tipped my chin up gently. "Hey, I'm sorry. I just...I'm a guy. I know when a guy wants a girl and he wants you."

"I think you're reading too much into it. He has a girlfriend."

"You sure about that?"

"I hear him talking to the same girl on the phone all the time, Dylan. I'm positive."

"Good, because *this* girl," he paused as he pressed me up against the wall and trapped my hands above me, "is taken."

I melted into him on contact, moaning into his mouth and aching for more. I'd missed him so much and I'd been hurting for a long while, for much longer than I cared to admit. I couldn't contain the emotion, crying when he ran his free hand up and over me.

"No, no, no...Don't cry, baby. What's wrong?"

"It's too hard."

He shushed me in a soothing tone, shaking his head. "We knew it was going to be tough. I'm trying so hard to keep it together, too. But I need you, Kasia, and I miss you so damn much."

He kissed me, and in that moment I needed him more than I'd ever needed him before. "Please," I pleaded, and he knew exactly what I was asking for. With one hand he undid his pants and then had my skirt around my waist, never taking his rough grasp off the hands he held captive above me. He hitched one of my legs up around his hip, pushed my underwear aside and then thrust into me without stopping to get a condom. It was primal and desperate, hard and fast. Dylan was sated afterwards, but I wasn't. Straightening my clothes, I was frustrated and pained but said nothing.

The frustration wouldn't ebb—not on the drive home and not during Dylan's homecoming dinner with my family that dragged on for hours. I wanted to go home with him that night, not wait until the morning. I wanted to be with him, live with him, prove to myself that I was still meant to be with him.

He pulled me aside at one point. "Talk to me. Are you all right?"

"No, I'm not. I'm tired, I'm frustrated and I need you. I don't want to sleep alone tonight, Dylan."

He rested his forehead against mine. "Do you know how happy I am to hear you say that? What a relief it is?"

"I didn't even get your Christmas present yet! It's like I'm so far away from you that I don't even know what you want or what you need anymore."

"*You* are what I need. It's not some stupid present, it's you. Please don't get me anything." He laughed when he added, "I can guarantee you're going to hate what I bought for you."

He held me close for a moment, stroking my hair before he whispered, "Tomorrow morning I'm going to be here at seven. You'll be ready. I'm going to take you back to my apartment, we're going to lock the door and we're not coming out all day, understand? Just you and me. No phones, no business-related shit, just us. And when we're away next week together, *that's* our present to each other."

I sank into him, relieved.

And Dylan kept his promise. The next morning I felt like we were two kids running away, except that I said a proper goodbye as I grabbed some fresh babka and ran out the door. When I walked into his apartment, I stripped down within the first minute and didn't put a stitch back on until we were leaving to go back to Brooklyn at midnight. It was exactly what I needed. I needed him to prove to me that we were still meant to be together and that he still loved me.

Maybe I needed to prove to myself that I still loved him, too.

Chapter Twelve

DYLAN

The pieces of my life were falling back into place. Just being around Kasia grounded me.

This renewed state of happiness had a lot to do with our self-imposed rule: No talking business. At least not for the few precious days we had together. It felt like we were back in college, without the weight of our responsibilities pressing down on us and distracting us from one another.

That's not to say that I didn't have to field calls from colleagues, but I made calls while she showered, kept them brief, and didn't discuss the details with her afterwards.

Gwen called every day at four o'clock sharp, the same exact time she'd be down on her knees sucking my cock if we were back in Chicago. After giving me the day's briefing on what now looked to be an imminent labor strike, she'd rattle off a short but detailed list of the dirty things she wanted me to do to her when I got back to Chicago. Poor Gwen was out of luck, though, because the one and only thing I planned on doing was telling her it was over. Now that

I'd had a taste of Kasia again, the thought of being with Gwen sickened me.

No surprise, Kasia hated her gift. We both laughed when she held one of the oversized studs up to her ear. "I think this is bigger than my earlobe."

"I'm sorry. I just—"

"Don't explain, Dylan. It's ok."

"I'll exchange them for smaller ones."

"Just return them. I don't think I'm a diamond girl."

We both had to stifle a laugh when Kasia opened her gift from my parents: teeny, tiny diamond studs.

A few minutes before we were called for dinner, Kasia rushed over as I was talking to my father about business, specifically about the troubling news Gwen had relayed about the strike. I asked her to give me a minute but she shook her head. Her lips were trembling and her eyes were panicked.

"What's wrong?"

"It's the store. I just got off the phone with Alex. He's there with Jake trying to repair a broken water pipe. It's *totally* flooded."

Jeez, I thought someone had died or something. I was trying my best to be understanding, but really, a busted pipe? Her problems were so small, so inconsequential. "Relax, that's what you hired Jake for. You can't do anything about it, so let him handle it."

"I feel awful. It's Christmas Day and they're both there instead of—"

"I get that you feel that way about Alex, but as for *him*?" I made an exaggerated hand gesture moving my hand from top to bottom. "You are the boss, he's the employee. That's his job. It's not your job to worry about stupid little details."

Poor choice of words on my part.

"Excuse me, Dylan, if my *stupid* little problems aren't as *big* and *important* as yours."

"I didn't mean it that way." But she was already on her phone, walking out of the room and away from me. She didn't come back until my mother called everyone to the table. I pulled her aside before taking our seats. "I'm sorry."

"They're all there. My father and all of my brothers are at the store helping Jake. It's Christmas Day, I'm here, and they're all up to their knees in water."

I took a deep breath and did my best to look concerned, even though I was anything but. "Do you want to go back?"

She looked around the table and after a moment said, "No, I can't be of any real help there. I feel terrible, though. Like I *should* be there, you know?"

"When you run a business you can't be the one fixing, doing and controlling everything. That's why you hire good people and you trust them to handle their jobs."

"I know...I know you're right."

* * *

KASIA

The next morning I woke up just before five, crept into Dylan's room and told him I was driving back down to the city. I was beyond restless. I had to see the store.

Dylan was just trying to be helpful last night, I knew that, but I wanted to scream when he made that snooty comment about employers and underlings in reference to Jake. I didn't understand that point of view, that air of superiority. I saw Jake as an equal, my assistant, Marta, as an equal, and Tucker, the guy who made my delicious coffee every morning as my equal. Dylan and his ilk did not.

I made it back to the store by quarter after six. It was still pitch black outside but there were floodlights on inside. Jake was mopping the floor in dirt-smattered jeans, wet boots and a thermal shirt streaked with grease.

"Good morning."

"Hey." He looked tired but his smile was bright. "Ah, hot coffee. I guess you got those telepathic messages I was sending."

"Here, sit down. Stop working for a minute and drink," I said as I handed him the cup. "I want to apologize. I feel so terrible that you were here yesterday instead of having Christmas Day with your family."

He laughed. "I guess you haven't spoken to your mother."

"No, I haven't."

"I wound up having Christmas at your house."

I winced. "I'm *so* sorry."

"Sorry? Kara said it was her best Christmas in years."

I'd often hear him talking to someone named Kara on the phone. I never asked who it was, but with an odd ache, I realized this had to be the girlfriend. "Kara is your girlfriend?"

He laughed, shaking his head. "No, my little sister. Although I think your mother may be looking to adopt her after yesterday."

His sister?

"How did it all happen? I should have been here. I feel like I abandoned ship."

"Nah, don't be silly. I just had this feeling I should pop in yesterday morning...It was so weird. And when I suggested it, Kara jumped at the chance to get a peek at the place." I must have looked confused because he paused to explain, "She knows who you are, Kasia. I think you're a bigger deal than you realize."

"What do you mean?"

"She's into fashion, so she knows Sweet Betty Threads. The day I mentioned the name of the store I was working on, just in passing, she practically flipped out. She's been begging me to ask if you'll make a dress for her." He held up his hand as soon as the words left his mouth. "I told her absolutely not, so don't even go entertaining that crazy idea. Anyway, she wanted to come along for the ride, and when I walked in I was ankle deep in muck. You mentioned you were away for Christmas, so I called Alex just to let him know, and before I knew it, your entire family was here helping out. Even your Uncle Victor."

"Are you kidding me?" I laughed envisioning my eighty-year-old great uncle attempting to pitch in.

"Yeah, he's great. So your mother took Kara home with her and then they came back later on with dinner plates for all of the men. Kara went back there and spent the night. In fact, she's still there. I'll head over at around eight to grab her."

"I owe Kara that dress then. My nieces probably tortured her all day and night."

"I went there late night to get her, but she was curled up asleep on the pull-out couch in the den with both of them. It was a pretty cute scene. She didn't look like she'd been tortured."

"I feel so bad that you weren't with the rest of your family."

"Don't, Kasia," he said, shaking his head. "It's always just me and Kara. I know she loved every minute of yesterday. And when I went back at night I wound up sitting with your dad, brothers and uncles. Some vodka was consumed." He cracked a smile. "It was great, really. We haven't been part of a big Polish family gathering in a long time. Just hearing everyone speak the language, it..."

He was choking up a little.

Wait, he was Polish?

"I guess I should call you Jakub? How did I not know you were Polish?"

He shrugged. "I knew you were from day one, but it was easy for me...Kasia is a dead giveaway. I would have guessed anyway from your eyes and your skin, though." He cleared his throat and got up then, tossing his cup into the trash and grabbing the mop.

My mind went back to that first day we met. He pronounced my name correctly right off the bat, and it was beyond rare to meet someone new and not have to sound it out for them. How did that slip past me? Shaking off the confusion, I stood up and asked, "How can I help?"

"There's nothing for you to do. The pipe was from next door and it's been repaired. It's all good now. I don't need you to help me clean up, and you don't need to be getting your white cashmere sweater all dirty."

I looked down at my ensemble. Yeah, not the best clothes to get down and dirty in. I teased, "That's *winter* white cashmere, just so you know, and I *always* dress like this to clean."

He teased back, "Nooo, I've seen what you wear when you're cleaning. Those are your fancy threads."

"Maybe I'll go back to my house then and meet Kara."

"She'd like that...And it's Karolina."

Chapter Thirteen

JAKE

Damn, I had to get a grip.

I'd been here most of the night and I was bone tired, but I couldn't blame that near meltdown on fatigue alone.

I wanted her—knew that since day one—but the sight of her this morning nearly brought me to my knees. Saw her six days a week, every one of those days a temptation and a torture. Add to that being welcomed in by her parents yesterday and seeing Kara all wrapped up in the warmth of a family again. It was all too much.

I was relieved when Kasia left. The way her eyes were boring into mine, it was as if she could see every desperate thought running through my mind. By the time she finally turned to go I was doing everything in my power to keep from crushing my mouth to hers.

When she fell on the steps that first day, my eyes immediately went to her ring finger. Right then and there I decided I would ask her out. I'm not sure why, other than to say it was just a feeling that came over me, or more like a sense of knowing. And her name, Kasia, stirred a deep longing inside of me. Without even knowing her she had me aching for a part of my past, for what's familiar.

Five years with no more than a passing interest in women, of seeking connection only to satisfy a most basic, physical need. Five years of not wanting anything more, of not allowing myself to want or dream of anything more. The moment I saw her, though, all that changed. *Here she is,* I thought. *She's the one.*

When I realized she was the owner, the person who'd hired me, I had to school my expression and shake off the disappointment. You don't get involved with your employer, that's a given, even if she is the most desirable woman you've ever laid eyes on.

I told myself I could wait. She would be worth the wait.

And while her looks had me hooked from the start, I knew there was so much more to her than the beautiful package she was wrapped in. I couldn't help it, found myself watching when she wasn't looking. As she measured windows inside the store, hauled supplies from her car to her studio and walked around checking things out, I was checking her out, too. It didn't take long to see that she was generous and kind, which elevated her beauty to a whole other level.

I had plenty of experience with rich, entitled clients who thought they were the shit. The kind of people who assumed that since you worked with your hands, you were a blue collar neophyte who wouldn't know the difference between a cabernet and a pinot noir. I once had one client who would actually stop mid-sentence to define words for me. Words like *proportional*, as if a contractor wouldn't have that one down. Not gonna say it didn't piss me off, but I let it roll off my back because I had nothing to prove. I knew who I was.

Kasia was different. At first glance you knew she was cultured and sophisticated, but she never gave off that pretentious vibe. She had me that first day, when I asked if I should call her Ms. Mazur and she laughed as if that was the most ridiculous idea she'd ever heard.

But I soon came to understand that she spoke to everyone with respect. Didn't matter if you were the lowest man on the totem pole, like the guy who delivered our lunch from the deli, or that Fash guy, one of Kasia's most important business contacts. And she was nurturing, looking out for everyone on site by getting coffees, surprising us with homemade goodies from her mother, and even giving one of the guys a ride to the emergency room and staying with him to make sure he was all right after a mishap.

This morning she looked like some kind of Christmas angel, or more like a Christmas fantasy come to life. Her hair was pulled up in a ponytail and she was fresh-faced like she was most days, natural and beautiful. But with those jeans and that sweater hugging her curves, so soft and begging to be touched? I had to swallow and turn away at one point. Had to remind myself that Kasia belonged to someone else.

It burned.

Her boyfriend reminded me of someone I used to know. Soft hands that never saw hard labor, hair cut with precision by a stylist, *not* a barber, and clothes tailored to fit that one man alone. He reminded me of the guys I used to go to school with, the people I used to call friends, the guy who looked back at me in the mirror a lifetime ago.

And now he knew.

He paused in the doorway and witnessed that casual exchange between me and Kasia, so now he knew I was into her. Can't really blame him for acting like an absolute dick. If Kasia was mine and some other man was looking at her the way I'm sure I was, all covetous and greedy, I probably would have grabbed her and staked my claim just like he did.

When they turned to leave, he looked back over his shoulder and caught me staring. He smirked and then shook his head as if to say, *Don't even think about it.*

After they went upstairs, I set about ripping the back door off its hinges with my bare hands, needing something to lay into. I wanted to wipe that smug look off his face. I wanted to rip him limb from fucking limb. No one but me should be touching Kasia, kissing her, loving her body.

No one but me.

Chapter Fourteen

KASIA

It was still early when I got home, but my mother and father were already up, sharing a roll and drinking coffee together.

I'm lucky, I thought as I paused for a moment to watch them. My parents had an enduring kind of love. My father still looked at my mother as if she was the most precious, beautiful woman in the world, and my mother still spoke of my father with pride and tenderness. Side by side, they worked hard for their entire married life, and they'd achieved success. What they had together was priceless.

I joined them at the table, kissing them both before sitting down and tearing into some of the leftover desserts from last night. "I heard you had an eventful Christmas. I feel terrible that dinner was ruined and I wasn't here to help."

"You don't have such a good memory, myszka. That's not the first time a broken pipe has interrupted a holiday in this house," my father said softly, laughing as he patted my head. I would always be his *little mouse*.

Mama added, "Tata and I were actually just saying that yesterday was fun, in a crazy kind of way. It was like old times, with everyone pitching in for the emergency."

"I just stopped by the store and Jake is still cleaning up. Please tell me he wasn't there all night."

Mama smiled. "He reminds me of your father, that Jake. What a hard worker and so strong. And his sister Karolina, what a little treasure. She's still asleep in there. I threatened Olivia and Veronica that if they wake her up early, no babka for them."

"I always thought he was talking to a girlfriend on the phone. He calls her Kara."

"What a good brother he is to her," Tata said. "But that's how life is, you do what is necessary."

My mother nodded with sad eyes. "It made me cry after she went to sleep, knowing the two of them are on their own. That young boy giving up everything to take care of her."

"What do you mean they're on their own?"

"The parents are dead, Kasia. I didn't ask how but I did ask when...Six years ago. So he's been taking care of her since she's twelve and he's twenty. He was a young man."

My father scoffed at that. "Twenty is a man. I landed here at twenty with you, not speaking a word of English. You do what you have to do, no?" He looked directly at me then. "He is a good person, though. Treats his sister with great affection."

With that, a petite girl with light brown hair and green eyes came into the kitchen. I found myself feeling warm and protective towards her in an instant.

"You must be Karolina. I'm—"

"Kasia! I keep asking Jakub to let me come by while he's working so I can sneak a look at your studio and maybe meet you, but he keeps telling me no." She took on a deep voice and scowled, doing a poor imitation of her brother. "*Kasia's too busy, Kasia works too hard as it is, Kasia has no time to entertain you.*" Taking the seat next to me, she let out an exasperated breath. "He's so stubborn!"

Karolina was like a whirlwind.

"I told Jake that since I ruined your Christmas, I owe you big time." When she shook her head, I added, "Please, at least let me make you a dress."

Her eyes lit up but then she frowned. "No, you don't have to do that. Jakub says that he worries about you sometimes, that you're working nonstop getting the store up and running. Anyway," she continued, her face lighting up again, "I had a great Christmas! I just adore Veronica and Olivia. Little Michal and Dominic are cuties too."

Jake worries about you. That line made my heart ache. I'd be lying if I said I wasn't secretly pleased every time I caught him looking my way. Just like I'd be lying if I said I didn't care whether or not he even thought about me.

When I was sitting across from him drinking coffee in the store this morning, I found myself staring at his hands. Weather beaten and stained with dirt and grease from hard work, in that moment I wanted him to ruin my white cashmere sweater, run his hands over it and ruin me. That's when I decided to get the hell out of there.

I shook off the memory and took Karolina's hands in mine. "I won't take no for an answer. I'm going away for a few days but I'll be back on January second. Are you in school?"

"Yes, but I'll be home until January fifteenth. Only if you're sure it's no trouble, Kasia."

"Really, I insist."

"In that case, I would *love* a dress for my winter semi-formal."

Karolina went on to tell us about her experience so far as a freshman at Georgetown. She was obviously sweet-natured and intelligent, but there was something about her, something warm and happy that emanated from her like sunshine. It wasn't hard to understand why, after whatever tragedy had befallen his family, Jake would move mountains to take care of this precious girl.

* * *

DYLAN

The timing of this getaway wasn't great.

I was tense, tapping away on my laptop while Kasia sat in the seat next to me sleeping soundly. Glancing down at her head resting on my shoulder, I decided I shouldn't be sweating it. I told myself it was a long holiday weekend and only two of the days we'd be away were actually work days, but I knew better.

The union head, who'd been presenting himself as a reasonable man, was now spewing crap on nearly every news outlet claiming that Cole Industries was refusing to pay the American worker a fair living wage. He lied outright when he insinuated that we were threatening to move our entire manufacturing operation overseas. Not to be outdone, the governor spoke at a union rally mimicking the sentiment, sucking up to his constituents as he geared up for his re-election campaign.

All those months of hard work. It was all turning to a giant pile of shit.

My father was cooling off after his morning run when I came outside this morning. Fixing his eyes on my suitcase, his tone was cold when he said, "You're in Chicago Monday morning." Guess he wasn't pleased about the timing of this romantic getaway either.

"Are you ok, Dylan? You look like you have the weight of the world on your shoulders."

Smiling down at her, I said, "We promised no talking business, and I'm sticking to it."

She rested a hand on my chest, and her touch did soothe me. "Just think, one more hour and we'll be on the beach."

We were on a private jet, which cut the travel time considerably, and I'd booked a secluded resort with a private villa right on the beach. I didn't want to explore town, do any scheduled activities or even pick up a tennis racquet. I just wanted to kiss her, hold onto her and love her.

I wasn't imagining it—Kasia was slipping away and I needed to grab hold of her, to keep her with me. Considering the deceitful shit I'd been up to, I had no right, but I intended to do everything within my power to win where she was concerned.

I had murderous thoughts about that douchebag, Jake. The other day I was forced to listen, grinding my teeth to keep from landing a cheap shot as Kasia's brother Alex went on and on about how talented, knowledgeable and capable the guy was. Did I miss something? Jake was a construction worker, not an astrophysicist or a top hedge fund manager. He hadn't cured cancer for fuck's sake. The way they all but worshiped the guy was nauseating.

No man was taking her away from me. I would see to that.

"Baby, how's everything at the store going?"

"No business, remember?"

"Just want to know if Boy Wonder has a handle on everything. Will the flood wind up delaying the project?"

I tried to mask my jealousy, but from Kasia's reaction it was obvious that I'd failed. She met my eyes and kissed my cheek before saying, "Yes, Jake has it under control…No, it won't delay anything… And yes, I love you."

As much as I tried to just relax and enjoy the weekend, I couldn't shirk my responsibilities.

Kasia understood when I left the room every morning for an hour to answer my emails and to make some calls. She made a few calls herself, but she was mostly "working" by creating designs while perched on the shore gazing out into the ocean.

Whenever I came upon Kasia sitting with her sketchbook balanced on her lap, she blew me away. She was so damn talented it was scary. The woman could have been an artist in her own right, with her quick freehand sketches fit to hang in any gallery.

I found her on the beach in a skimpy bright blue bikini after finishing my latest round of calls, and vowed again to do everything in my power to make this work. There would be no more Gwen, and as soon as this labor dispute crap was settled, I was determined to spend the bulk of my time back in New York, no matter what my father's opinion on the matter was. Being away from one another wasn't good. I knew if we kept it up, kept up this pace, we would crash and burn. We were dangerously close to the tipping point right now.

Over dinner, Kasia insisted on breaking the no talking business rule. "Okay, we've had two days, Cole. Now I want you to fill me in on what's been happening."

I choked on a sip of my drink when she addressed me the same way Gwen did, but recovered quickly. "You're sure, Kasia? I like the no business, all pleasure thing."

She winked at me. We'd just had quite a nice romp back in the room. "I like it too, but it's not realistic. I want to support you, Dylan, and that means knowing what you're going through and trying to help you. I can see that you're stressed out. Don't shield me from your troubles."

I breathed a sigh of relief at her words. The truth was, I needed this. I needed a rock, someone outside of work who was there to listen. And Kasia listened.

For the next two hours we lingered over dessert as I laid everything out. It was so good to have someone as bright and insightful as Kasia to bounce ideas off of. She suggested using the union head's claim about moving operations overseas to our advantage by comparing costs publicly, and putting some pressure on the government to be comparable to other foreign governments in terms of tax incentives. She also suggested that I go on the offensive, taking the position that Cole Industries is the sole U.S. based manufacturer in that sector. Let them think you might bail, she said, call their bluff. I swear that if my father had been listening in on this conversation he would have tried to hire her on the spot.

I'd missed this, missed the way we used to be together.

With Kasia's blessing, I spent the entire flight home discussing strategy with my father and then checking in with my Chicago staff. I had an interview set for one of the major national Sunday news programs, taping live in New York the next morning, and would then be off to Chicago for what would probably be two grueling weeks.

It was time to play hard ball.

* * *

KASIA

I went back to the store Monday morning intent on reverting to professional Kasia: friendly yes, flirty no. Dylan and I had not only recharged our batteries, but I'd recommitted myself to him. I loved him, he needed me, and that was that.

I walked in at nine, which was beyond late for me, with coffee and pastries for everyone.

My brother Alex was there to greet me when I walked in. "Nice tan, Kasia," he commented when he kissed my cheek. "How was the trip?"

"It was great. Just what I needed."

Just as I said that, Caitlin came bounding in the front door. "Kasia, I love it!"

"You love it? It's still studs and wires, you freak."

"But I can already envision it. And I love this area...Sooo much better than tired old Manhattan."

Caitlin was a force of nature and she liked to make an entrance. Every man in the store took notice, and who could blame them? It was January in New York, and here she was strutting her stuff in a super short skirt, knee-high boots, and a snug, cropped leather jacket. She had a figure to envy and a great sense of style.

I introduced Alex, who soon made his exit, and then introduced her to the workers as I toured her around the space.

Caitlin's eyes lit up when Jake came walking through the door carrying supplies, his shirt riding up to reveal that rock hard torso, his face screwed tight in concentration—or was it anger? He shifted the heavy load from where it was balanced on one shoulder and rested it on the floor. He didn't even get a chance to stand up before Caitlin was off to the races.

"Well, Kasia doesn't need to introduce you. You *must* be Jake. She didn't do you justice."

He slowly raked his eyes over Caitlin from head to toe and then smiled as he stood and extended his hand. "Jake Wozniak."

"Caitlin Richards. What you're doing here looks great so far, Jake."

I cringed listening to her pour it on. Caitlin had a talent for saying even the most ordinary things in a way that oozed sex, so at that moment she wasn't speaking to Jake, she was basically purring. And if it was possible to make someone feel as if you were licking them simply from the greedy, ravenous look in your eye, then yes, Caitlin could pull that off, too.

I was fighting the urge to turn her around and push her out of the store, push her as far away from Jake as humanly possible.

He smirked and eyed her playfully. "Thanks, I bet you'll be really impressed when we actually have some walls back up." He looked to me then, the humor that was in his eyes a moment ago long gone. "Kasia, how do you and Caitlin know one another?"

His tone was casual and fun towards her, but clipped and sharp as a dagger when he spoke to me. After a moment I stammered, "Uh, Caitlin is my, my...She's a friend from Chicago."

"Who may be moving to New York *very* soon," Caitlin chimed in as she nudged me in the ribs.

Caitlin's brazen seductress act was grating on me. It was obnoxious. She was being too familiar, borderline aggressive and presumptuous. Did she think she could have Jake just because she wanted him?

What was the matter with me? I was looking to set Jake up with someone great, right? But Caitlin no longer seemed good enough for Jake. He needed someone kind, someone who would take care of him the way he took care of others. I couldn't listen to them flirt, knowing it would lead to nothing more than a casual hook-up for Caitlin. But maybe Jake wanted that too. The look on his face when he blatantly checked out her body made me want to cry and rage at the same time.

I needed to leave.

"Um, I have to go. I mean, I have to do some stuff upstairs. Caitlin, meet me up there whenever you're ready, all right?"

She smiled, eyes sparkling as she teased, "I think I'm going to watch Jake manhandle some other heavy things down here for a few minutes. No offense, but that's a lot more entertaining than watching you sew."

I walked into my studio, slammed the door behind me and slid down against it, letting my head rest in my hands as my ass hit the floor.

"Kasia, are you ok?"

I raised my head to see Karolina sitting at the kitchen island, a look of absolute dismay on her face. "Today isn't a good day. Jake was right."

"Ohmigod Karolina, no! I just…Never mind, don't pay any attention to me. I was expecting you today, and I enjoy making custom dresses, especially for people I really like." I was rambling on like an idiot. "I'm sorry, I didn't know you were here already and I was just… having a moment." I picked myself up off the floor and made my way over to her, tossing my scarf and hat on the counter as I sat down next to her.

"Are you certain?"

I smiled at her and took her hands in mine. "I'm really happy to see you, Karolina. I'm *certain*."

There was a knock on the door and then Jake came in with Caitlin trailing close behind. And when I say close behind, I mean she was practically brushing up against his ass.

"Sorry, I forgot to tell you I had Kara with me. I told her it probably wasn't a great day for this." His jaw tightened. "You just got back from your trip and all."

"No, it's fine. Karolina and I have an appointment for today. We're good."

Caitlin looked between me and Jake a few times and then said, "I was just asking Jake about coming out with us tonight to meet Rene and Caleb. You're still coming, aren't you, Kasia?"

Caitlin was my friend and she was a good person, so I was feeling guilty about the hateful thoughts I'd been having. I wasn't being fair. Jake was a good man and he deserved happiness. Maybe Caitlin could give him that.

I looked to Jake when I said, "I don't think so, Caitlin. You two should go, though."

His lips, always smiling and so full of expression, were drawn in a tight line. "I can't tonight. Sorry, but I already have plans."

Caitlin didn't look overly disappointed. "No big deal." Within a minute she was on her phone speaking to some guy named Mick and inviting him to come along.

Jake turned and walked out the door without another word.

The ache in my chest eased the more time I spent with Kara. She made me and Caitlin laugh all morning, telling us about parties and some of the awful dates she'd been on this year.

"Speaking of men," Caitlin asked, "what's up with that hot brother of yours? Does he have a girlfriend or what?"

Kara looked out the window. "No, not that I know of. He has girls calling him and he goes out sometimes, but there hasn't been anyone serious in years. Jake put everything on hold for me. Sometimes I just want to scream at him."

I stayed quiet, giving her hand one gentle squeeze, but Caitlin dove right in. "Wait a sec, I'm lost here."

Karolina let out a soft, cheerless laugh when she looked back at Caitlin. "My parents died in a small plane accident when I was twelve. Jake was a sophomore in college at the time...At Georgetown, like me. We didn't have any close relatives nearby, but my aunt and uncle in Seattle offered to take me in, move me out there and let Jake finish school. Jake knew I didn't want to go. I mean, I hardly knew them. So he left school and started working to support us both, and he left everything behind. I can't stand the thought of it sometimes, you know?" She paused to wipe at a stray tear. "He had a girlfriend back then and I know they were serious. He had a life just like every other twenty-year-old college boy and he dropped it all for me."

Caitlin now had both elbows on the counter, chin propped in her hands, hanging on Karolina's every word. "What happened to the girl?"

Karolina rolled her eyes. "Her name was Hannah. I shouldn't be hating on her, it's really not fair, but he was devastated when she broke it off. I mean, who does that? A guy loses his parents, has to drop out of school and start working two jobs to take of his sister, and *that's* when you dump him? That's cruel, right?"

"What a bitch!" I heard myself say.

"Yeah, what a bitch!" Caitlin repeated. Tapping Kara's hand, she added, "He's better off. You know that, don't you?"

"Absolutely. I just wish he had someone special in his life, someone who makes him happy. He deserves to be happy more than anyone else on the planet. The boy works like crazy, goes to school at night, always helped me with my homework...He even taught himself to cook so that I would eat properly after my parents died."

"He's really proud of you, Karolina."

She smiled with downcast eyes. "I know, but I owe everything to him. Without him pushing me I never would have done as well in school as I did. And I never would have gotten a scholarship without his SAT tutoring." She let out a soft laugh, rolling her eyes. "Jake was more like a dictator than a tutor." Karolina was serious again when she fixed her eyes on me. "He's just the best brother...No, he's the best person I know."

With that, Jake knocked and asked if everyone was decent before he came in. "Hi, ladies," he said, the harsh edge from before now gone. "The guys are breaking for lunch. Just wanted to know if I should get Kara out of your hair."

"Stop talking about me like I'm a nuisance," she snapped as she threw a spool of thread at him.

He put his hands up in surrender and laughed. "Sorry!"

"She can stay as long as she likes."

"Actually, I have to go soon, Kasia. Looks like I'm taking over as your replacement."

"I don't follow."

"I'm babysitting for your nieces this afternoon. Any tips?"

"Oh, yeah. Tie that beautiful hair up unless you want it to be braided into knots, and do *not* let them handle scissors. They like to play hairdresser, and believe me, they won't think twice about cutting it off."

She looked horrified. "They seem so sweet."

"They are, but they take their beauty and fashion hard-core serious. And when they team up, they're dangerous."

Jake gestured to the fabric samples when he asked Karolina, "So how did the dress thing go?"

She teased, "The dress *thing*? You mean the fitting? It was awesome! I felt like a young ingénue having an up and coming designer fit me for my movie premiere."

Jake rolled his eyes. "Jesus, Kara, you're so dramatic."

We were all laughing then. As Kara was getting ready to leave, Caitlin made her way towards the door. "I'm going back downstairs to get a good look around again." She turned to Jake. "I was too busy drooling over you before."

Jake's cheeks flamed, and Kara poked him in the side, laughing as she breezed past him. He went to follow Kara, but then turned back around to me as I approached the door. We were alone, and my breath hitched as we stood with our faces only inches apart. Without thinking, I found myself breathing in deep to fill myself with his scent.

He covered my hand that was resting on the doorknob with one of his own. "No more, Kasia. No more trying to set me up with your friends. I don't want any of them." He lowered his eyes and watched as he slowly slid his hand off mine before turning to leave.

My breaths came in deep and left my body fast. My heart hammered in my chest. And just from that one touch, my body was on fire, lust-drunk and needy.

He's off limits...

You have a boyfriend...

What are you thinking?

Was it even forty-eight hours since I'd convinced myself that Dylan was right for me, since I committed myself to making things work?

I repeated the words, told myself again that I was in love with Dylan.

So why did I feel like Jake owned me?

Chapter Fifteen

DYLAN

Sunday was a success. I had them on the defensive now, had them on the run. Public opinion and the opinion of the union members were swaying. Those lazy, dimwitted public officials and union bosses had lost control of their base. The governor had come out swinging to justify his misguided policies, and the union's mouthpiece was scrambling. They wanted a fight? Now they had one.

Monday we were behind closed doors all day, the four of us, the main players. Mike, Bill, Gwen and I went out for drinks after our marathon day to let off some steam. Tomorrow afternoon we were meeting with union officials and the mediator at three, and wouldn't be coming up for air until a deal was hammered out. I told everyone not to come in until lunchtime tomorrow because we were in for a long week, but as is typical of the work hard, play hard crowd, they took that as an invitation to let the liquor flow.

Bill was the first to bail at around midnight, while Mike had some girl pressed into a corner with less than a centimeter of space between them last I saw. That left just me and Gwen.

I was three or four whiskeys in by that time, never mind the wine we'd consumed during dinner. Still, I managed to start in on the agenda I'd set concerning her. I was sitting on a barstool and she was standing too close.

"Listen—"

"Please tell me you're not doing this *now*. I knew it was coming, but this week? Seriously, Cole?"

"What does it matter if I do this now, next week or next month? We can't see each other anymore, Gwen. She means a lot to me. I'm going to marry her."

She stepped in closer, so close that my thigh was pressed up against her cooch. Jeez, this girl needed to get off more than anyone I knew—more than Melanie, who held the world record in my opinion.

"So marry her," she whispered in my ear, "and fuck me. There's no need to change our arrangement. Fuck me whenever you need me, whenever I need you." Her gaze snapped up then and her tone changed. "Excuse me. Are you enjoying the performance, asshole?"

"Yep, you're both very entertaining. I'm dying to know how this is going to play out. What's it going to be, *Cole*?"

My throat was in my ass at that point. I knew before turning around that Kasia's brother Tomasz was behind me. I was so fucked and I knew it. Didn't mean I wasn't going to try and talk my way out of this mess. I gently pushed Gwen back and turned to face him. "Tom—"

"Forty-eight hours, asshole. That's how much time you have to fess up before I tell Kasia myself."

I stood up. The towering over people thing usually worked in my favor, but not this time. Tomasz and I stood eye to eye and he laughed in my face. "Are you fucking kidding me? Puffing out your chest as if you'd be able to intimidate me? I'm not some fucking peon who worships at the altar of Cole Industries, you dick."

"Tom, you don't understand."

He looked over my shoulder. "Help me out, Gwen. Did I *understand* you correctly? Are you fucking my sister's boyfriend?"

Gwen took her coat and stormed out of the bar. I looked back to him, defeated. "Please don't do this, Tom."

He pushed me full force and I let him. I was drunk and I was busted. And that, as they say, was that.

He had his finger in my face. "Never! I'd never let my sister stay with a lying cocksucker like you, and you're *never* going to marry her, you got that?"

Great, Tom must have heard that part too.

"At least let me tell her. I can't be home until the end of the week. Please, I'm fucking begging you."

"I never liked you, you know that?" He paused, shaking his head as he grabbed his coat off the barstool. "Forty-eight hours and I won't even promise you that."

The next morning I woke up with a raging headache that had nothing to do with the booze I'd consumed. Blinking against the light streaming through my window blinds, the events of last night came back to me like a knockout punch. I grabbed for my phone in a panic to see if Kasia had called. No calls but there was a text marked early this morning:

Good luck today, Dylan!

On my hands and knees, I slumped over the toilet and emptied my gut.

I'd completely, irrevocably fucked it all up.

* * *

KASIA

I woke in the middle of the night, perspiring and out of breath. Sitting up with a start, I grasped at the threads of my memory, reaching for the dream before it slipped away because I knew it was a good dream—one that I wanted to keep hold of.

I was back on my island beach, naked, and his body was slick from the ocean, the hard and heavy weight of him so welcome when he moved on top of me. My fingers gripped his hair when we kissed and he moaned when his hand slipped down between us. He broke the kiss to look at me as he eased his way in.

It wasn't Dylan staring down at me.

I avoided the store on Tuesday. Between that dream and what had transpired between us yesterday, I couldn't face him. I met up with Caitlin, Rene and Darcy for lunch instead. We met uptown near Darcy's school so she could sneak out during her break.

Caitlin had us all laughing, giving us the play by play of her night with some guy she'd nicknamed *Mick with the Magic Dick*. "Thank goodness for Mick or else I would have been a third wheel."

Darcy asked, "What happened to that tasty treat Kasia was hoping to hook you up with?"

"Jake? No, I think Jake has the hots for someone else, right Kasia?"

"What do you mean?"

"I mean he's crazy about you."

"What?" Darcy blurted out.

"You're wrong, Caitlin." I hushed her. "You're wrong."

"Take it easy, Kasia. I was teasing, but he's definitely into you." She weighed her words for a moment and then spoke softly. "The way he looks at you...I'm pretty sure he's in love with you."

I started to cry, and everything I'd been holding inside came out in a torrent. The uncertainties, the doubts I had about Dylan, my love for Dylan, and the pull I was feeling towards Jake.

Rene took my hand. "It's ok to be confused. Look at the year you've had, would you?"

Darcy added, "You're working non-stop, your business is exploding, and you and Dylan are on two opposite sides of the planet most of the time."

Direct as always, Caitlin asked, "Who is it that you want?"

I choked on a sob when I whispered, "Both of them."

I walked around the city for a few hours before making my way back to Brooklyn. Walking into my house, I heard the girls' happy little squeals and I was relieved, so desperately in need of a distraction. Olivia and Veronica had Kara sitting on the floor in the living room. One was putting lipstick on her while the other was dousing her in perfume.

I all but whined, "Hey, I need a makeover too."

They both screamed my name and hugged me as they pulled me down to sit.

"Did you come here to rescue me?"

"No way. My aunt says you have them under control. They're going to miss you when you go back to school next week."

Veronica chimed in, "No we won't 'cause Mama said we can go visit her when we go to see the president."

"That's very nice, Veronica." I turned to Kara when she laughed. "She's very persuasive. Don't be surprised if they show up for the cherry blossoms this spring."

Kara's eyes went wide. "That's a great idea!" She went on to tell the girls about the *beautiful pink flowers that go on for miles and miles*, as they listened, transfixed by this beautiful girl. She was wonderful with them. And damn, that got me thinking about Jake becoming Kara's guardian at such a young age. It made me want him even more. It made me see him as a man in the best sense of the word —a man who took care of what was his, who protected those around him, who would sacrifice everything for family. That was pretty damn hot.

I stiffened when I heard his voice, an unfamiliar combination of fear and anxiety taking hold. I was scared of wanting him, and scared of what this would mean for me, for him, and for Dylan. And I was insecure. I regretted things about myself, things about my past. If Jake knew everything, everything I'd been and done with Dylan, would he still want me? Would he see me as damaged goods, experienced in a way that was off-putting? I don't even know why those ridiculous thoughts were swimming around my head. I mean, I'd been with only two men my whole life, while some of my friends—Val came to mind—had been with so many they'd most likely lost count. I was judging myself harshly for those few times when I played a role for Dylan, pushed myself beyond where I was comfortable to please him. It was never his fault and I didn't place any blame on him, but those experiences had changed me, and maybe not for the better.

I felt Kara's curious eyes on me. "Kasia? Um, Jake's here."

Maybe I'd been sitting there lost in thought for longer than a moment.

He came closer and put his hand on my shoulder. "Are you all right? I was worried when you didn't come in."

I nodded. "I met the rest of my friends for lunch before Caitlin flew back to Chicago. I'm going to pay for it, though. I have so much work to do." I got up and took a few steps towards the door, wary of being so close to him. "I'll head over there now...Grab a few things I can take back here and work on later tonight."

"I'll drive you."

"No. I don't want you to go out of your way."

He looked away, fixed his eyes on the floor. "The other day... When you called me Jakub...I liked that."

I took in a ragged breath and looked around to see that Kara and the girls had left us. "What are we doing?"

"Come, take a ride with me."

I followed after him without another word, without protest.

We drove in silence for the ten minutes it took to get to the store. We climbed the stairs. My hand shook when I tried to work the key. Jake's hand came to rest on mine.

"Let me," he said, unlocking the door with his hand steadying mine.

I sat at the kitchen counter and he took the seat next to me, his knees brushing against mine. When I looked to him, he was looking right back at me.

"Do you love him?"

"I don't know. I was so sure that I did, but how can you love someone when you're thinking about someone else at the same time? What kind of person does that make me?"

"Kasia," he said as he took my hands in his, "I'll back off. I don't want to hurt you or make you feel bad about yourself. You need to work this out on your own. But I want you to know that I'm in love with you." He stood and rested a gentle hand on my cheek. "I'm not telling you that to pressure you, and it's probably stupid to say all that while I'm still working here for you." He was pulling away but his touch had me closing my eyes and wishing for so much more. "I'm just not good at hiding my feelings, and I don't want to where you're concerned." He took a deep breath. "I'll meet you in the truck and I'll take you home."

I stood and reached for his hand as he turned to leave. "Not yet."

Oh, and I felt that kiss everywhere. I pressed in closer and he matched me with each stroke of his tongue. I couldn't get enough. I silently willed him to move the hands that were cradling my face, to move them and touch me everywhere. When I took his hands in mine, he let me have my way when I smoothed his hands down the sides of my neck, across my collarbone to my shoulders and down. But when I rested his hands alongside my breasts, practically begging him to touch me there, he pulled back and whispered my name on a breathy exhale.

I dropped my head, scolding myself in silence.

He tipped my chin up so that I had no choice but to look at him. "Are you ok?"

"A little embarrassed, that's all. Kind of just begged you to feel me up…Not my finest moment."

"Embarrassed? Don't be. I'm pretty much fist pumping the universe right now. The fact that you want me to touch you has me more turned on than I've ever been in my life." He moved in so close that I could feel the hard ridge of his erection pressing into my thigh, could feel his warm breath on the shell of my ear when he whispered, "I want to, so bad it hurts. But when I touch you, I'm the only man who's touching you. I don't share, Kasia."

Damn if that didn't just turn me into a puddle of want. And now there was nothing to do but surrender. I wanted him so badly that everything ached, my heart and my body.

"I want to be yours, Jakub."

He leaned in and kissed me again. "I already know that I'm yours."

Chapter Sixteen

DYLAN

Back in my office and gearing up for the long day ahead, no one would ever guess that a few hours ago I was coming apart at the seams.

I called my father first thing and told him about my plan to fly home late tonight before making a turnaround back to Chicago tomorrow morning. When he asked why, I told him the truth.

"Son, you'll get through it as a couple if it's meant to be."

I fucking hated him sometimes. "We won't get through it."

"Then—"

"I'm going, Dad. We're nothing like you and Mom. Kasia's definitely not like Mom. She won't turn a blind eye and let me fuck around for the next twenty years. I'm taking the last flight out tonight and I'll be back first thing tomorrow."

"You. Are. Staying. *You* are the point person in this labor dispute, so *you* will be dealing with the unions and the government officials. *You* Dylan, so grow the fuck up. You won't be leaving the bargaining table for the next three days for so much as a shower, so you can just forget about flying back east to reassure your weepy girlfriend.

"You have millions of shareholders and thousands of employees who rely upon you. *This* is what it means to run Cole Industries. Do you understand, Dylan? It's about your name, your family and your responsibility to the firm." His voice softened then. "Your life is no longer your own."

In that moment I realized my father was right.

Above all else, I had a job to do.

Gwen was smooth and composed when she entered my office a few minutes before the others were scheduled to arrive. She closed the door behind her and sat on the edge of my desk. "Do we need to discuss anything?"

"No. I'll brief you when the others get here."

"I was referring to last night."

"I said everything I wanted to say and it still stands."

"Understood."

Gwen got it. We weren't lovers in any sense of the word, and she knew I didn't see her as a confidant or a shoulder to cry on. She also understood that we were done. It was over, and the affair would never impact her position or reputation at the company.

We were cut from the same cloth.

I wondered if she liked what she saw when she looked in the mirror because I sure as shit didn't.

* * *

KASIA

On the way back to my house, Jake had one hand on the wheel and one hand holding mine. I'd done a complete one-eighty that was beyond all reason, but it felt so very right. I wanted Jake and there was no one else. It was as if my head and my heart were finally on the same page.

"It's only seven o'clock. I want to fly out there tonight."

"Fly where? To see him?"

"I need to talk to him…To tell him in person."

"Don't do that for me. I've been waiting for months so I can wait a little longer. Talk to him when he gets back to New York."

"But *I* can't wait. I can't talk to him on the phone or respond to his texts as if nothing has changed. I'm not a liar."

I couldn't look at him once those last words left my mouth. Even when he nudged my hip, I kept my gaze fixed out the passenger side window. He slowed and pulled over.

"Kasia, talk to me."

"I *am* a liar. I've been with him this entire time while I've been wanting you." I shook my head, so ashamed. "I've wanted you since that first day, but I've been with him. Do you understand? I was *with* him a few days ago."

"Please stop beating yourself up. He was your boyfriend. I pushed my way in, forced something even though I knew you were with him. I'm not so innocent in all this. Listen," he said as he drew me closer and rested his forehead against mine, "we'll take things slow, all right? I can wait for you."

I nodded and swallowed to ease the lump in my throat. "I still want to go tonight. Is that all right with you? Will you take me to the airport?"

"If that's what you really want, Kasia, but I'd like to come with you." My eyes went wide and he smiled in response. "I don't want to be sitting in the room when you break the news to him, but I don't like the idea of you alone in the city late at night. I need to know you're safe."

"I'll be fine. I'll take a cab straight to his place and then I'll head right back to the airport to get the earliest flight out tomorrow morning." He wasn't happy about it. "Jake, I don't know what else to do. I feel awful telling him while he's in the middle of this big mess at work, but what's the alternative? Wait two more weeks? Break it to him over the phone? I can't do it."

"Your parents—"

"I'll call them from the airport."

* * *

JAKE

Dropping her off at LaGuardia was nothing short of torture.

Putting loved ones on planes had become nearly impossible for me to do, and add to that the fact that she was flying at night and would be navigating the streets of Chicago on her own. I was so uneasy about the whole thing that I nearly told her no, but I knew that I had no right. Kasia made her own decisions, and her strong, determined nature was one of the many things that drew me to her.

When she told me she was mine, I wanted to whoop and holler, to hold her tight and never let her go. So watching her pass through airport security on her way back to see him was agonizing, but I told myself that I'd already endured months of waiting. I could make it a few more hours if it meant she was coming back home to me.

I'd been on edge since that boyfriend of hers walked into the store last week. And when she came back from vacation looking all tan and relaxed, it was like having the truth of the situation shoved in my face. Kasia belonged to Dylan. I had to accept it and move on.

Anger and misery were steady companions those days when she was away. The only positive was that I got a shitload of work done on the project. I needed to keep moving, keep doing, and above all else, stop thinking. So I worked fourteen, sixteen, eighteen hour days, beating myself up physically so that I'd fall into bed exhausted every night, too tired to even dream.

But that first day I saw her back at the shop, I knew it. Knew I still had a chance.

My Kasia was jealous, she was angry, and she was confused. I was angry too, vengeful even. I wanted to hurt her that morning. And it was satisfying at first, to watch her suffer as her friend practically stripped down and threw herself at me. I couldn't help but fuel the fire, getting off on the murderous look in her eyes when I licked my lips and studied her friend from top to bottom as if she was a perfectly cooked porterhouse and I was a starving man.

Caitlin was pretty, no doubt about it, but she didn't do anything for me. No, I only wanted one girl, and she was on the verge of tears by the time she left to go upstairs.

There was no comfort in hurting Kasia, and no sooner did she leave than I was racing upstairs to try and make things right. I knew deep in my soul that she was drawn to me, but I couldn't make this decision for her. And although I knew moving on would hurt like hell, I had too much pride to wait this out any longer. No, Kasia had to choose.

And she chose me.

Kasia texted when she landed in Chicago at eleven o'clock, and texted again when she was in a cab on the way to his apartment.

After I got Karolina home, I sat on the couch watching late night television and infomercials. No way in hell was I going to sleep. Kasia never indicated that Dylan had a temper, but as I sat there regretting my decision to let her go alone, I was tense, envisioning every possible negative scenario.

I just had to pray that she was safe, and hope that after spending time with him, that she was still mine.

* * *

DYLAN

I never returned her *good luck* text.

There was no way to handle this, no strategy to employ, no tactics that would generate a positive outcome. My brand of shady bullshit would never fly with Kasia. It was over.

Who was going to be the one to drop the axe, me or Tomasz? That's the only question that remained.

He obviously hadn't rushed home to tell her. If he was really sticking to his asinine forty-eight hour deadline, then I had until Wednesday night, maybe Thursday morning? The whole ordeal was passing in and out of my consciousness because, callous asshole that I am, I was also fully engaged at work.

We called it a night at nearly one-thirty with plans to resume talks at nine the next morning. I had a suite at the hotel where we were hosting the labor talks, so I had no intention of venturing home. My plans changed when I saw a text from Kasia sent at midnight.

She's here. Here in Chicago. I can't do this tonight.

The elevator pinged as it sped past each floor, and with every jarring beep I knew I was one step closer to the executioner's block.

"I'm sorry I couldn't get here earlier, Kasia. It's been so crazy today with, with...with everything. I'm just so sorry. I don't know what else to say."

"Stop apologizing, Dylan. It's ok. You've been tied up with work, you're under a lot of pressure and you must be exhausted. I should be the one apologizing. I've been sitting here for the past two hours thinking that I shouldn't have come."

I sat on the couch and dropped my head into my hands. Why was she being so nice? I'd fucked her over royally and she was still more concerned about my well-being than her own.

"I messed up, and I just...I don't know what I can say to fix this."

"Dylan," she said as she dropped to her knees in front of me. "I'm the one who's sorry. Being apart all the time has been so hard.

I've tried, I really have, but it's not working. I don't want to lie to you. That's why I'm here."

"You've never lied to me."

"I feel like I'm changing. I care about you, so much, but I can't help what I'm feeling."

I was dog-tired, but that couldn't explain the confusion, the utter haze I was in. What the hell was she talking about? Why was she pleading with me instead of slapping me?

I lowered my hands and sat back. "I don't understand."

She took a deep breath and covered my knees with her hands, as if to brace me. "I can't see you anymore, Dylan. I didn't intend for anything to happen, and nothing has, but my feelings for—"

"Jake? Holy motherfucking shit. It's Jake, isn't it?"

She didn't answer and there was no need. I already knew. That motherfucker had outmaneuvered me, slithered in like a dirty snake and took advantage of the distance between us.

When Kasia rested her head back on my lap I began to stroke her hair. The urge to comfort her was automatic.

I was a mess, and for the first time in my life I wasn't above begging. "Listen to me, Kasia." I had to clear my throat, so tight with emotion that my voice didn't sound like my own. "I love you. You're all I've ever wanted. And I already have it worked out that I'm going to be in New York full-time. No more of this long-distance bullshit." When she went to raise her head I doubled down. "I don't even care if something *did* happen with Jake. We can get through this. Both of us, right?"

Maybe, just maybe, I thought, she could forgive my cheating now that she'd admitted to her own infidelity—even if hers was merely the sin of thinking of someone else.

"I can't. It wouldn't be fair—"

"You want *him*."

"Dylan, I want to get my head together. I don't want to hurt anyone. You didn't do anything wrong. You've always been good to me."

"Fuck...Just stop." I couldn't listen to this. "We both know I've never been good enough for you."

"Look at me." And when I did, the loss of her hit me soul deep. "I know you've always tried for me. You've wanted things." When I went to speak, she raised her hand, silencing me. "You have. You need things that I can't give you, and you've always been patient. You're a good man. You've taken care of me, loved me, and always tried to help me. I love you for that. What I'm doing hurts now, but in the end it will be better for both of us."

"No one will ever be better for me. There's no one but you."

She rested her head back in my lap and I went back to stroking her hair. We were both out of words.

I wanted to tell her. Wanted to confess it all, going all the way back to that first time in Palm Beach. I wanted her to comfort me, as she was doing right now. Wanted her to tell me that it was ok, that she understood me, and that she knew I'd never meant to hurt her. But I kept my mouth shut, hoping against all reasonable odds that she'd never find out. And if she didn't find out what a dishonest prick I was, then maybe I could convince her to change her mind. Maybe I wouldn't have to let her go.

It was wishful thinking and faulty logic brought on by a combination of fatigue and desperation. Tomasz wouldn't miss out on his chance to nail me to the cross. I'd already sealed my own fate.

"Is there anything I can say to change your mind?"

Standing up, Kasia shook her head. She kissed my cheek and told me she was sorry once more, fighting back tears as she turned and walked out the door.

I sat there until the night gave way to morning, punchy from lack of sleep and confused. I went over everything she said, again and again, in an effort to make sense of it all.

At the end of the day, only one fact remained: Kasia chose another man over me.

For the first time in my life, I got exactly what I deserved.

* * *

KASIA

Is there anything worse than breaking up with someone?

I was wrung out and boneless by the time I slumped into the back of the cab. I stared out the window as the driver sped back to O'Hare, but there was nothing to see in the dark of night.

The airport was lit up but lifeless at three in the morning. A few porters were working, mopping floors and emptying trash cans at a snail's pace, and one or two stragglers were sleeping in chairs. Passing through airport security, one TSA officer eyed me curiously while the other asked about my lack of luggage. I didn't feel entirely safe when I took a seat at the boarding gate. With not so much as one news kiosk or coffee stand open, it was like an off-limits zone in the aftermath of a zombie apocalypse. I had to use the bathroom but the thought of danger lurking in dark corners kept me in place. I could hold it a while longer.

I texted Jake, not expecting a reply, and was so relieved that I cried when he texted me back immediately.

He was waiting up for me.

And I couldn't wait to get back to him.

Chapter Seventeen

KASIA

It was nearly eight when I walked out of the terminal to find Jake leaning against his truck, worry etched into his features as he looked off into the distance.

It occurred to me sometime this morning that maybe I'd taken advantage of his easy going nature. It couldn't have been easy to stand by and watch me take off like that, knowing I was going to be with Dylan. I hoped he understood that caring enough about Dylan to tell him in person didn't mean I still had some lingering desire for him. I didn't.

And taking Jake in now, I thought to myself that he was beautiful in a way that had nothing to do with his looks. He was kind and he was good in the purest sense of the word—that's what made him irresistible.

If I was lucky enough to capture his heart, I knew he'd never give me a reason to regret my decision. I was sure of it. I also knew deep in my soul that staying with Dylan was wrong, and that someday he would destroy me. It could be next week, next month, or twenty years deep into a marriage marked by ups and downs, but one day Dylan Cole would break my heart beyond repair.

"Thank you."

He reached out to touch my cheek. "For what?"

"For worrying about me, for letting me go, for staying up all night...You look as tired as I do." He smiled when he rubbed at the stubble covering his cheek, taking my bag with his free hand. "Thank you, Jakub Wozniak."

"Anytime, Mazur." After I was situated, he went to start the truck but then turned to me and took my hand. "I've been thinking," he smiled before adding, "*all* night long. I just want you to know there's no pressure. I'm not expecting you to be my girlfriend right this second or anything." He shook his head. "Wait, that came out wrong. I sound like I'm in eighth grade or something."

"Is it ok with you if I want to be your girlfriend?"

He kissed my hand. "I think I could be ok with that."

"But like you said the other night...Maybe we can take it slow?"

"I told you, Kasia, I'll wait for you."

Instead of going straight to the store, we sat at a nearby diner and I basically told Jake my life story. I told him about growing up in Greenpoint, about Patryk, my adventures at Prep and at UV.

I told him about Dylan—the PG version—but Jake understood me when I said there were a few experiences I regretted. He held my hand across the table whenever I faltered or needed a moment, but it wasn't all that hard to open up to him. I told him everything, including all the wonderful things about Patryk and Dylan, because I had so many happy memories from both relationships. They were both good men. They weren't perfect, but no one was.

He did a double take when I ordered a second cup of coffee and muffin after polishing off my omelette, but I was ravenous and there was still more to say. I wanted him to know about my past and to know how I envisioned my future. I wanted him to know me.

And then I wanted to know him.

"Now it's your turn."

* * *

JAKE

I knew what made Kasia different.

When she told me about her life, about her past, she never once lingered on what was negative. I gathered from listening to her talk about Patryk that he was a bit of a control freak, someone who had to be on top in a relationship, so to speak, but she skated over that. She wasn't blind to his faults, it ended their relationship, but she chose to focus on his best qualities. And with Dylan it was the same. I'd bet my entire life savings that he'd screwed around behind her back—everything about the guy screamed entitled, narcissistic prick—but Kasia saw him as a man who tried his best. According to her, he tried to change, to be better, to go against his nature just to please her.

We were on our third round of coffees when she put me on the spot. I was out of practice with the whole opening up to people thing. Karolina was too young to burden with my worries, and for a long time there was no one else. So I started off easy, told her about my childhood, my happy days as a kid growing up in Wallington, New Jersey, another Polish-heavy enclave close to New York City. The excitement of Kara's birth, which I'm sure was a total *oops!* moment for my parents. The sense of well-being I had growing up with family and financial security. Told her about the big house, the vacations, the private schools.

She smiled and laughed along with me, but then topped my hand with hers when she sensed my story was about to take a turn for the worse. So it wasn't all that hard to keep going, to tell her about the day the rug was pulled out from under me. The devastation of not only losing my parents, but of finding out in the days and weeks that followed how my father had spent way beyond his means and hadn't secured the basics to protect us, such as life insurance.

"Sounds like you never thought twice about what to do, Jake."

"I didn't, but it was all because of Karolina. I still wonder, though, if what I did was selfish or if it was best for her."

"Selfish? How could you say that? Look at her today. You couldn't be anything but proud of her, and if you listen to her tell it, that's *all* thanks to you."

"But those first two years…" I pinched my eyes closed just thinking about it. "She went from living in a four-bedroom house to a studio apartment in a neighborhood that wasn't exactly safe. Had to leave her friends behind and switch from an all-girls private school to a noisy, overcrowded public school. I had to take any job I could find, which meant long hours away from her and working for shady contractors who cut corners. Those first few years I questioned my decision every day. But Kara was always smiling, she made friends at that new school, didn't complain about our crappy apartment…"

"She does seem like a little piece of sunshine, right?"

"Yeah, that's my nickname for her—"

"Sloneczko." She smiled at me. "That's my brothers' name for me."

"Yeah, it fits."

I couldn't get enough of this girl. I wanted to spill my soul to her, share everything I had with her. I never wanted to let her go.

I was always busy working, planning, saving—looking ahead. I realized sadly that up until now, I didn't have anyone to talk to. And Lord, it felt good. Didn't know just how much I needed this, needed her.

"You sacrificed so much. You had to leave school, throw yourself into working full-time, and you had to take on the role of being a parent, too? It must have felt overwhelming"

"It was like I was on autopilot, you know? You just do what you have to do. I couldn't have afforded the room, board and tuition, even though I had a partial scholarship. Maybe I could have worked and stayed in school, but then I wouldn't have been able to keep Kara and," I cracked a weak smile, "like I said, I'm selfish. I couldn't let her go live on the other side of the country. I couldn't..."

When I paused, she rubbed her hand along my arm, urging me to go on. "You couldn't what?"

"I couldn't stand the thought of being all alone."

I bared my worst self when I admitted that, but Kasia just leaned in and raised both of my hands to her lips, laying a tender kiss on one and then the other.

After a moment, she asked, "How serious were you with Hannah?" My surprised expression led her to confess, "Kara told me."

I shook my head and smiled. "That figures."

It took me a minute to gather my thoughts, because me and Hannah? It felt like a lifetime ago.

"At the time it seemed like we were in deep. And if nothing had changed, who knows, maybe we would have gone the distance. But she did cut ties within a month of my parents' funeral, so the whole *for better or worse* thing obviously wasn't for her. That was pretty harsh."

"Harsh is one way to describe it."

"But I get it...Hannah was only twenty and she didn't sign up to help me raise a teenager. And we had absolutely nothing in common anymore. I became a different person. I had no interest or patience when she was yammering on about the latest parties or some silly disagreement between her and her friends. I was damn near drowning. I'm trying to take care of Kara at the same time I'm sifting through overdue bills, trying to teach myself estate law on the fly, and cleaning out my parents' house so we could sell it before foreclosure proceedings started."

Kasia wiped at a stray tear. "You had no one."

"I had Karolina, and that kept me going. And I don't want to make Hannah out to be totally heartless because she wasn't. She tried, she'd ask how I was doing, but I couldn't...or wouldn't talk about my parents with her, so I can't really blame her for not comforting me."

"Are you still in touch?"

"No." I shook my head and laughed. "She started banging my roommate a few weeks after we broke up. At least that's when I found out about it. I lost touch with most of my friends. I was too busy and I didn't fit in with them anymore. I'm only in contact with two of them, Henry and Kyle. They both ended up in New York after Georgetown so we reconnected."

"And Hannah, is she still with your roommate?"

"No, he's married and living back home in Rhode Island. I don't know who Hannah wound up with. She's living somewhere in New York, though. Kyle saw her at some alumni function recently."

"Oh no, I have competition?"

"She's probably been here for a few years now, Kasia. I haven't looked her up and she hasn't tried to find me. She wouldn't be interested in the person I am now."

"What's that supposed to mean?" She looked offended on my behalf, which was cute. "What's wrong with the person you are now?"

"Nothing. I'm good with who I am. But she wouldn't see beyond the scuffed boots or the clothes I wear to work. She's more for the Huntsman suit, Testoni shoes...For the Wall Street guy I was on my way to becoming. Hannah liked money. Once she understood I was going to be struggling financially, she was out."

"Nice."

"No, Kasia, she was more honest than most people are. I mean, she didn't say it straight out, but she also didn't string me along, make me think that she still loved me. I don't harbor any bad feelings towards her. And I don't regret anything. Everything I've been through has brought me to this day, right? And I'm pretty damn happy today."

"I'm pretty damn happy, too."

I swallowed and looked away for a moment. I hadn't worn my heart on my sleeve in a long time and it had me choking up there for a second.

"So how do we do this? I've already told you that I love you and I haven't even taken you out on a first date."

She threw a sugar packet at me, pretending to be annoyed while stifling a laugh. "Yeah, that's messed up!"

"It really is. Can I take you out Friday night?"

"Yes, I'd like that."

Chapter Eighteen

KASIA

Radio silence from Dylan.

I don't know why I was surprised. Dylan was right in the thick of a difficult situation at work, more high-stakes and contentious than I'd originally been led to believe, so I knew he was under a tremendous amount of pressure. But still, it was odd. Other people saw Dylan as cold and impenetrable, as a man capable of turning his emotions on and off like a faucet, but I knew him, and knew that nothing could be further from the truth.

When my phone rang Thursday morning with Anna's name flashing on the screen, my heart ached. When you end a relationship there's a ripple effect. Over time Anna and I had grown close, so the thought of her drifting away and out of my life truly hurt. And wasn't it inevitable, wasn't this only the beginning? Anna was one of many people in my life with close ties to Dylan. Would I remain close with Darcy, being that Tom was one of Dylan's oldest friends? Would I lose Trish and Brian too?

My voice was weak when I answered, "Hey, Anna."

"Ohmigod, whatever Dylan did to fuck this up, please give him another chance. I know what he's like, but he loves you."

"He didn't do anything wrong. It just wasn't working."

"I just spoke to Aunt Margot and she's beside herself."

That was hard to believe. "Really?"

"Uncle Vince told her Dylan was trying to fly home to you Monday night but he wouldn't let Dylan go. He was trying to tell you himself, Kasia."

"Tell me what? I don't know what you're talking about. I went to see him in Chicago Tuesday. We broke up. I'm really sorry, Anna, but it's over." I paused before adding, "I haven't heard from him since."

"I wish things were different. I wish *he* was different."

"Don't. Dylan is a great person. Our lives just don't fit together anymore. There's someone else out there for him, someone who will make a better match than me."

"No way! Who would be better, CeCe or that twat, Melanie? I don't think so."

Melanie. CeCe. The thought of him with either one had me blinking back tears, but Melanie Pierce? That would be tragic. I didn't want to be with him anymore, but emotions aren't convenient things. I would still hurt for him if he was hurting, and I'm sure I'd feel at least a pang of jealousy when some other women invariably came along and replaced me.

"I don't want you thinking this is on Dylan. It's one hundred percent on me. He's been nothing but good to me, ok? And please, I don't want you to disappear on me. Promise me that?"

"Kasia, it won't be the same." I agreed but didn't want to say the words out loud. "I was hoping you'd be like my sister someday soon."

"Me too, Anna...Me too."

After I took a few moments to collect myself, I called Darcy and told her everything. She was totally supportive, and I don't know why I expected anything less. We made plans to meet for lunch on

Monday after she returned from Connecticut for the weekend. Rene and Maureen already knew, and while they didn't shout it from the rooftops, I could tell they were both happy for me. Those few times when Dylan met us for a bite to eat after spin class, or when we met as a big group for Sunday brunch, the girls seemed way more at ease around Tom and Caleb than they did around Dylan. It bothered me, but I just told myself that it was to be expected. Dylan, by the very nature of the life he was born into, was intimidating. Or who knows, maybe they saw something that I was too blind to see.

I'd like to say I was eagerly anticipating my first date with Jake, but I was still on a messed up emotional rollercoaster. Maybe I should have asked Jake to hold off on starting any kind of relationship with me until I was single for, I don't know, maybe one entire week?

We saw each other every day at work, just like always, and even though I was a hot mess, Jake kept things light so it wasn't awkward.

We still had our chats over coffee in the morning, not delving into anything too deep like we had that morning in the diner. We talked business during the day. He went home after work and I went home. There were no naughty moments in the upstairs apartment. We kept things entirely platonic.

Friday afternoon he came up and knocked on the studio door at around four. "Can you be ready by six tonight?"

"Sure. What am I wearing? I mean, where are we going?"

"I got us a court at the tennis center in Prospect Park, then I figured we could grab a burger afterwards. Does that sound good? Michal told me you're pretty decent."

"He used the words *pretty decent*? I'll have you know that he hasn't beaten me since I turned eighteen."

"Damn, I hope I don't get my ego crushed tonight."

I was glad the date was more casual. I don't know how I would have felt about dressing up and going someplace fancy. It would have been too stuffy, too formal, and too similar to my dates with Dylan.

It was just after midnight when I fell back onto my bed, smiling to myself and rubbing my fingers over my lips in an effort to revisit his goodnight kiss.

If I was asked to grade my first date with Jake, I'd give it an A-plus. Choice of activity was perfect, he looked good enough to eat, and the conversation flowed as easily at it always did between us.

He didn't let me win, ramping his serve up to full speed when I whizzed a return shot down the alley that left him shaking his head. So he beat me—just barely—and I could tell he was surprised that I'd made him run as hard as I did.

My father taught us all how to play, and as a kid I competed mostly against my brothers, boys who were bigger and stronger than me. I played at Prep, which was another factor in earning me the disdain of Samantha Paulson. I beat her out for the top singles position, even though she'd had years of private instruction and I grew up playing on the raggedy, unkempt public courts at McCarren Park.

Over burgers and beers, Jake and I laughed a lot and shared more about ourselves with one another. The night was light, though, nothing heavy—no talk of exes or other sad topics.

When he dropped me off, we lingered on my front stoop and he kissed me once on the lips. It was all very 1950's. The air felt heavy around us, like the universe wanted more, but I was happy he held back. I wanted to be closer to Jake before anything happened in that department.

Deep down I felt like this was it, he was the one, and I could wait for the goodness that was to come.

* * *

JAKE

Now that was a good first date. No, I take that back—it was so much better than good.

There was no song on the radio, but I was tapping my fingers against the steering wheel and grinning like a damn fool on the drive back home to my apartment. I laughed, replaying the match in my head, impressed with how hard she played me. For a skinny little thing she was strong, and damn, I'd never seen anyone wear a tennis skirt the way she did. Her legs. Lord, I couldn't stop thinking about running my hands over her legs, kissing up the insides of her thighs and claiming every square inch of her body. I drifted off to sleep dreaming of the day I'd finally have her beneath me, loving every part of her.

"Hello?"

"It's Tomasz Mazur. How are you?"

"Good. What's up?"

"I just stopped by the house to talk to Kasia but she was up and gone already. My father said she was out with you last night?"

What was with the all-business tone? Was he upset with me for taking her out? Did he disapprove? If so, then too fucking bad. "Kasia was out with me. I dropped her off at around eleven. Is there a problem?"

"No, there's no problem. I was just confused and I need to talk to her. Did she seem ok?"

"Yeah, I guess. Is everything all right?"

"I don't really know. You have any idea where she might have gone today?"

"No idea. She's not answering her phone?"

"No."

"I'm heading to the site. If she's there I'll tell her to call you."

"Thanks....And Jake?"

"Yeah?"

"I'm glad she was out with you."

She wasn't at the store and I didn't hear from her all day. If not for that odd conversation earlier, I wouldn't have given it a second thought. By five, though, I was restless.

Since my parents' accident, it was hard to shake the feeling that something bad was always looming on the horizon. Poor Karolina, she could barely cross the street without a warning or a lecture on street safety from me. And when she started dating in high school, she was subjected to threatening glances directed at every potential boyfriend, ridiculously early curfews, and me pacing the floor until she came home. I was over the top but I couldn't help it.

When Kasia walked through the shop's door sometime after six, I breathed out a sigh of relief. "You left your phone at home."

"I did?" She checked her bag and then smiled at me. "Oops. Were you trying to call me? Were you looking for a rematch or something? I was actually just meeting with my tennis pro to get some tips on my net game. You're going down next time, Wozniak."

She was so damn adorable. "Bring it on, Mazur. And although I do enjoy talking to you several times a day, it's Tomasz who's trying to track you down."

"He was trying to get me yesterday but I missed him. We were playing phone tag and then I didn't want to answer when you and I were out together last night. I'll see him when I get home. You want to come back with me? I was just grabbing some paperwork to look over later. Karolina is babysitting again today and," batting her eyes she teased, "I'm sure my mother is cooking a *big* Polish dinner, moj drogi (my dear)."

"You slay me when you speak Polish, Kasia."

"You like?"

"I love."

It was weird walking into her house. Mr. Mazur gave me his usual bear hug and then Mrs. Mazur greeted me with a kiss on both cheeks, fussing over me like she usually did. They treated me the same. It's not like I was expecting some *Welcome to the Family* speech, but the fact that everything *had* changed and it went unspoken felt odd.

Michal rolled in just as we were about to eat dinner, and his arrival took the focus off the elephant in the room. Tomasz came in then, giving me a big happy grin when he saw me at the table. Then came Uncle Victor, then Aunt Agata with her husband and her little boys, then...Patryk and his parents. What the hell? It was like an open house at the holidays. Kasia and her mom jumped up to make extra plates, and then Kasia introduced me to her ex and his parents, all of whom regarded me with cross expressions. She introduced me as her friend, not her boyfriend, but I was all right with that. It didn't really matter anyway, as Kasia made it somewhat obvious in the way that she smiled every time I caught her eye.

And just when the night couldn't get any more bizarre, who knocks on the door but Dylan. The elephant in the room? Try a herd.

Suddenly the air was thick with tension. Mrs. Mazur greeted him warmly but with a pained expression, Uncle Victor was calling out to him, welcoming him in Polish, my sister was staring at Dylan wide-eyed, Patryk's mom was looking at Kasia with disdain, and Kasia looked as if she was going to be sick. For a split second there, I actually felt bad for Dylan. He looked like hell.

I stopped talking to Michal mid-sentence. There was nothing to do but sit back and watch, to take in the whole scene.

When Dylan caught sight of me, he shook his head and laughed. "You're already invited to family dinners? That's just great."

Tomasz barged in from the kitchen at that moment. "Are you fucking kidding me? You actually have the balls to show your face in this house? Get the fuck out of here!"

Mrs. Mazur was confused, yelling to quiet Tomasz, Mr. Mazur was trying to hold Tomasz back, Agata was ushering her boys into the kitchen, and both Michal and Patryk were making their way to Kasia but I wasn't having that. I got there first and moved to stand in front of her so that she didn't get hurt in the melee.

Dylan was pointing his finger at Tomasz. "Mind your own business, Tom. You imagined all that shit, and now you're going to ruin it for Kasia and me? You're going to root for this...this fucking nail banger to have her?"

I gestured for Kara to follow the rest of the women into kitchen, but kept hold of Kasia's hand. And although her lips were parted in a surprised O, she was still sensitive and unfailingly kind, which almost made me laugh. When Dylan threw down the nail banger comment, Kasia made sure to squeeze my hand in solidarity.

"I imagined it?" Tom looked to Kasia apologetically before turning back to Dylan. "I didn't hear that woman say that she still wanted to be with you, and she didn't care that you had a girlfriend? And I imagined you telling her it was over, that you couldn't do it *anymore*? Couldn't do what, Dylan? What couldn't you do anymore?"

"You got it all wrong, Tom." Dylan looked at Kasia, pleading. "He's wrong."

Tomasz settled down and his father released him. Everyone in the room stood in stunned silence for a moment before Tomasz said, "Even if I heard nothing, your body language with that woman said it all. Gwen, was it? It's pretty obvious that she knows you well." Tomasz looked to Kasia again. "I'm sorry, I didn't mean to tell you like this."

Kasia whispered, "Gwen," in a way that didn't indicate surprise or disbelief. She nodded to reassure me before crossing the room to Dylan. When she took his hand there was nothing romantic about it, it was more of a comforting gesture, but I still found it hard to watch. She turned back to look at all of us, but focused her gaze on me when she said, "Can you give us a minute?"

Dylan kept his head down, avoiding eye contact with everyone in the room as she led him outside.

* * *

KASIA

Dylan kept his eyes on the sidewalk.

"Are you all right?"

"How can you ask *me* if I'm all right? Your brother just...Were you even listening?

"I heard every word." Gwen, Dylan and Gwen—I was listening but I was still numb, still processing the entire mess.

"I'm so sorry, Kasia. I can't even imagine what's going through your head right now."

"I'm not surprised, I guess. And it hurts, but I hurt for you more than anything. I know you loved me, Dylan."

"I love you. Present tense."

"But I can't accept that kind of love."

"I swear on my life that I'll never do it again. I already broke it off with Gwen. She means nothing to me. Nothing."

"You know how ridiculous that sounds, don't you?"

He nodded, defeated. "Do you love that guy, Jake?"

"I think I do." I squeezed his hand when I added, "So really, I'm no better than you are."

"Yeah, I beg to differ."

"Can I ask you something?"

"At this point you can ask me anything."

"We're not getting back together, we both know that, so can you just come clean with me? I don't want to have to keep wondering if I was crazy or not."

"I don't follow."

"Can you please just tell me…How many times?"

"With Gwen?"

"No. How many women were there?"

He took a deep breath and looked me square in the eye. "Three. Melanie and Cecilia Tate in Palm Beach last Christmas break, and then Gwen. We started up in October. I'm sorry, Kasia. You know it's me, right? You were perfect, so perfect for me."

"But not enough for you, apparently."

"We both know that's all on me. I'm the fucked up one here."

I smiled up at him. "I knew who you were from day one and I loved you."

He laughed, echoing my words, "But not enough, apparently."

"I need to be the only one."

"You're the only one I love." He let out a breath. "But I know what you mean. You deserve to be the only one."

"Friends?"

"Maybe someday." He gave me a weak smile but then shook his head. "I'll never just want to be friends with you."

We hugged then, holding on for a minute before breaking away.

He got into his car and drove off.

It was final. It was goodbye.

The room fell silent.

"Show's over, folks," I said, trying my best to muster up a smile. "Really, I'm fine, so go ahead and eat."

Patryk and his parents were gone when I came back inside, thank the freaking heavens above. I'm sure Patryk's mother loved every second of that debacle. I could practically hear her clucking her tongue in disapproval, assuring her baby boy he could do better and was fortunate to be rid of a girl like me.

Oh well.

Jake came to me and took my hand, gesturing towards the den with his chin. As soon as he sat on the couch, I sank into his lap.

"I swear, family dinners around here are usually pretty boring."

"Good to know. I don't know if my heart could take that much drama on a regular basis."

"I've been beating myself up for hurting him while he's been lying to me all along. I feel like such a fool."

"You're trusting and loyal. Nothing wrong with that."

"This sounds weird, but I'm kind of relieved. Deep down, it's like I always knew he would be unfaithful, and now I don't have to suffer through that with him."

Jake was rubbing circles on my back, holding me close. I desperately wanted to know what he was thinking but was too afraid to ask. Maybe he was having second thoughts, and who could blame him? That was one messed up family dinner.

"Do you want me to get you out of here, Kasia? You can come back to my apartment with me."

"No. I should just clear the air with everyone, and I need to talk to Tomasz. Anyway, Kara's leaving tomorrow. You should spend the night hanging out with her."

"I want to see you, Kasia."

I joked, "Still, after witnessing that mess?"

"Absolutely."

"You want to give me another shot at the title tomorrow?"

"Sounds good." He nudged me playfully. "And don't think I'm going to go easy on you because of all this."

"Of course not."

He squeezed me tight before shifting me off his lap and getting up. As he turned to leave, he said, "I'm dropping Kara off at the train at noon. I'll come to get you after?"

I nodded and then called after him, "Jakub?"

"What?"

I was shaking all of a sudden. "Are you sure?"

"About what?"

"How could you want me after...everything?"

He came back and pulled me close. "How could I want you? Are you serious? Do you think everything happens according to some kind of perfect timeline, Kasia? Sometimes the timing is awkward or the timing just sucks. Would it have been nice to meet you when you weren't involved with someone else? Sure. But life isn't perfect and I don't care how or when I got you. I'm just grateful that I've got you. Understand?"

I relaxed in his arms and let his strong embrace reassure me. After today, I was afraid he'd think I was too much trouble. Or worse, that he wouldn't want to be with a girl that he knew had been intimate with some other guy just a week ago. The thought made me cringe. I didn't feel worthy of Jake. Despite knowing that Dylan had been cheating on me since the beginning, I felt like a cheat myself. Dylan was *inside of me* not much more than a week ago, and I was already desperate to be with Jake in that same way.

I was desperate for Jake to want me. To love me.

Chapter Nineteen

DYLAN

It felt good to come clean.

After everything, after this crazy, absolutely fucked-up night, I sat on the plane heading back to Chicago feeling oddly relaxed, as if a burden had been lifted off me.

I knew Kasia got at least one thing she deserved from me tonight. After everything I did, and for as much as I loved that girl, I owed it to her. I knew that being honest with her was what she wanted and needed the most.

It wasn't easy. It was more in my nature to lie. And I guess it would have been smarter to stick with that strategy, but in my heart I knew we were done. I had absolutely nothing left to lose.

I'm convinced there's not another woman on the planet who would have reacted to that news the way Kasia did. I fucked around behind her back, lied to her for more than a year, and I would have tricked her into marrying my deceitful ass if I hadn't been caught. Forgiveness and understanding, that's all she gave me in return.

No one knew me the way she did, and I do believe that she loved me, but she put herself first when she left me. That's how this was supposed to end. I would have ruined her and we both knew it.

It's not like I was wishing Kasia and that dickhead Jake all the best. If I could have gotten away with it tonight, I would have wrestled him to the ground and knocked every tooth out of his head. I felt nothing but pure hatred for that guy. Didn't matter that he was solid, honest, hardworking and faithful—that he was better for her. The irrefutable fact that he would soon have the pleasure of fucking my Kasia made me hate him with every cell in my body.

So where to now?

The thought of being with Gwen made me sick. She was as heartless and disloyal as I was. A string of meaningless hook-ups wasn't appealing either, as I noticed my well-dressed seat companion looking over at me in earnest.

As I drained the last drop of my third gin and tonic, I scrolled through my contacts and landed on her name, but my trigger finger stalled. She was familiar, and I was looking for the sort of comfort she'd be more than willing to provide, but still I held off. Did I really want to do this, to settle for the role I was born to play?

I'm landing at O'Hare at eleven. Can you meet for a late drink?

And with that one text I set it all into motion. I settled for second best.

Chapter Twenty

JAKE

I can't remember that far back, back to a time when I steered the pace in a relationship, took it slow. Every girl since Hannah had been a hook-up, or someone with potential that I didn't click with for one reason or another. But this time I wanted the whole courtship experience: dating, developing a commitment to one another, easing into the physical side of the relationship one step at a time.

Kasia was it for me. I had no second thoughts. I'd seen her at her best, at her most vulnerable, and in her angriest, most stressed-out states. I loved every side of the woman.

I saw a lot of her mother in her. Now that Kasia and I were together, I was spending more time with the family. Sunday dinners at their home became routine, and for many reasons those evenings were special to me. It was a connection to my parents and to the life I once had, where people sat around the table enjoying one another's company, speaking the first language I was ever exposed to, eating foods that tied me to my heritage. And Kasia's family was what every person hopes for in life. When you had a seat at their table, you were surrounded by warmth and love.

Your first impression of their family dynamic was of the father as breadwinner and mother as a homemaker, but nothing could be further from the truth. Kasia's parents ran their business as a true partnership, with Mrs. Mazur making as many decisions regarding finances as Mr. Mazur. She was traditional in certain ways, but listening to her talk business was like getting a glimpse of Kasia twenty years down the road.

Kasia was keeping up the same crazy pace as before, but she was starting to reap the benefits of her hard work already. When the shop opened in March, there was a big party with family, friends, her suppliers, business contacts, other shop owners and some local press. I don't want to pat myself on the back, especially because the design of the place was all thanks to Kate Donovan and Kasia, but the store looked great and I was proud of my hand in that. I literally couldn't take my eyes off Kasia that night. Besides looking breathtakingly beautiful, she just had this way about her. Watching her move from one group to the next, poised and confident as she greeted friends and big shots alike, left me a little awestruck. There was no doubt she was going to make this business into a success.

That next week she was contacted by New York Magazine for a story they were doing on Williamsburg. When the issue was released in early May, Kasia was the featured business owner. A large photo of her standing outside the store along with several pictures of the store's interior accompanied an article about Sweet Betty Threads. The timing couldn't have been better. Kasia had just secured a manufacturing deal the month before, so she was prepared for the dramatic increase in orders she was getting from both the website and the increased foot traffic in the store. She hired more employees, and made the transition from college graduate to successful business owner look easy, even though nothing could be further from the truth.

Life changed after I was done renovating the store. I was running my own construction company now, and supervising my project sites could have me in any one of the five boroughs on any given day. Our hours were long but we never went more than one day without seeing one another, even if it meant just having dinner at her parents' house and sitting on the couch together talking for an hour or two afterwards.

Kasia would regularly run issues and dilemmas by me, just as she became the person I relied on when I wanted feedback on my business. She was my equal. I could feel us changing from two people dating to two people in a loving partnership. When I looked across the dinner table and saw her father take her mother's hand in his, or noticed the looks that passed between the two of them, I couldn't help but want that life for us.

* * *

KASIA

Taking things slow had its advantages.

After that night at my parents' house when all *three* of my boyfriends were under the same roof at one time, I was an emotional wreck for a solid week. Jake, who would always have my best interests at heart, put the brakes on us for a while. It was exactly what I needed.

We dated. Tennis and burgers became a routine, as did long walks and coffee shops, or meeting him for dinner after his night classes. We did lots of talking, lots of laughing, lots of kissing and...that's it. I still hadn't stepped foot in his apartment, and the upstairs office at the store wasn't used for anything other than business.

Was my body burning with desire for him? Yes, and I knew there were times when the snail's pace was killing him too. But the anticipation made it all the sweeter. The time spent getting to know Jake made the idea of making love to him something more meaningful. I could see into the future with him. I wanted to be his wife, to raise children with him, and to spend the rest of our days together.

The first time he invited me to his apartment was a full two months later. And in the span of those two months so much had changed for us both. Sweet Betty Threads was a full-fledged business, thanks to the exposure I was getting from magazine articles, web buzz and the exploding scene in Williamsburg. Jake passed all of his licensing requirements and was now out on his own as a general contractor. Kate and Luke were generous with Jake, referring all the jobs they couldn't take on to him. But I knew they did this only because Jake's work reflected on them, and Jake's work was impeccable. I also made sure to reference him any time the store got press, and he would tease that he needed to cut me a commission on the retail and commercial jobs he got as a result. It made me feel good to do anything I could to help him, not only because I loved him but because he was becoming my rock. Jake always had good ideas and his input on pricing and contract issues was invaluable. He also provided me with a constant stream of encouragement and support. In the span of a few months, I'd gotten to a place where I could no longer imagine my life without him.

When he gave me the grand tour of his one bedroom apartment, it was just as I'd expected: neat as a pin. You could see Karolina's influence in the artwork that adorned the walls and the goofy expression magnets on the refrigerator, but this was Jake's space. Nothing was out of place, everything was perfectly organized, and every square foot of the small apartment was utilized in the most efficient manner.

My eyes watered when I noticed that even though Kara was now only home for school breaks, her room remained closed when she was away. Jake had been sleeping on a pull-out sofa bed in the living room for the past six years. It was probably because I was burning up with lust to begin with, but in that moment, the hardships and struggles he'd endured made me want him all the more. I wanted to snap open that pull-out couch and show him just how much I wanted him. But no, Jake had some more sweet, slow torture in mind.

He sat next to me on the couch, taking my face in his hands and kissing me, but I was restless—decided before I came here that I wasn't going to be denied. I straddled his lap, thanking the powers that be for the warm March weather when I hiked the flimsy fabric of my skirt up and over my hips so that there was only the friction of his jeans between us. I couldn't help but arch my body, wanting nothing more than to press in closer, closer, closer. Jake matched the pace of my movements, kissing me deeper, and then used one strong hand to tug both of mine behind my back. With his free hand he explored my body, and I nearly cried out when his fingers grazed my breasts over the fabric of my shirt.

He broke the kiss and gestured to my clothes. His voice was commanding when he rasped out, "Let me see you, Kasia."

I took my time unbuttoning my shirt, and Jake looked like a man who hadn't eaten in days when he took me in. As I undid the front clasp and slid the straps of my bra down my arms slowly, I never took my eyes off him and he never took his eyes off my tits. After a moment, he whispered, "Damn, Kasia."

I watched as he took one and then the other in his mouth, sucking, kissing and gently tugging my nipples until I was literally in pain from wanting him so badly.

"I need you."

"I know, baby," he whispered as he continued the slow torture of kissing and touching me. He reached behind me and pulled my ass up so that he could slide my skirt and panties down, and I was more than eager to make the job easier. I shimmied out of those in seconds flat. Then I was in his lap, completely naked while he still had all his clothes on. It made me feel exposed, like I was his to do with as he wished.

My heart hammered in my chest, my breasts were achy and I was wet with desire. He pushed my hand aside when I went to touch myself, and I moaned when he took over and cupped me between my legs.

"Mine," he whispered as he worked me over. I moved against his hand, rolling my hips and riding his lap. The sensation of him sucking my breasts and touching me had me coming undone quicker than I ever had.

But I needed more, so much more.

He kissed me tenderly and then rested back, nodding when I undid the buttons on his shirt and pushed the fabric aside. It wasn't the first time I saw him bare chested, but now all those rippling muscles and smooth skin were mine to touch. My hands slid over his shoulders, across his chest, down the ridges of his abs and lower, and then it was his turn to moan as I eased him out of his jeans. He was a sight to behold and I was a woman possessed. I kissed down his torso and moved my naked body down to kneel before him. I looked up at him as I took him in my hands and in my mouth, feeling powerful. His head fell back and he gripped my hair gently when I took him all the way in. I loved hearing him moan and whisper my name, as if no one had given him pleasure like this before. He warned me before his release but I wasn't having it. I kept at it and took everything he gave me.

"Come here," Jake said as we left the bathroom a few minutes later. He shucked off the remainder of his clothes, laid back on the couch and then laid me right on top of him so that we were lined up from head to toe. He ran his hands over my back and bum. "Kasia, I love you." He smiled and teased as he gripped my ass, pulling me closer to him, "I love your ass, I love your tits, and I love your mouth, your very talented mouth."

Wanting him so badly, I shifted my body up a bit so that he was pressing against my entrance. I *wanted* to say, "Then fuck me, Jake. Fuck my mouth, my tits, my ass," but, yeah, I didn't think breaking out the dirty talk on day one was such a good idea. Didn't want to scare the poor boy off, so I toned it down big time. "I need you."

He flipped us over in one smooth motion, and then he was above me, lowering his head to worship at my breasts again before he went lower still. I was gasping and writhing because damn, he was good. He snaked his way back up my body, and without much warning he slid on a condom and thrust fully into me. Talk about being worth the wait. Jake filled me and took me, alternating between gentle and powerful. When he came, I could feel him pulsing inside of me, and I didn't want to let him go when he went to pull out. With my hands still gripping his hips close to mine, he looked down at me and whispered, "I'll never get enough of you, Kasia."

Ditto, I thought dreamily, too wiped out to actually speak.

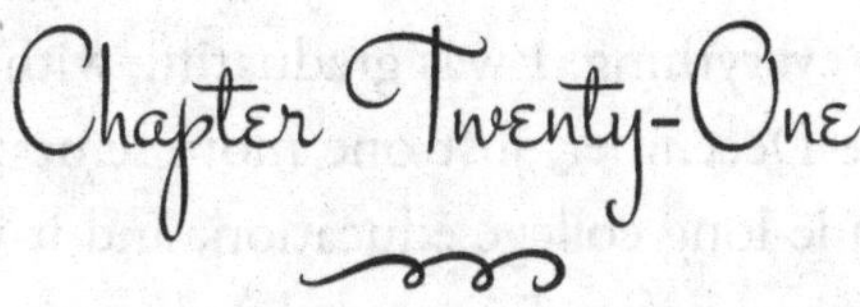

Chapter Twenty-One

JAKE

It didn't feel like summer. I was working so many hours that the days sometimes passed by in a blur. Now it was *me* farming out jobs to other guys who worked as my project managers. And as Luke had done with me, I mentored some of my best workers, priming them to go out on their own one day.

Between jobs, I was busy keeping my eye on Kara as she worked her first real nine-to-five job in the city as a summer intern, and I spent every spare moment I had with Kasia. My life was full in the best possible way.

Kasia was busy too, but she managed to make me feel like I was her number one priority. It's hard to explain, but every little thing she did sent the message that I was loved, truly loved. She would light up when I walked into a room, happy just to see my face. And when we were at her family's house for dinner, I'd notice her heaping extra veggies onto my plate. When I'd look over to her and smile, she'd shrug and say something like, "You eat too much meat." When she did things like that, cared about what I ate, bought me gloves that she read somewhere protected your hands in sub-zero weather, or sent my sister care packages at school, it brought me to my knees. I loved her, I knew that, but it was like I could no longer imagine my life without her.

I was ready to marry her yesterday, but I wanted to be able to provide her with everything. I was graduating with my bachelor's in engineering come December, just one more semester to go in what was a nearly decade-long college education, and it was important to me to have that degree before I proposed. I also needed a new place to live.

In my business, the opportunity to scoop up distressed real estate often presented itself. I'd been making this a priority lately, and had looked at several sites in Brooklyn. Kasia's dad came with me a few times, joking that he'd try to outbid me if the property was really great. I wanted his opinion on structure, neighborhood details and that sort of thing, but I also wanted his unspoken approval, which he gave to me. Without me saying it outright, he knew that I was looking for a place where Kasia would want to live.

When I came across a brownstone in Park Slope in September, I knew I'd found our home. It was the one dilapidated eyesore amid well-kept houses on a tree-lined street. There looked to be a lot of young families, and I liked seeing the kids on the block riding scooters and playing outside. A little research told me that the nearby public school was one of the best in the city, so I was sold.

The place had to be completely gutted and would probably take me the better part of a year, but I didn't care. I negotiated a good price and was working with Kate to draw up the plans and apply for permits a week after the closing.

I didn't tell Kasia. We'd only been dating for nine months, so buying a place for *us* seemed more than a little presumptuous on my part. I decided to show it to her after it was finished, and if she didn't react the way I hoped she would, I'd lose nothing by keeping the place as an investment property or even flipping it.

As I walked through it again with Kate one afternoon, though, it was as if I could see our future. I could smell food cooking, I could hear the sweet voices of a toddler calling out and a baby babbling, and I could see my beautiful wife walking down the stairs to welcome me home.

Chapter Twenty-Two

KASIA

It was all happening so fast that sometimes I had to pinch myself to believe it was real.

I was walking on air as I made my way down Madison Avenue, fresh out of a meeting with a buyer from Nordstrom's. Corporate had flown him all the way in from Seattle, and we'd just signed the contracts at my attorney's office. Trent—he was one of those first name only kinda guys—had gushed over my resort wear designs when he visited the Williamsburg store yesterday, and today he made a commitment to carry the entire spring line. He said he'd been following me for at least two years, and as proof, pulled out one of the first dresses I offered up for sale on my website. I was floored.

If this deal went through, it would catapult Sweet Betty Threads into an entirely different stratosphere. Once Nordstrom's started carrying the line, other high-end retailers were within my reach. It was exhilarating and frightening at the same time. There was a strange comfort in being small and lesser known—a simple store, a simple life. This kind of move could change my life drastically. Did I want that?

Lost in thought, I didn't notice them until I just about ran smack straight into Mrs. Cole and Melanie Pierce. I was taken by surprise and still bubbling with excitement from my meeting, so my reaction didn't match what I truly felt for either one of these women.

I smiled and practically chirped, "Ohmigod! Hello!"

"Kasia dear, how *are* you?" Mrs. Cole's tone dripped pity and compassion. I was confused for a moment, but then it dawned on me. Right, she only knew that Dylan had been caught cheating. She thought of me as the devastated, jilted ex-girlfriend.

Melanie gave me her usual head-to-toe once over, then smiled appreciatively when she said, "You look fantastic."

Over time my feelings towards Melanie had softened, especially now that I was no longer with Dylan. I still didn't want to be friends with her, and we wouldn't be meeting for lunch ever in this lifetime, but there was no resentment. I still had my doubts, but maybe only someone like Melanie could give Dylan what he truly needed. And there was no room in my heart for negativity where he was concerned. More than having once loved him, I would always care about Dylan and want what was best for him.

There was an awkward moment before I replied to them both, "Thanks, and I'm doing well. How is the magazine going, Melanie?"

"I'm done there. It wasn't for me." Working in general wasn't for girls like Melanie. "I'm too busy traveling between here and D.C. to see Christian. I'm thinking about designing jewelry."

I cringed when people said things like that, as if you could be a jewelry or clothing designer without any artistic background or anything remotely related to experience. I tried my best to sound sincere when I said, "That sounds great, Melanie. Good luck with that."

The last time I heard from Dylan was a text congratulating me after the feature in New York Magazine. I was sure I would have seen him at Darcy and Tom's wedding, and I agonized in the days and weeks leading up to it. I didn't want to hurt him by bringing Jake as my date, but I also didn't want to hurt Jake by deciding to go solo. I was going to reach out to Dylan beforehand until Darcy told me that he had to decline due to a major crisis involving one of their European subsidiaries. He told Tom that he had to be overseas, but I couldn't help but think he wanted to avoid me. Some people still didn't know we'd broken up, so there were a few uncomfortable moments that day. Fielding *Where's Dylan* questions as Jake stood by my side was all sorts of awkward.

I'm human, so I did follow what was written in the press about Dylan. There was no regret, no longing to rewrite our story, but from time to time I wanted to know how he was. I was happy to read that Cole Industries had come out on top in that whole labor mess, and wondered if the success, coupled with the timing of our break-up, had driven Dylan and Gwen closer. Standing here right in front of me, I thought, was my opportunity to find out.

"How is Dylan doing?"

Melanie's eyes were saucers. "You two aren't in contact at all?" She recovered quickly. "I mean, I know you broke up, but I just thought—"

Mrs. Cole interjected, "He's doing well, dear. Work has him traveling nonstop lately."

Melanie, of course, couldn't go all Sally Sunshine on me—she was still a certain percentage bitch by blood. She smiled when she added, "But CeCe has been traveling with him, so he's managing."

It didn't feel like a kick to the gut, but it did sting a little. I nodded my head and smiled back. "I glad he's happy and doing well." And I meant that.

Mrs. Cole looked pained as she took Melanie's hand to signal their departure. "I'll tell him we saw you, Kasia. I know he'll be pleased to hear that you're doing well. Goodbye, sweetheart."

Those words were as close to genuine affection as I'd ever get from Margot Cole, and I was ok with that. I knew that in her own way, she was fond of me. She may not have wanted me for her son, but I think that deep down, she really didn't want Cecilia Tate for Dylan either.

Was I surprised? Yes and no. I knew by choosing Cecilia, Dylan had settled on the girl who would best fit into his Cole Industries world. She was born into that lifestyle. She was also a girl who would submit to his every whim and desire. I knew Dylan would never be completely happy with someone like Cecilia, though. She didn't challenge him. After the novelty wore off he'd have a different woman at his beck and call in every city he visited for business. There was probably already a shapely young assistant in place of the middle-aged woman I'd met in Chicago. I pitied both Dylan and Cecilia.

Walking off in the opposite direction, I pulled Anna up in my contacts. I felt bad that I'd never followed up on my promise to keep in touch with her, and remembered that I hadn't responded to the message she sent me a few weeks ago after a Sweet Betty Threads dress was featured in CityStyle Magazine.

Hi! So glad you saw the article. How is school going so far?

I got a reply a nanosecond later:

Seems like SBT is blowing up-congrats!!! School is great. I'm loving Boston.

I was glad she sounded so happy.

Any hot guys?

With Anna, you never knew, she could be dating the provost.

Actually an old flame has rekindled.

I smiled to myself. When I commented *interesting*, she texted back:

Very interesting. I miss you, K. Wish D didn't fuck it all up for my sake :)

No, I never wanted our break-up to affect the way she
saw him.
Not his fault...Plz pop in when ur in NYC.

It was inevitable that Anna and I would drift apart. If we saw
each other occasionally that was one thing, but I wouldn't pursue
meeting up with her because she was a close link to Dylan. And even
though it wasn't direct contact, it still might send a message to him
that I didn't intend. To me, closure was a good thing. I didn't
honestly believe you could be friends with an ex. You could be
cordial, you could care about their well-being from afar, but keeping
in contact would be misleading to Dylan and disloyal to Jake. And I
had no intention of being either one of those things.

Chapter Twenty-Three

KASIA

When my alarm went off, I was in the middle of a very sexy dream starring my boyfriend. It was a regular occurrence, and one that helped me make it through those long nights sleeping without him.

I was madly, deliriously, happily in love with Jake. My life was on track in every area, and I credited him, with how he made me feel.

Maybe I did the same for him—I hoped that was the case. I was so proud of Jake the day he rolled up in front of my house in his new truck with the company's name and logo painted on the side. Tata took a picture of me and Jake standing in front of it, and when I had it printed, it may sound corny, but I envisioned the picture hanging somewhere in our home years from now.

Going out on his own was a huge accomplishment for Jake. It was the result of hard work, meticulous attention to detail, long hours and dedication to his customers. The fact that he parented Karolina *and* worked his ass off taking extra classes at night to finish his degree just floored me. In my eyes, there was nothing the man couldn't do.

My best moments each day came in the evenings when we were able to sit together and talk, holding hands. Take that back—my *best* moments were at the end of the day when I was able to either sneak away with him to his apartment or to my upstairs studio.

Rene and I went to Chicago to meet up with Caitlin for a few days this past September—a combination business trip and girls' getaway. While I was gone, Jake surprised me by renovating the studio. He carried the design theme from the store throughout the space. He had large work islands installed, better lighting put in overhead, and utilized a once-wasted nook to provide display-like storage for my numerous rolls of fabric. It looked fantastic, and was now a place I could proudly meet with potential buyers and other business contacts. The best change by far, though, was what he did to the small back room. It was crammed full with spare garment racks, fabric rolls and clutter, but now it had a fresh coat of paint, well-organized, decorative storage, and also had a plush futon that looked like a couch but easily unfolded into a queen-sized bed. Jake said he was contemplating putting an actual bed in there, but worried that my father might choke him if he saw it.

I loved it when he walked into the store after finishing his day's work. The sight of him in his work clothes would never get old. The boy was gorgeous. His jeans hung perfectly on his hips, and his shirts weren't too tight, but gave just the subtlest hint of the powerful muscles that lie beneath. The dust and paint on his clothes just added to my lustful fantasies. I would laugh to myself when I noticed the reaction Jake elicited from the women *and* men browsing in the store. He was downright edible.

On a Friday night late in November, I sat on the train thinking to myself that tonight would be the first time I would see him in a suit. He had to attend a Georgetown Alumni Association function to show his support and thanks to the people who funded the scholarship Karolina was awarded. A few of his old friends were going to be there, and he was excited for me to meet them.

I was running late. Two women came into the store right at closing, but it wasn't in my nature to turn away a sale. As I made my way into the crowded club room bar, I didn't see Jake at first. When I did see the back of a head and broad shoulders in a navy blue suit jacket that screamed his name, I stopped in my tracks. He was seated on a barstool and a raven-haired beauty was leaning in close to whisper in his ear. That sick feeling I occasionally had when I was with Dylan washed over me. What can I say, the boy had conditioned me to think the worst. I took a moment to collect myself, threw my shoulders back, took a deep breath and made my over thinking: *Screw this.* I tapped her shoulder and smiled when she took me in, clearly annoyed by the interruption. Then Jake turned his head and smiled at me, looking more than a little relieved. It wasn't the cat that ate the canary look of a cheater, but then again, Dylan never got caught because he was always too smooth to look guilty.

"Kasia, what happened? I was getting worried."

"There were a few last minute customers. I got tied up."

I would have kissed him hello but this chick had scarcely backed up enough to give me room. She was too close and she wasn't moving. I didn't care if this girl introduced herself as the modern-day Mother Teresa, I did not like her.

Jake introduced us. "Uh, this is Hannah Moore. Hannah, this is my girlfriend, Kasia Mazur."

I wasn't that much younger than Hannah—four years if she was the same age as Jake—but she cocked her head to the side as if she was talking to a preschooler when she said, "Kasia...What an unusual name. It's *so* nice to meet you."

What was I supposed to say back to that? *Hannah, what a stupid palindrome you have for a name.* And it's against my religion to say *Nice to meet you* when I do not feel that way. I won't do it. So I nodded and went with, "Oh right, Hannah...Jakub's mentioned you."

I did everything in my power not to feel jealous, but damn, I was about to turn a Hulk shade of green. I'd never felt this territorial about anyone before and it unnerved me. The fact that Hannah was special to Jake at one time just—well, for some reason it made me want to cry.

When she still hadn't moved to leave a respectable amount of distance between her body and Jake's, he stood up, pressed closer to me and kissed my cheek as he took my coat.

"What do you want to drink, cranberry and soda?"

Hannah teased, "Aren't you legal?"

I teased back, wide-eyed, "Is eighteen legal?" I laughed at her shocked expression. "I'll have a vodka cranberry, Jake."

He wasn't saying much. I think he knew he was standing between two women on the verge of baring their claws, and he wasn't entirely familiar or comfortable with this type of scenario. As he handed me my drink, he was tapped on the shoulder by a guy who was most likely Kyle, from the way Jake had described him. Jake urgently gestured for me to join them, but as I went to move away from Hannah, she leaned in close and grabbed my upper arm.

"I was his *first*."

Pushing her hand off my arm, I snapped back so that only she could hear, "Yeah, and he said you fucked like a dead fish."

What the hell? With not even one sip of my drink! Never in my life had I said something so crude and I immediately regretted it. Not only did I lower myself to her level, I'd given her the upper hand. She knew I felt threatened.

Hannah threw her head back and laughed before narrowing her eyes on me. "He *definitely* did not say that, Kayla. *That*, I can guarantee."

Kayla? Ok. I straightened my shoulders and glared back. "I think we're done here."

Making my way over to Jake and the others, she called after me, "I'm done with you, but I am *not* done with him."

I didn't take the bait this time, but because of that witch I was just so over this night. I wanted to tell Jake that I had a terrible headache and just hop on the next train back to Brooklyn, but I'd only been here for five minutes.

He took my hand and smiled as he introduced me to Kyle, his girlfriend Madeline, and Henry. They were all outgoing and friendly, but I'm sure I made a lackluster first impression. I was still a little shell-shocked from my encounter with Hannah, and didn't make conversation as easily as I normally would have. Why did I let her get to me so easily?

When I had Jake to myself for a moment, I whispered, "I think I'm going to go. Is that ok? I just—"

"Are you all right? Did Hannah upset you?"

"I don't know," I said, suddenly eager to lash out at him. "If you walked into a bar and saw Dylan whispering in my ear with his body pressed up against me, would it upset you?" Shaking my head, I knew that was a low blow and wanted to take it back immediately. I was just making a total mess of it every time I opened my mouth tonight, and apparently I couldn't stop. As I drained my second vodka cranberry, I said, "She's still very interested in you, Jake."

He put his hand on my cheek and gently turned me to face him. "She's nothing to me. Do you understand? She's nothing, you're everything."

"I feel like a fool."

He pressed his forehead to mine. "C'mon, you ready to go? I've shown my face for long enough. We can get out of here now."

Jake and I stopped at a pub close to his apartment, and I had at least three more drinks. He was sucking them back too, and soon we were laughing about nonsense and having fun again. I texted my mother to tell her I'd be staying at Jake's because it had gotten so late. I laughed wondering how that would go over. Jake looked scared for a split second before breaking out in a fit of laughter. "Oh shit, your father!"

"It's late, Tata's already asleep and Mama probably won't even tell him. Anyway, my father thinks of you as his fourth son. He'll forgive you." Jake's loopy, emotional expression made me laugh and warmed my heart at the same time.

As Jake fumbled with the lock on his apartment door, I wrapped my arms around him low on his hips and stroked him through his pants. "You look fucking delicious in a suit, you know that?"

"You'd better watch your mouth, sweet Kasia, or else I'm going to have to punish you."

"You don't like when I say *fuck*, Jake?" I purred as I stroked him harder. "What if I tell you to fuck me, Jake? If I say that I want you to fuck me hard and deep…Is it ok if I use that word then?"

The door opened and he dragged me inside and pressed me back against it as it closed behind us. He had a wicked gleam in his eyes. "Say it again and see what happens to you."

I trailed one hand down my body, lingering on my breasts before moving lower and landing between my legs. "First I want you to fuck me right here, Jake, and later I want you to fuck my mouth."

I guess I unleashed a man possessed, because next thing I knew I was turned around, my dress was around my waist, my underwear was ripped off me and he was in me with such force that I was bracing against the wall and arching back to take him even deeper. He drove into me hard, and I was so desperate for it that I was moaning his name and begging him for more.

We woke up the next morning to my phone ringing. We were curled up together on the couch, naked with no blankets covering us. My head ached a little but not too bad.

"Hi Mama, sorry I texted you so late last night."

"I didn't tell Tata, ok?"

"Thank you."

"Are you coming home soon?"

"I'll be home in an hour."

"Tell Jakub I'm making gulasz, to come for lunch."

"Ok, I will."

When I hung up, Jake pulled me in close. "Gulasz is the perfect hangover food. That sounds good."

I got up and used the bathroom, then laid back down after putting on one of his t-shirts. "I feel kind of embarrassed about last night."

"Why? Please don't say you're embarrassed about what happened back here. I liked last night," he said as he nudged his hips into mine.

"I don't know. It's like I was trying to claim you as mine or something. I nearly begged you to do me, and we didn't even stop to use a condom."

"Yeah, I know. You're still on the pill, though, right?"

"Yes," I answered, even though I hadn't exactly been religious about it since we always used condoms.

"And I can't believe I let Hannah get to me. I've never been a jealous, whiny girl, and she reduced me to that in seconds." I was full-on pouting by then. "You didn't tell me she was so pretty."

"She's not pretty, Kasia. Only being interested when things are looking up for a guy, running out when shit gets tough, sleeping with your best friend...Believe me, that's not pretty." He ran his hands up underneath the t-shirt and caressed my stomach and breasts as he nuzzled into that space just underneath my ear. "It's not like I'd want to see that side of you very often, but I have to admit that knowing you're jealous because you want me is kind of hot."

Licking my lips, I slowly dragged the thin fabric up and over my breasts. "I do want you, and I want to be the only one you want."

"You're the only one I'll ever want, forever."

* * *

JAKE

"Why did you take off so early last night? I wanted the four of us to go someplace for dinner after."

"Kasia just needed to get out of there. Hannah said some stupid shit to her last night."

"After you left she was asking me all about Kasia. Wanted to know what she did for a living, where she went to school, how you two met, how serious you were. Kept asking if you were happy. She was like a goddamn investigative reporter."

Too little, too late.

Even though Hannah didn't deserve my discretion, I would never bad-mouth her. I never told anyone besides Kasia that Hannah had basically dumped my ass the moment she realized I was penniless. Before Hannah knew what kind of shit storm my father had left behind, she played her part, acted like she was still in it with me. But she could hardly mask her shock when I told her I'd taken a job working construction, and then when I told her the house was going into foreclosure and I was looking at studio apartments for Karolina and me? That's then she was officially done. She stopped returning my calls.

I didn't blame her for wanting out—I could understand that she hadn't signed up for that kind of life. But I couldn't forgive the fact that Hannah just cut me off without so much as an explanation. One day she was my girlfriend and the next day I was nothing to her. I went two weeks without a word back from her before I stopped reaching out. A week later I found out she was with my roommate, my closest friend. It was like she had a hollowed out empty space where her heart was supposed to be, like she didn't notice or care that I was suffering. And she had no instinct whatsoever to reach out to my sister. In fact, she never once asked how Kara was doing in those days and weeks right after my parents died. *Not if she was the last woman on earth.* Those were the odds of me and Hannah ever reconnecting. The fact that she was sniffing around now, only because I was doing well for myself, left me with an even poorer impression of her.

Kyle snickered. "Must be nice having two hot girls duking it out over you."

"Not really."

"I feel like I'm to blame. A few months ago I mentioned in passing that you'd just started your own firm and you were killing it."

"That explains her renewed interest."

"And when I told her you just bought a brownstone in Park Slope and were going to be my neighbor," he laughed, "then she seemed obsessed with knowing every last detail concerning you."

"Next time she asks about me, make sure to tell her that I'm *very* happy with Kasia. Let's do dinner one night next week. Wait, the week after would actually be better for me. Kasia feels bad that she didn't get a chance to talk to Madeline."

"Definitely."

Right after hanging up with Kyle I got a text:

**It was sooo good to see u last nite. Having pple for the Giants-Redskins game tomorrow...Lots of Hoyas will b there who miss u. Plz come.
1875 York Ave-8E.**

I texted back that I couldn't make it. By the end of the week, Hannah had texted me three more times, and when I called to basically tell her to stop contacting me, she played it off like she was in the subway and the reception was poor. I wasn't playing this game. I texted what I intended to be our final communication:

It was good to catch up with you last week. Life is busy between work, school and Kasia. I wish you all the best. Take care.

The month of November was the busiest I've ever had. I was juggling projects that spanned from Bay Ridge in Brooklyn, to the Upper West Side of Manhattan, up to the Riverdale section of the Bronx. All the while I was supervising the crew that was currently gutting our place in Park Slope. All of my jobs were top priority, but I was spending extra time at the brownstone to ensure that everything went smoothly. I planned to be on site as many hours as possible, from the time the first room was gutted until the last light switch was installed. It had to be done right and I didn't want any neighbors inconvenienced by the work, as I hoped to be living next door to these people someday.

I was running at least sixteen hours a day but I was energized by the work. I was careful when I did my hiring, which made supervising easier, and was pleased to see that everyone from site managers to basic, unskilled laborers was doing their job well. It kept me in the good zone where I was busy but not stretched too thin.

When I got a call in December to price out a job in the Gramercy Park area, I declined at first. I always wanted to have enough clients, but not so many that I wasn't able to give my full attention to the work. Overbooking led to mistakes. When she insisted that she could wait for the work to start in the spring when my schedule opened up, I agreed to give an estimate.

The woman who opened the door looked to be around my age, but she dressed with a level of opulence that made her appear older. She literally looked like she was being weighed down by the amount of gold hanging around her neck and wrists.

My initial appraisal, looking at just the exterior and the foyer, was that the place was pristine. Most of my clients didn't *need* work done, they just wanted work done. And I wasn't complaining—people like this lady kept me in business.

"Hi," she said as she took my hand and led me in, "you must be Jake."

"Jake Wozniak. I have to say, Mrs. Kildaire, your home looks beautiful from what I can see so far. You mentioned a complete reno-vation. Are you sure you need that?"

"Please call me Ashley. And wait until you see the kitchen, it's *so* dated. I'm really just looking to have work done on the first floor. New kitchen, the two baths remodeled, and the closet off the foyer expanded. I hope this job isn't too small for you, Jake."

"No, I didn't say that. But you do understand that I'm not avail-able to start until the end of March, early April, right?"

As we were walking down the corridor leading to the kitchen, she explained, "A friend recommended you and said it would be worth the wait, that you do beautiful work."

And who was sitting at the kitchen island, a glass of wine in one hand while the other fingered a silver heart-shaped pendant on a chain?

"Jake! I told Ashley you were the *only* one she should hire. It's so hard to get good, reliable people and she's been burned in the past." As I stood there stunned, she kept at it. "You look great, as always."

Are you fucking serious right now?

Do I look like a moron to you?

My molars were grinding with the effort to be cordial when I said, "How are you, Hannah?"

She was giving me a look that was meant to hold some deeper meaning when she answered, "I'm good now."

Doing my best to school my expression, I walked around the kitchen inspecting the cabinets, counters and the general condition of the space.

I ignored Hannah, addressing Ashley directly, "What exactly are you looking to do in here?"

She showed me pictures of a friend's kitchen with a more contemporary design scheme, and then took me to the bathrooms she wanted gutted and remodeled. I spent a third of the time I normally would have taken to assess the smallest of jobs. I didn't even bother to take measurements.

"All right, I have a good idea of what you want. I'll be in touch."

And when I said, *I'll be in touch*, what I meant was: *I'll be in touch with the name of another contractor. There is no way in hell I'm working for you.*

Ashley was definitely in on this. The doorbell rang with takeout before I could leave politely, and then she was asking me to stay and have a bite with them.

Hannah cocked her head and smiled. "Jake, please stay for a few minutes and have a beer. I want to hear about everything you've been up to."

I used to love that smile. I bought that stupid heart necklace because I used to be crazy about the girl sitting in front of me, but that was literally a lifetime ago. Hannah was a part of my old life, and she had no place in my life now.

"Ashley, could you excuse us for a minute?" When Ashley left, I looked directly at Hannah and there was no smile on my face. "I don't know what you're trying to pull—"

"I'm not trying to pull anything! I knew Ashley was remodeling and I wanted the work to go your way. Is that so terrible?" Before I could answer, she was standing within a foot of me, taking my hand as she looked down and said, "Do you know how long I've been beating myself up over what I did to you?"

"Hannah—"

"No, Jake, hear me out. I was scared. I was so afraid. I mean, Jesus, I was only twenty. I couldn't be what you needed and I hated myself for that. I loved you so much."

"I didn't expect you to drop out of school like me and leave everything behind. You know that. But kicking me to the curb right after I had to *bury* both of my parents? That was fucking heartless." I backed away. "What you're trying to do here? Don't waste your time. I have a different life now. I moved on from you a long time ago, and I love Kasia with everything I have. So don't beat yourself up over what you did to me because I'm good...I'm better than good now."

Chapter Twenty-Four

KASIA

With just one week to go before Christmas, I was a wreck.

Between the crazy hours I was putting in at the store to help with the holiday rush, overseeing the web-based operations, managing production details for the upcoming season's garments, and worrying over the fact that my period was four days late, I was on the verge of hysteria.

I would shut it right down whenever my mind veered in that direction, but when it did, I would lose track while ringing up a sale, or I might find myself absently staring off into space. I'd count the number of months we were together, scarcely eleven, and fret over the conversation I'd be forced to have with Jake.

Day five was the worst, and by the time we closed the shop's doors and I collapsed onto the futon in the back room of the studio, I was in tears. But just then—*hallelujah!*—I felt the tell-tale cramps that I always despised but was now doing a happy dance over. After I verified my state and situated myself, I laid down and the tears came on again. I was totally exhausted, I was probably PMS-ing hard, and I was...disappointed?

Jake walked in a few minutes later. When he saw me, his smile dropped as he sank down next to me and took my face in his hands.

"What's wrong, moja milosc?"

When he called me *my love* in Polish, I started full-on sobbing. He pulled me against his chest and stroked my hair until I could catch my breath. "What's wrong, Kasia? You're scaring me."

Between sniffles and wiping my runny nose on my sleeve, I sat up and choked everything out. He inhaled deep when I said my period was late, and then when I told him that everything was ok, that I'd just gotten it, he leaned his head back and let out the breath he'd been holding, presumably very relieved. When I wiped at my eyes again, he kissed my forehead and asked, "So why are you sad? Wait," he pulled back and studied my face, "did you think I would have been angry with you? Upset about it?"

I looked up at him through wet lashes. "Would you have been?"

"Surprised, yes, but angry? No, definitely not angry. I know I sound crazy, but I think I'm actually a little disappointed right now."

I laughed when I blurted out, "I am too!" but then a fresh wave of tears came on like a torrent. He held me and rocked me in his arms as if I was a child, comforting me as he whispered in my ear, telling me how much he loved me and how someday we'd have lots of babies together. I've never felt more loved in my entire life.

Once I was all cried out, Jake took me to the bathroom to wipe the messy streaks of mascara off my face. "I know it's late, Kasia, but can we take a ride somewhere? There's something I want to show you."

I asked him at least five times where he was taking me, but he just kept shaking his head, smiling. It was probably close to eleven by then, and I was so tired that I couldn't even protest. He pulled up one of my favorite streets in Park Slope, where well-kept houses were dressed with beautiful Christmas decorations or twinkling blue lights and menorahs for Hannukah. He stopped the truck outside a brownstone that had much of the brick façade removed and permit stickers prominently placed in several of the downstairs windows. A sign for **BR All-City Construction** was affixed to the door. I smiled whenever I saw the sign, as it reminded me of Jake's tender heart. He chose BR to represent his parents' names, Benedykt and Rachela.

He sounded nervous leading me through the front door. "Now I know this place looks awful, but you have to imagine how it will be. The neighborhood is great and the schools are the best. There's a small backyard, and it's even got a driveway."

I was speechless, turning in a circle and looking around dumbfounded.

He shook his head. "Too much? I didn't know how to tell you. I knew buying a place with us in mind was insane." He shrugged and smiled. "I'm doing this all wrong, but here goes." He kissed my hands as he lowered himself onto one knee. "I know that I want you to be my wife. If you *had* been pregnant, believe me, I would have been overjoyed. The thought of you having my baby makes me feel..." He wiped at his eyes before he looked up at me again and went on. "I didn't buy you a ring yet, so the timing is all messed up, but will you marry me, Kasia?"

I sank down next to him and hugged him so tight around his neck that I probably risked cutting off his air supply. "Yes, yes, yes, yes, yes! I'll marry you, Jakub!"

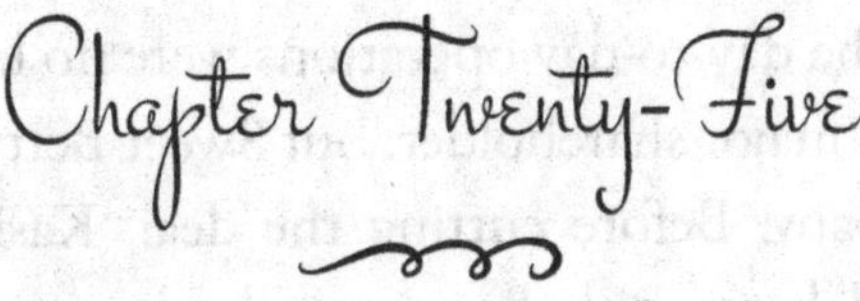

Chapter Twenty-Five

Five years later...

JAKE

Getting to the park used to be so easy.

Balancing one on my shoulders, I was pushing one in the stroller while keeping my eye on the daredevil riding alongside me on his scooter.

We were giving Mom time to rest this Sunday morning. That was our routine. It was a joke, really, because by the time we got home, not only would Kasia not be resting, but she would already have the house straightened and there would be a giant stack of blueberry pancakes waiting for us to devour.

Since we got married, Kasia had blessed me with three beautiful children and a life better than any man could ever hope for. Little Jakub was four now, Tomasz was three, and baby Rachel was just five months. Our life never really slowed down enough for my taste— there were times when I wanted to lock us all in, ignore the phone and just be with them and no one else—but life with Kasia would always be a moving train and I was ok with that.

Kasia's business basically exploded after the better-known specialty retailers started carrying her pieces, and licensing offers soon followed. While she still maintained some measure of creative control over the brand, the day-to-day operations were no longer her responsibility. She was a major shareholder, but Sweet Betty Threads was no longer her company. Before cutting the deal, Kasia made sure the employees who'd been with her since the beginning were offered equity stakes, as well as iron-clad employment contracts with the parent company so they would be well taken care of.

Kasia now worked out of the home studio I built for her. She never stopped. She gave mothering our three children her full effort, but used what little spare time she had to develop and market Betty Bumps, her maternity wear line.

Kasia has never looked sexier to me than when she's pregnant. She swore it was her designs, but it wasn't. The thought of my woman with our baby growing inside of her, a life the two of us created together, was the biggest turn-on ever.

The children went happily between our house and Mama and Tata's, and they were doted on by their uncles and aunts. They saw a lot of their Aunt Karolina, who liked to bounce back and forth between making me very proud and driving me crazy.

After finishing school last year, Karolina moved in with us. Kasia was the one to suggest we renovate the basement and turn it into an apartment. My Kasia did that for me, knowing I couldn't relax unless I was sure my little sister was safe. Having Kara close by allowed me to keep an eye on her, but it also drove me insane when she stayed out late in the city with her friends or her new boyfriend. The jury was still out on that guy as far as I was concerned.

We spent most of our free time with family. Little Jakub and Tomasz asked to see Michal and Sophia's boys practically every single day as soon as they woke up. It was pretty cute. But we were still close with a small circle of our old friends. We saw Kyle and Madeline a lot, as they had kids around the same age and were practically neighbors. We also got together with Caleb and Rene, Tom and Darcy, Jenna and Dan, and Caitlin and Mick regularly. When we were all together at the big house we rented on Cape May for a week every summer, it was mayhem, with a total of seven boys and five girls between us.

There were times when I couldn't believe my good fortune, couldn't believe how happy I was.

I thought of my parents often and missed them when I would see our children with Kasia's parents. I knew they would be happy looking down on us from above, seeing how things had turned out for me and for Karolina. But I also thought of my parents when Kasia and I paid off the mortgage on our home early, when we set up college funds for the children, when we purchased life insurance, and when we wrote our will with every conceivable worst-case scenario planned out.

Kasia teased, calling me Doctor Doomsday sometimes, but she understood. She knew it wasn't pessimism that drove me, but my need to protect them. I felt a crushing, overwhelming sense of love for her and for our children. The thought of them struggling financially or suffering in any way could keep me up at night.

Taking care of them was a responsibility I'd never take lightly.

They were my life.

* * *

KASIA

The boys were excited, but they settled in about halfway through the thirty-minute drive down to Darcy and Tom's beach house.

Taking in the pink balloons tied to the front steps and the fence posts, and the many cars lining the street, I thought of him. Dylan and I were like a divorced couple who shared custody of our good friends. In a roundabout way, I would find out if he was going to be at the smaller gatherings or he would find out beforehand if I was going to be there. One of us would politely decline and Darcy knew better than to push. It was just better that way.

The last time I saw him was at Brian and Trish's wedding. Class reunions, weddings—there would be times when running into one other was inevitable, but you could lose yourself more easily in a crowd of two hundred.

Today was the Baptism of Tom and Darcy's fourth child, a girl they named Clare Rebecca Donovan. Jake had to tend to an emergency at a job for his most particular and demanding client: my father. I left Rachel with my mother but had the boys with me.

When we pulled up, I just barely cut then engine before they were jumping out of their car seats and running into the house with me trailing behind. They loved the happy chaos of being with all of the kids, and Darcy and Tom's home was a dream for little boys. Their huge, fenced-in backyard had a treehouse, a jungle gym, soccer nets and a basketball hoop. Like I said, every little boy's dream.

I always felt so relaxed here. Through Darcy, the women sitting around the kitchen table with me had become my closest friends. Talking and laughing with Darcy, Rene, Caitlin, Jenna, Kate, Darcy's step-mom and Tom's mother always left me with a good feeling. They were an interesting and supportive group of women.

After Dylan and I split up there were some casualties in my social life. I never met up with Anna in person, but we would trade occasional texts when she saw something about me in a trade paper or I heard mention of her work as an associate at Kate's architecture firm. We followed one another's lives from afar. Another hard loss was Brian and Trish. I think Trish felt guilty when she became close to Cecilia, which was silly on her part. Bernadette told me they often vacationed together, the two couples, and I knew from Darcy that Trish flew in last year to help Bunny Tate host Cecilia's bridal shower.

I didn't know Cecilia well, but she came off as somewhat kinder and more sensitive than the girls she associated with. I could see how Cecilia and Trish became close friends.

As for Bernadette, she lived in Portland now and was busy with twins and a baby on the way, so we kept in touch here and there through email and text. And Valerie? If anyone told me at graduation that she'd be the one who would still be sister-close to me years later, I wouldn't have believed it. Valerie was still doing her own thing, living single in a coastal South Carolina community where there were a lot of other creative types like her. I was beyond proud when her debut novel did so well that she had the freedom to pursue writing full time. Val described herself as being allergic to marriage, but she was never alone. She'd been through a string of guys since Cooper, but her newest flame, one of her former graduate professors from Emory, seemed like the real deal. Two or three times a year she flew up to New York to meet with her agent and editors in person, and when she did, she always stayed with us. She spoiled our kids with gifts every time, always signing them: *From you pal, Val*. My little ones adored her.

"Mama, I want to bring Rachel a shell," Tomasz pleaded as I was zipping their coats and getting ready to leave. It was early December but not too cold, so I agreed to walk down to the shore before we left.

The ocean was a dark ominous grey, and while the waves weren't so big, each one landed on the shore with a pounding crash. Tomasz and Jakub searched the shoreline for intact shells, but most of them were broken by the rough surf. I didn't mind waiting. Being near the ocean was soothing, and I always found the beach in this kind of turbulent state just as beautiful as the calm, blue waters of the summertime.

I was lost in thought, focused on some news I'd learned this morning when I felt a hand on my shoulder. I knew the touch before I turned to see Dylan's face.

"I didn't startle you, did I?"

I put my hand to rest on top of his, still on my shoulder. "How are you, Dylan?"

"I'm good, you?"

"Good."

"What's your name?" Jakub asked as he scampered over. He was already turning into a protective little man.

"My name's Dylan. I'm an old friend of your mom's," he said, crouching down to Jakub's level. "What's your name?"

"I'm Jakub Wozniak."

"Oh yeah? How old are you, Jakub?"

"I'm four years old, and my brother Tomasz is three, and my sister Rachel is nothing."

"Not nothing, Jakub." I shook my head and laughed. "She's just not one yet."

"I know, Mama, she's a months old."

"Close enough," I said as he ran back to where his brother was throwing stones into the ocean.

Dylan looked down at me and smiled. "You've been busy, Kasia. They're cute."

"When did you get here? I know we never talk about it, but it always seems like either you come to these things or I come, right?"

"Is it ok that I'm here?"

"Of course, Dylan. I'm really happy to see you."

Jakub and Tomasz ran over and gave Dylan a rock, wanting to see how far he could throw it. After he spent a few minutes showing off for them, he turned his attention back to me.

"I have a confession to make. I was on the phone with Tom this morning, and when I overheard Darcy telling him that your Jake couldn't make it, I decided to pop in. Cecilia is in Paris shopping with her mother."

"Oh." I didn't know how else to reply to that.

"I just...I still think of you, Kasia, and I wanted to see you, to see how you're doing. And," he laughed as he threw another rock far out into the waves, "you look as good as I knew you would."

His words didn't make me blush, but they did make me smile.

"So how are you?" I asked. And before he could toss back some stale variation of *fine* or *good*, I added, "I want to know how you're really doing. I'm not asking just to make polite conversation."

"You never waste time on bullshit. It's one of the many things I remember fondly." After a pause, he said, "I'm doing well. The company is doing great. My father has all but stepped aside, so it's mine to run my own way."

"You must be traveling all the time."

"Not as much as I was, but yeah, I'm overseas at least six or seven times a year." He bent down to pick up a stone, smoothing his thumb over its surface a few times before asking, "Are you happy?"

"Yes," I nodded, "I'm very happy."

"I already knew what your answer would be. You look happy."

"Are you?"

"I'm as happy as I can be. My life is complicated. I'm complicated, as you well know," he teased as he bumped my shoulder.

I couldn't help but ask, "Are you happy with Cecilia?"

"That's a complicated question. Best answer is that I'm happy enough. We got married last year. Did you know that?"

"Yes, I did. Congratulations."

He smiled, but his voice lacked enthusiasm when he said, "Thanks." His eyes were fixed on my boys running along the shoreline when he added, "I'm not *un*happy. CeCe is a good person, she's beautiful, she puts up with my shit. She plays the role of perfect little corporate wife to a tee, and we both know you would have hated all that crap." When I nodded, he rolled his eyes and said, "Margot thinks I made a *fabulous* choice."

"Yeah, I think Margot and I would have spent the next thirty years butting heads."

"Probably. But she liked you, Kasia. She even bought one or two of your dresses when you were just getting established."

"Really? I'm shocked."

"And Anna pretty much dressed in nothing but Sweet Betty Threads before you sold out of the business. Cecilia was convinced Anna was doing it just to piss her off, but I think she really loved your clothes...And she missed you."

"She's doing well, I hope?"

"Anna's great. I tried to convince her to come and work for me after she graduated, but she wanted no part of it."

"Kate says she's so talented."

"She really is," he said, beaming with pride.

The boys walked over then, each carrying one unbroken shell. I was impressed they unearthed them on a day like today.

"Boys, lets head back up now, ok?" They walked a few feet ahead of us, stopping every few seconds to pick up a piece of sea glass or a rock that caught their eye.

"I'm so glad I got a chance to see you, Dylan."

"So am I." Bumping my shoulder again playfully, he asked, "Do you think we could have made it work?"

I was thinking, *No, absolutely not*, but didn't want to hurt him. "It's hard to say. I think it's probably for the best that we let each other go."

We were standing next to my car as the boys climbed into the backseat.

"That's the problem," Dylan said as he lowered his eyes to the ground. "I think there's a part of me that won't ever let you go."

He gave my hand a quick, affectionate squeeze and then walked across the street and got into his car without looking back.

I kissed Jakub and Tomasz as I buckled them into their car seats and then set off for home. The upbeat tunes on the radio didn't match my melancholy mood. Every single day, Jake and my children surrounded me with love and happiness. I got my happily ever after, but I wasn't sure if ever Dylan would.

Pulling up outside of our house, I smiled when Tomasz and Jakub called out in excitement, "Look, look!"

I took in the festive wreath on the front door and the mass of multi-colored lights that were hung with precision from every window of the brownstone. "Ooh, isn't it pretty?"

Walking in the door, the boys hollered happily, jumping and clapping when they saw the tree set up in the corner of the living room. Smiling, Jake shushed them and whispered, "Keep it down," as he pointed to Rachel resting peacefully on his chest. *Yum*, I thought, that was a pretty picture. He laid Rachel down in her cradle as he made his way over to me and then the boys, kissing each one of us.

"How was the party, guys?"

They spoke over one another, relaying details about a soccer game, playing in the treehouse, and about the giant pink frosted cake. Tomasz said, "And we met a friend of Mama's."

"Yeah," added Jakub. "Dylan throwed the rocks really, really far."

"Oh, yeah?" Jake asked as he grabbed Jakub and lifted him up towards the ceiling. As our oldest son squealed in delight, Jake looked to me with a smile and raised eyebrows.

I chimed in, "You know, Daddy can throw them *much* farther, right?"

Little Tomasz asked, "You can, Daddy?"

Before he could answer, I waggled my eyebrows and said, "Of course! Daddy can do it *much* better because Daddy is *much* bigger and *much* stronger."

By then he'd put Jakub down, and in response to what I'd said, the boys were both jumping up and down, flexing their little toddler-sized muscles.

Jake grabbed me, flung me over his shoulder with one hand and joined the boys in jumping up and down. They thought that was hilarious.

"Whoa, gentle with Mommy!" I pleaded. Jake slid me down his body then, so slowly that I could feel his desire for me.

"I missed you today, baby."

"I missed you too. Everyone was asking for you."

"I can think of one person who was probably happy I wasn't there," he teased. "How is Dylan?"

"He's good, I guess. I don't think he's found the kind of happiness I have," I teased back, poking his ticklish underarm area, "but he's ok. It was actually nice to see him."

He nodded and then kissed me tenderly before turning his attention back to the boys. "Guess who's coming to help us decorate the tree tomorrow night?"

"Who, who, who?" they both yelled as they pounded on Jake's legs.

"Grandmama and Tata," the boys whooped and cheered as every name was said, "Auntie Karolina, Auntie Sophia, Uncle Michal, Uncle Alex, Uncle Tomasz and his Annabelle." He purposely left out Sophia and Michal's boys, knowing that would cause a near riot.

Jakub yelled, "What about Christian and Lucas? You didn't say them, Daddy!"

He opened his eyes wide. "You're right! I forgot all about them! Should we call and ask them to come?"

They both yelled, "Yes!" running into the kitchen to the house phone. Jake coached them through the call, telling the boys to tell their cousins that Mommy was going to make meatballs and spaghetti, we were going to bake Christmas cookies, and we were going to decorate the tree.

After he had them settled watching a show, he came and flopped down next to me on the couch. Studying his face, I thought to myself that he was the most handsome man alive.

"What are you thinking, moja milosc?"

"I'm thinking that I have to give you some news before I tell my mother tomorrow."

He kissed my head and tugged me close into his side. "All right, I'm listening."

"You know how we were planning to take a trip to Bermuda this summer, just the two of us?"

"Yeah, and?"

"Well," I stretched out the words, "we might not be able to do that."

He turned and tilted my chin so that I was looking up at him. "We won't be able to go because we'll be having a baby?" I nodded, tears at the corners of my eyes as I smiled back at him. He laid a seriously hot kiss on me, but then pulled back with a worried expression. "Why'd you let me fling you over my shoulder like a damn caveman before?"

"I'm fine," I reassured him. "He or she is like the size of a lima bean right now."

"But I take care of *my* lima beans, woman," he said as he rested his hand over my stomach. "Can we tell them?" he asked, gesturing towards the room where the boys were watching television.

"I'll be nearly three months on Valentine's Day. How does that sound?"

"Perfect. Everything is perfect, Kasia."

Yes, I thought, everything *is* perfect. Jake was perfect for me and I would never let anything or anyone come between us.

I would never, ever let Jake go.

The End, *for now...*

* * *

A Note From Lily

Thank you for reading *Let Me Go*. Dylan's character took hold and grew roots as I was writing the first book in the series, *Let Me Be the One*. When I sat down to write his story, it was as if the book wrote itself. I hope you enjoyed the escape.

And if you're jonesing for some more Dylan Cole, you'll be happy to know he makes cameos in the two books that follow, and that Dylan's story concludes in the sixth and final book of the series.

Anna and Declan's story, *Let Me Heal Your Heart*, is up next. *RT Book Reviews* hails it is as "a heartbreaking story of first love and adversity."

One hockey phenom, destined for the pros.
One summer he'll never forget.
One girl he'll never stop loving.

Visit the website to learn more:
LilyFoster.com

9 780990 594147